For Amy.

ACKNOWLEDGMENTS

WITH THANKS as always to the All-Star Fun crew, without whom this book would not exist; to Laura, for her insightful alpha read; to Liz, whose wonderful edits I'm finally learning to accept without ego.

And to Brandon, who's always been my rock.

Readers love
ASHLYN KANE

Fake Dating the Prince

"As sparkling as a diamond engagement ring, this contemporary delivers."

—*Publishers Weekly* Starred Review

"It's that sparkling, sweet romance you remember and will reread when you need a lift."

—Scattered Thoughts and Rogue Words

Hex and Candy

"I'm just going to say it, I adored this clever little romance by Ashlyn Kane. *Hex and Candy* is clever, humorous, captivating and an absolute feel good novel."

—The Novel Approach

"Everything about this novel's presentation is unique, sharp and witty. It's also as sweet as its candy store hero, exactly the kind of novel for a light pick-me-up."

—Kimmers' Erotic Book Banter

His Leading Man

"If you are looking for a fun, romantic book then I highly recommend this one."

—Love Bytes

By ASHLYN KANE

American Love Songs
With Claudia Mayrant & CJ Burke: Babe in the Woodshop
A Good Vintage
Hang a Shining Star
The Inside Edge

DREAMSPUN BEYOND
Hex and Candy

DREAMSPUN DESIRES
His Leading Man
Fake Dating the Prince

With Morgan James
Hair of the Dog
Hard Feelings
Return to Sender
Winging It

Published by DREAMSPINNER PRESS
www.dreamspinnerpress.com

THE INSIDE EDGE

ASHLYN KANE

Published by
DREAMSPINNER PRESS

5032 Capital Circle SW, Suite 2, PMB# 279, Tallahassee, FL 32305-7886 USA
www.dreamspinnerpress.com

This is a work of fiction. Names, characters, places, and incidents either are the product of author imagination or are used fictitiously, and any resemblance to actual persons, living or dead, business establishments, events, or locales is entirely coincidental.

The Inside Edge
© 2020 Ashlyn Kane

Cover Art
© 2020 Paul Richmond
http://www.paulrichmondstudio.com
Cover content is for illustrative purposes only and any person depicted on the cover is a model.

Trade Paperback ISBN: 978-1-64405-895-4
Digital ISBN: 978-1-64405-894-7
Library of Congress Control Number: 2020943495
Trade Paperback published December 2020
v. 1.0

Printed in the United States of America
∞
This paper meets the requirements of
ANSI/NISO Z39.48-1992 (Permanence of Paper).

PROLOGUE

"I, KELLY Marie Ng, take you, Caley...."

Nate Overton had been to plenty of weddings in his time. He'd even stood up in a lot of them—playing professional hockey led to the kind of intense friendship that lent itself to groomsman duties.

But this was the first time he'd held a bouquet as he stood up for a bride.

Just a few feet away, Kelly slid the ring onto Caley's finger and wiped away a tear, her smile so bright it almost hurt to look at.

The two of them were embracing even before the officiant finished pronouncing, "You may kiss your bride.

"Please rise for the newlyweds!"

Nate let out a quiet breath that he hoped went unnoticed, and applauded with everyone else when Caley retrieved her bouquet. Then it was just the private witnessing of the certificate to get through and he could have a drink and relax.

Kelly insisted she talked enough at work, so there weren't any speeches. Nate couldn't say he minded, since he was in the same boat. Besides, it was nice to enjoy the meal without an hour of other people failing to prove they could've had a career in stand-up.

Instead, he got to ride herd on his co-bridesman, who was currently peeking up at him from under the tablecloth.

Nate bent down to speak to him in a stage whisper. "You know, there's no green beans under the table. But there isn't any cake either."

Carter Ng stared back at him thoughtfully. At three and a half, he was painfully shy and just getting to that age where vegetables were the enemy.

Nate had been the favored team babysitter for the thirteen years he'd played in the NHL, and he wasn't above bribery to keep the kid on the correct side of the table, at least until the photographers had pictures of him dancing with his mom and stepmom. Then he could get as dusty as he liked. "If you come up here and eat two more bites of vegetables, I'll eat the rest and tell your mom you did. And then you can have cake."

Carter considered this wordlessly for a moment before climbing back into the chair between Nate and Kelly, who threw him an amused but grateful look and then returned her attention to Caley's great-aunt something-or-other, whose pontificating Nate had tuned out.

"So much for no speeches," he said sotto voce to Kelly when the woman finally—blessedly—left.

On Kelly's other side, Caley smothered a snort in her hand. He was pretty sure Kelly would've smacked him good-naturedly, but Carter was in the way.

"At least we're the only ones who had to hear it," she said, and then the emcee was calling them up for their first dance as a couple.

Nate surprised himself by making it through all of the ceremony, dinner, and the official dances—including a very short one where he swayed around the floor with a toddler giggling in his arms—without a single traumatic flashback or bittersweet memory. But when he put Carter back down, it was like he'd set down his shield against reality. He looked around quickly to ensure no one would miss him and then let himself outside for some fresh air.

Immediately he found it easier to breathe, which was stupid. He didn't have anxiety or asthma. He didn't have a reason to struggle with witnessing the beautiful wedding of two of his very dear friends.

Unless you counted what he had to do tomorrow.

The door behind him squeaked open, and he sighed. Caught.

"Hey," Caley said, coming to sit next to him on the bench outside the door, heedless of her pretty white dress. "I thought I might find you here. It's all too much, isn't it?"

Nate tried to frown at her. "You're missing your party. You should be celebrating."

"I will." She nudged closer until their shoulders bumped. "When I'm done checking on you."

There was nothing for it; she hadn't been the captain of multiple gold-medal-winning Olympic women's hockey teams for nothing. He sighed. "I'm fine. I promise."

"Forgive me if I'm concerned about the well-being of my friend, who's putting on a very good front of being happy for me despite the fact that he's about to fly to Texas tomorrow to sign divorce papers." She leaned her head against his. "The timing sucks, I know."

"We've been separated almost three years," Nate said. Part of him thought repeating that should make it suck less, but no dice. "It's past time. Not your fault there's a scheduling conflict. I could've asked to push it back."

"You should've," Caley said darkly. "Just been conveniently busy until the delay would've ruined *his* wedding plans. I'm just saying."

Nate smiled, tilting his head back. "I'm not going to say I didn't think about it."

"Pretty presumptuous planning a wedding before you've even got the ink dry on your divorce, if you ask me."

Nate had suspicions about what Marty had been up to before their separation, never mind before their divorce, but he didn't have any proof, and in the end it didn't matter. They wouldn't have lasted anyway. He'd only delayed filing for so long because it felt like giving up.

Nate's parents hadn't raised a quitter.

"I appreciate your support."

"There's an open bar, you know," she told him unnecessarily. Then her voice turned teasing. "And you know, Kelly has this cousin...."

Oh no. No, Nate was not ready for that. But before he could protest, the door opened and Carter ran toward them, followed a few seconds later by Kelly.

"Uncle Naaaaaaate," Carter said, patting Nate's knees. "They're doing cake!"

"Cake!" Nate said, standing and swooping Carter into his arms. He tossed him once, just a few inches, and caught him. "Cake sounds much better than this conversation. What a nice guy you are. Did you know I needed a rescue?"

Kelly indulgently watched the three of them. "I see you've successfully threatened him into a good mood."

Caley grinned. "What can I say, it's a gift."

Nate craned his head back so he could look Carter in the face. "God help you when you're a teenager in a sulk, kid. I'll make sure you have my number."

But he let Kelly and Caley flank him on the way back into the hall, and his maudlin thoughts didn't catch up to him for the rest of the night.

THE PHONE call came in just after Aubrey finished in Makeup, but long before he had to be on set. Had it been any other day or any other person, he probably would have ignored it. He hadn't met his co-star yet and he was supposed to be on the air in an hour. It was his first day on the job; he didn't need to be taking calls at work. He was having a hard enough time wrapping his head around the show, which was mostly news, analysis, and women's game coverage during the week, with a featured play-by-play on the weekend.

But it was his mother calling from home in Vancouver, and she called infrequently enough that he was inclined to take it.

And maybe a tiny part of him held some hope that she was calling to wish him well and let him know she'd be watching—though he didn't know how she would, since she didn't live in their broadcast range.

"I'm sorry, I've got to take this," he said to the makeup tech. "Thanks, though—I look great."

The man laughed and shooed him out of the room.

Aubrey took a deep breath and answered the call. "Hi, Mom."

"… no, I think the roses if you want traditional and the gerbera daisies if you want something a little more fun. Lilies are a bit morbid for a wedding— Oh! Aubrey?"

He could already feel his hackles rising. "Yeah, Mom. You called me, remember?"

"I'm sorry, I was distracted. I've been helping your cousin choose flowers for the ceremony."

Aubrey glanced at his watch, counting down the minutes. He hoped his mom didn't want to chat for long. He couldn't remember the last time he'd had a conversation with her that didn't end with one or both of them frustrated or angry. "It's all right," he said, trying to be patient. "So, why'd you call?"

Can't a woman call to catch up with her only son? he half expected her to say. Lord knew he'd been burned by those words enough times. They inevitably led to invasive questions about his love life, followed by *Mrs. Society So-and-So has a gay son about your age*, or *Your father and*

I miss you; when are you going to move back home? As if they'd ever spent time with him when he lived there.

If he was really lucky, she'd find a new facet of his life to disapprove of, like his diet or—

"Well, like I said, I'm here with Rachel, and she tells me you haven't sent in your RSVP for the wedding yet."

Aubrey's stomach soured. "The wedding."

Right. His cousin was getting married. Well, Rachel wasn't actually his cousin. She was more like the kid his mom had always wanted, the daughter of his parents' friends. Aubrey had won multiple Grand Prix events, two World Championship figure-skating titles, and an Olympic silver, along with a handful of junior medals. None of it had been good enough. Why did he have to go clubbing so often? Wasn't he interested in a more rewarding long-term relationship? Didn't he want to take some business classes so he could take over his parents' hospitality business one day?

Why couldn't he be more like Rachel, basically.

He'd always been jealous of Rachel's relationship with his parents, but when her mom and dad were killed in a car accident four years ago, it added a healthy dose of self-loathing to the mix. Because how could he be jealous of an *orphan*?

"It's December 23," his mother reminded him. "RSVPs were due last week."

"Well, we both know I can't do anything right, so it can't surprise you that I forgot."

Aubrey winced. That was a little more combative than he'd meant to be, but he couldn't take it back now.

His mother sighed. "For God's sake, Aubrey. Just tell me if you're coming. Your father and I would like to see you."

"Sorry, I don't think so. The NHL plays until the twenty-third. I'll probably have a game to cover."

"Fine," she said, her tone frosty. "Was that so hard?"

Aubrey gritted his teeth. He'd even reminded her about his new job, which was starting today, and she couldn't take two seconds to wish him luck? "I've got to go, Mom. I'm needed on set. Unless there was something else?"

"No, that was all." She sounded resigned. At least he wasn't the only one. "Goodbye, Aubrey."

The call disconnected before he could say anything else. "Goodbye," he said to dead air, fighting the urge to bang his head against the wall. Next time she called, maybe he could do that instead. It would be less painful.

For now, though, he had a job to do. He summoned all the good cheer he could muster and headed toward the sound stage. His mother might consider him beneath her notice, but Aubrey could get the attention he thrived on elsewhere. All he had to do was show up and be charming. And charm was something that came very naturally to him—as long as his mother wasn't around to see it.

CHAPTER ONE

NATE TIPPED his driver extra; the guy had made it from O'Hare in record time. He sidestepped around the office workers in the plaza like they were opposing defenders and entered the enormous revolving door as the big lobby clock struck the hour. It almost felt like beating the buzzer—he was going to just barely make it in time for makeup and a brief rundown, but barely was good enough and far better than he'd hoped, after spending an hour waiting for a gate at the airport. The stress of being late—Nate hated tardiness in himself as much as in others—was only eclipsed by the situation at the network.

"Don't worry about it; it's handled," Jess had told him in their too-brief call before the flight took off. That didn't make him feel better. The few subsequent messages they exchanged during the flight hadn't helped, especially as it felt like he was also getting texts from everyone he'd ever met—all variations of the theme: *So what the hell is up with John Plum?* Not that he'd answered. Nate had already gotten a very firm, if unnecessary, voicemail form his agent that he should not, under penalty of torture, say anything but "no comment" about the situation.

What would he even say? *Sorry my cohost is a xenophobic misogynist douchebag with no control over his basest impulses?* Silence was the better part of valor.

"You're late," Gina the PA told him, falling into step next to him as he beelined for Makeup. "I sent a rundown of tonight's show to your phone. You have time to look at it?"

Nate shook his head. "It died halfway through the flight. Too much Candy Crush. Forgot the charging cord in my hotel room." He glanced around as they walked. "Is Jess around? She told me not to worry, but—"

"Yeah, on second thought, maybe I better let her tell you in person. I think she's with—uh." Gina pasted on a smile. Good thing her work was mostly behind the camera, because she didn't convince Nate. "You know what? I'll just go tell her to find you."

That didn't inspire confidence, but Nate didn't have a lot of time to argue. He had a call in… well, basically now. "All right," he agreed, but Gina was already scampering down the hallway, talking on her headset.

Jess didn't come in while he was in Makeup, and the usual chatter was suspiciously free of office gossip and sports talk, focusing exclusively on the relative merits of different varieties of Girl Scout cookies. Nate happily shared his opinion (Samoas best, the peanut butter ones disappointing), but he found it weird that no one was even referring to the elephant that was no longer in the room, and that made him feel wrong-footed. Someone had passed him a portable charger for his phone, so he was able to read through the rundown he was now expected to do by himself. It might be a little flat with just one body behind the desk, but they were going to cut away to the game in Brampton, and Kelly was always good. Maybe they'd use this as an excuse to give a little extra time to the women's game. John would hate that. Nate couldn't resist smiling at the image of him fuming about it.

"You're done." Samira batted him on the shoulder as she finished. "Now get out of my chair and y'all have a great show."

Y'all. Plural. Was that significant? Nate turned to ask, but Samira had already scooted out of the room.

Something strange was definitely going on.

"*Nate Overton to the set.*" The voice over the PA made it clear he didn't have any more time to wonder. In fact, he barely had time to change—he unbuttoned his shirt on the way to Wardrobe, where Tony was already waiting to help him into its replacement.

"Little behind today?" he asked, turning to grab the jacket and tie—helpfully already tied—while Nate buttoned up.

"O'Hare," Nate said grimly.

"Say no more." Tony held the jacket for him. "Not going to miss your old cohost's wardrobe peculiarities, you know?"

Nate figured Tony wouldn't miss him, period. "Maybe his replacement will be easier on the eyes."

Tony opened his mouth to say something, but Nate didn't have time. He took the tie to go, waving his thanks over his shoulder.

"Cutting it a little close," their primary camera operator commented as Nate stepped onto the soundstage.

Jeez. You get twitchy about people being late a few times and you'd never get any slack. "Yeah, yeah," Nate said. "Point taken." He took another three steps—

And stopped.

Someone was sitting in his chair.

A handsome—*very* handsome—dark-haired man had his elbows propped on the desk as he leaned forward, grinning at something Carl the camera operator was saying. Carl gestured with his hands, and the handsome brunet laughed, tossed his head back, and turned a million-watt smile on Carl. If Nate didn't know better, he'd think the guy was flirting with their straight, married, sixtysomething grandfather of three. Whatever. The guy was in Nate's chair, and Nate needed to politely inform him of the fact and give him the opportunity to move... and maybe to introduce himself, since no one else was going to tell Nate who he was. Where did they get him from? Nate squinted as he approached. The guy looked vaguely familiar. Local news? A weatherman maybe?

"Nate!" Carl intercepted him before he could make his case to the usurping newcomer. "Glad you made it! I thought I was going to have to join Aubrey up in front of the cameras tonight," he joked.

"Uh, yeah." Nate pasted on a smile, more confused than ever. He tamped down on a surge of change-induced panic. "You kn—"

"And Emmy would've loved that," Carl continued, still chuckling.

"Well, I'll make sure she gets that autographed picture," the guy—Aubrey—said. "Always happy to hear about a fan. Give her my love, Carl."

There was more batting of eyelashes until Carl ambled back to his station.

"Hi."

And now the guy was making eyes at Nate. Nate, who'd just spent twelve hours in travel with a dead phone. Nate, who hadn't been able to wrangle a straight answer out of his producer all day. Nate, who had *no fucking idea* what was going on and needed to be on the air in *minutes*.

Right now Nate didn't care if Aubrey was the only other gay man on the planet. He wasn't going to flirt with him. Definitely not at work, and *especially* not while he was sitting in Nate's chair. "You're in my seat," Nate said.

The eyelashes stopped fluttering and instead narrowed around clear gray eyes. "My apologies," he said smoothly, and all the warmth of his initial greeting faded. "Ms. Chapel told me to sit here."

Why would she do that? Nate knew ratings had suffered with John. Had Jess decided to go in a totally different direction? Would she call him to set just to fire him?

The guy in Nate's chair leaned back, eyes still narrowed in assessment. The movement drew Nate's eye to his suit—cut very close, expensive too, and Nate knew expensive suits. This one had a silver line of stitching around the lapels. Flashy, but with class. John would've hated it.

"I'm Aubrey Chase, by the way," the guy said, holding out a hand, and oh. That was why Nate recognized him.

"The figure skater." It came out sounding a little more cringeworthy than Nate intended. He had nothing against figure skaters. He knew what kind of tremendous athleticism the sport demanded. But this was a hockey show. "Uh, nice to meet you," he offered belatedly and shook the guy's hand. "Nate Overton."

"My pleasure." Aubrey's smile was polite, if not warm, as if he could read Nate's thoughts. "You're the senior now, so I guess that's why you get John's old spot. Kind of surprised it looks just like a normal chair, you know? It's not like it's velvet or ermine-lined or anything."

Nate adjusted his earpiece since he couldn't manage to adjust the nagging sensation of disorientation.

"Two minutes," Gina's voice said in his ear.

Nate glanced over the paper in front of him. To his right he noticed Aubrey smoothing his own sheet and shrugging and shaking out his shoulders a bit as if he were about to step into a spotlight on the ice. He was getting ready for his audience, obviously. Just Nate's luck that after all the times he'd dreamed of getting rid of an overbearing bigoted buffoon like John, the replacement would be a different sort of diva.

"I see we're hashing out Kazakov's new contract."

"That's what it says," Nate replied. He hated that he felt he'd gotten off on the wrong foot, but somehow blaming Aubrey for his own lack of grace made him feel better.

"Five and a half by five. That's going to be a squeeze with Dallas's cap issues," Aubrey offered.

"Well, it's not like top-four defenseman grow on trees, and Popov's not getting any younger." Nate probably sounded more definite than he felt about the issue, but it had been a long day.

"Dallas wouldn't know if they did grow on trees, unless they were trees in Russia. They can't seem to draft one from anywhere else." Aubrey clicked his pen for emphasis.

Nate swiveled on his chair to glare at the handsome but misinformed face. "They traded for Svensson at the last deadline!"

"Trading for a thirty-four-year-old isn't the same as developing or draft—" Aubrey insisted, but Gina's voice interrupted.

"Forty-five seconds."

Nate felt like his nose was going to hit the desk in forty-five seconds. He should have chugged an energy drink or three, and now a figure skater was trying to debate him on the finer points of building a blueline.

Worse, he wasn't entirely off base. At the very least he was competent, which was better than John, and unlikely to spout some of the more offensive bile that seemed to fall like flowers from John's mouth. Nate needed to focus on that and on staying awake and alert, and then he could apologize to his new cohost and try to start over.

"I really need a coffee," he grumbled, and Gina piped in over his earpiece.

"I'll get you one for commercial break."

"*Thank you*," Nate said fervently. He made a mental note to buy her something really nice for Christmas this year.

"Thirty seconds."

He took a deep breath. He'd be fine. He could talk about hockey in his sleep. He had, in fact, done so on enough occasions that he'd chased Marty out of bed to the guest room, which probably hadn't helped when everything went to hell. And wow, he needed to think about something else. *Anything* else.

"Are you okay?" Aubrey asked, one eyebrow raised. "You look a little… gray."

Despite himself, Nate prickled. Now Aubrey was calling him old. *Great.* As if he needed a reminder that he'd just stepped into the senior role. Nothing like feeling your age. "I'm fine," he snapped. "Let's just get this over with."

"Live in ten!"

"I love your enthusiasm," Aubrey deadpanned. But then Gina held her hand up for the countdown, and Nate could see the moment he switched into broadcast mode. He sat straighter, corrected his posture, and his features relaxed into something open and friendly instead of just openly hostile. He brushed a hand through his hair and somehow avoided messing it up. Instead it looked like he'd just paid a hairdresser a hundred dollars to do it. Nate would have sworn his *skin* even looked nicer, which was patently ridiculous.

Of course. On top of being a charming, shmoozing flirt, his new cohost was hot. Fuck Nate's life.

The red broadcast-indicator light came on and Gina gave them the signal—they were live.

"Good evening and welcome to *The Inside Edge*. I'm Nate Overton and this is Aubrey Chase. Tonight, the Chicago Snap take on the Toronto Furies. We'll have that game for you live, as well as news updates, scores, and highlights from around the leagues. The puck drops in ten. For now we're going to our women's correspondent, Kelly Ng, live with Snap Captain Dominique Ryan. Kelly?"

CHAPTER TWO

WHEN THEY broke for commercial, Aubrey let his smile relax and eased back in his chair. Samira, their makeup and hair tech, swooped in to check for strays, casting sideways glances at Overton every now and again.

Aubrey didn't blame her. Their animosity had to be obvious, and she'd only just met Aubrey. She couldn't exactly ask him about it. But maybe she was judging whether she could ask Overton.

Probably not, he decided, if his own read of his cohost could be trusted. The guy was shut down, mask in place. Handsome but unapproachable.

Aubrey didn't know what he'd expected. More professionalism, yeah. And a smile wouldn't have killed the guy. A little more recognition— *the figure skater*, really? Aubrey was vain, all right. He liked to know people recognized him and his accomplishments. He liked to be looked at—not just looked at but checked out the way he'd checked out Overton. Not lecherous but appreciative. Aubrey couldn't help that Overton was his type.

Married, though, he reminded himself. Like a model gay. Straight-passing haircut, conservative suit.

Ass that wouldn't quit.

Still, some show of solidarity might be nice.

Maybe they just got off on the wrong foot. Aubrey'd had a day or two to get used to the idea of being on the program with Nate, but according to Carl, Nate hadn't even known Jess fired John until this afternoon. Maybe he was pissed she'd left him out of the loop, and Aubrey being in the know just made it worse.

"Hey," he said tentatively as Samira shifted over to Nate. "Look, I'm sorry if, uh, you were expecting someone else or whatever." Hell, Aubrey would be surprised he'd gotten this gig too, if he hadn't filled in for John once before.

Overton didn't look at him—couldn't, as Samira was touching up his makeup.

"Sixty seconds!"

"Who else would I have been expecting?"

Aubrey shrugged. "I don't know, maybe one of your old hockey buddies wanted the job. Hockey's an old boys' club. I know how it works."

Overton scoffed. "You don't know Jess, obviously."

"Hey, she let John Plum sit in that chair for eight years despite the excrement that spewed out of his mouth—"

"Forty seconds!"

When Nate didn't react, Aubrey pushed on. He didn't want his cohost to hate him. "I'm just saying, I didn't mean to step on any toes, but I also didn't get here through nepotism. I'm good at this job, if you think you can unclench long enough for me to prove it."

A muscle worked in the corner of Overton's jaw. Aubrey bet he ground his teeth at night. Probably drove his husband nuts. "If you're done insulting me—"

Samira finished with him and scampered off. He reached for the water bottle the PA held out.

"Insulting—?" Damn it, where had Aubrey gone wrong? Did Nate think Aubrey was implying *he'd* gotten the job through nepotism? Talk about delicate. "Excuse me for trying to make conversation. You know, you could stand to loosen up," Aubrey said, then added under his breath, "Someone needs to get laid."

The set went dead quiet, and Aubrey remembered for the first time in twenty seconds that he was wearing a hot mic. Everyone had heard him.

The blood drained not just from his face but from the entire upper half of his body. *Fuck* his stupid temper and his own sensitivity about being overlooked. Fuck, fuck, *fuck*.

The PA called, "Thirty seconds!"

Overton took a long, deep breath. He didn't look at Aubrey. "We have an update on the Nielsen situation?"

Gina answered from just off camera. "Bob McKenzie is reporting the ask is Simmonds and a second-round pick. Not sure if they're going to take the bait yet."

"Keep refreshing his Twitter feed and get ready to call him if this goes through. I want a soundbite."

"Ten seconds!"

Aubrey couldn't even open his mouth to apologize, not that Overton would look at him anyway. Not that Aubrey *blamed* him. Shit, was he going to ignore Aubrey unless the camera was on? That would make this even more uncomfortable. Probably only for the next two hours or so, though. Good thing Aubrey didn't actually need this job.

The show's theme played, and the teleprompter counted down the seconds to air. Aubrey sat up straight again. If this was going to be his only show, he at least wanted it to be an entertaining one. "Welcome back to *The Inside Edge*. I'm Aubrey Chase. If you're just tuning in, the Chicago Snap leads Toronto 2-1. Puck drops for the second in five minutes. Meanwhile, around the league...."

They played a few clips from yesterday's and tonight's games, including the Colorado-Dallas shocker, and Aubrey managed to find the same reserves of professionalism that let him get up and keep skating when he missed a jump, even though inside he was dying.

"I expect the Stars will announce a partnership with Cuisinart, as the coach gets out the line blender at the first sign of trouble," Aubrey quipped.

Apparently Nate didn't find that to be terribly substantive, but instead of trying to make an in-depth response, he just went with, "The line blender works." Yawn. Boring.

Aubrey couldn't let it go. "Yes, turning a 5-0 deficit into a 5-4 regulation loss is progress which—let me check—you still get *zero* points for."

"And those are points the Avalanche need more than the Stars now," Nate asserted. Was this guy joking? It was the second week of October. A little early for the playoffs race. But he doubled down with, "Let's pull up the Central Division standings."

It was going to be a long night.

NATE WAS still bristling when he closed the door to Jess's office behind him.

Jess raised an eyebrow and gestured to the chair in front of her desk as she lowered herself into her own. "Have a seat, Nate."

She was playing it cool, so Nate was probably about to have his ass handed to him for being a dick. And he probably deserved it. Who the hell talked about the points race not even two weeks into the season?

People who were so disoriented from having their show rearranged immediately after their divorce they didn't know which way was up, that was who.

He sat.

But instead of taking him to task for the clusterfuck of an episode, or even better, addressing Aubrey's heinously inappropriate comment, she just asked, "How was Houston?"

Damn it. Nate slumped in his chair and rubbed a hand over his face. He could feel the makeup smearing. He should've taken it off first. Instead he'd sat in his dressing room, stewing.

"That good, huh?" Jess said sympathetically.

Nate pulled his hand away and drew a deep breath. "I mean, what do you want me to say, here? I went. I signed the papers. It was a long time coming."

"It's less about what I want you to say and more about what *you need* to say." Jess loved to pull lines like that, ones that sounded straight out of a Psych 100 class. Unfortunately she actually meant them.

Even more unfortunately, Nate fell for it every time. "Marty's getting married." It didn't hurt exactly. It didn't feel *good*—the ink hadn't even touched their divorce papers when Marty made the announcement—but they'd been separated for years. Nate didn't love him anymore.

But seeing his ex comfortable in his gorgeous new house with his gorgeous new husband-to-be, getting ready to start the family he'd put off having with Nate—Nate was never home, he said; they could wait until Nate retired, he said, except somehow they never made it that far—okay, Nate could admit it. It hurt.

"Ouch." Jess winced. "And then I sprung these changes on you while you were gone. I thought I was giving you time and space to sort out some personal things, but I should've called. Are you okay?"

No, Nate thought. He was thirty-six and he'd spent the best years of his life with a man who'd left him as soon as Nate started being home more often. He'd done everything right, and it hadn't mattered in the end.

"I'm fine," he lied. "Let's talk about the show." Because yes, she should've called, though he knew why she hadn't. The internet gave people a forum to show their whole asses, John had done it, and Jess had to react to that in a certain period of time or risk being seen as endorsing his behavior. And obviously she didn't want to bother him while he was taking personal time to *get a divorce*. The timing just… sucked.

"Wow, you really don't want to talk about it." Jess shook her head. "Fine, let's talk about the show. You want to tell me what your problem is? I could tell you had a chip on your shoulder even before it all went truly to hell. I thought you'd be grateful to get rid of John, move up to the lead role."

"I am. But is Aubrey Chase the right guy to replace him?"

For a long moment, Jess held herself absolutely still, inscrutable. Then she slowly leaned back in her chair. "You know I can't comment on the discussion I had with him, but I promise you that I've addressed it, and if it happens again, he's gone, no questions."

In his three years in the industry, Nate had heard a lot of horror stories. "Thanks." Aubrey didn't strike him as that kind of problem—more like a guy who sometimes had trouble holding his tongue—but it comforted him to know Jess had his back.

"I'm more concerned about his qualifications," she went on shrewdly. "You think he doesn't know hockey?"

"I'm just saying—I know John had to go, he was awful, I hated working with him. But we already alienated a lot of people when we got rid of him, and now...."

"Now I've replaced a conservative windbag with a flamboyant figure skater?" Jess suggested.

Nate had to be on the only mainstream sports news show with two gay hosts—and probably the only gay guy to question whether that was the right decision. And he couldn't figure out how to object without feeling like an asshole. Without *being* an asshole.

"Look, we're not alienating anyone by hiring Aubrey that we didn't already piss off when we let John go."

With a slow exhale, Nate admitted to himself she probably had a point. But in the meantime, Nate's divorce was bound to become a minor news item in the near future now that they'd signed the paperwork, and he knew it wouldn't take much for people to jump on Aubrey as a possible reason. Marty and his new fiancé weren't famous; they'd easily fly under the radar.

People online will think we're dating and that annoys me would not fly as a legitimate objection, unfortunately. "All right," he said finally.

"And we're hoping to tap into a new market," she reminded him. "Young, left-leaning viewers who are tired of hockey being an old boys' club"—he wondered if she were throwing Aubrey's words back at him intentionally—"and want a little less xenophobia with their sports commentary. Not to mention Aubrey's got a horde of Twitter followers from his skating days, and hey, maybe they'll follow a new sport if we get a hip, hot, visibly gay athlete to feed it to them."

"You're a mercenary," Nate said glumly, nonplussed at the implication that he was neither hip nor visibly gay. Then, "Things are that bad?" Because he loved this show, but with video-streaming services on the rise, with entertainment budgets in the tank, advertising revenue took a hit, and so did their profit margins.

For the first time, he noticed the dark circles under her eyes. He'd been so involved in his own problems he hadn't even seen them. "Things aren't great. But that's why we're making changes, okay?"

He nodded, mostly because he could tell she needed him to believe her for now. "Yeah, of course. I trust you." And if the show flopped, it wasn't like he'd be out on his ass. He hadn't been the best-paid hockey player of all time, but he'd played professionally for over a decade and managed to avoid major financial disaster. He didn't need to work. "Just keep me posted, okay?"

"Promise," Jess said, flashing a quick, brittle smile. "All right, that's it. Get out of here. Let's go home."

CHAPTER THREE

MIRACULOUSLY, AUBREY did not get fired, even if, as he stood on the sidewalk waiting for his Lyft ride, he could still hear Jess's clipped words ringing in his ears.

Or maybe that was his phone.

He barely glanced at the caller ID before picking up just as his car arrived. He got in and confirmed his destination with the driver.

"Jackson," he said finally, doing a little mental math. Just after ten thirty on the West Coast. "Shouldn't you be on the ice right now?" They'd been giving score updates during the show.

"Game's over. We won. No points for me, but Fishy scored on a penalty shot, so I ducked out while everyone was talking to him to call my best boy. How'd it go?"

Aubrey leaned back in his seat and stared at the ceiling of the car. "Well, Jess Chapel didn't pull me into her office immediately after the show and fire me, so I guess it wasn't that bad." She did bawl him out for inappropriate conduct, though, which he deserved enough that her anger actually made him feel better.

"What! Man, I am glad I set my DVR. What did you do?"

Aubrey explained in as much detail as he dared while sitting in the back seat of a car where he might be recorded. Fortunately the drive only took a few minutes at this time of night, so by the time Aubrey was waving goodbye to the driver, he'd only just gotten to the good part.

"And I just kept... trying to make conversation, but it was like talking to a wall, like the guy had the world's biggest chip on his shoulder. So I figured, fuck it, he doesn't want to talk." He waved to his doorman as he went inside. "And that would've been fine! Okay! But it was my first day of work, and I was kind of hoping to actually get along with my cohost, and when I got frustrated I, uh, I did something dumb."

There was a pause as Jackson digested this. Aubrey thought he was thinking about what Aubrey might have said—it wasn't a secret that Aubrey hated to be ignored, and while Aubrey had been working on how he handled that, sometimes he backslid—but instead Jackson asked,

"You managed to piss off Nathan Overton?" His voice hit a register that indicated extreme incredulity. "That guy is *so nice*."

Oh hell. "You *know* him?"

"Yeah, didn't I tell you? We did that PowerPowder Camp—God, that must've been, what, six years ago? I was still green as grass, couldn't keep weight on to save my life. Donut gave me a couple tips, helped me get the hang of altitude training."

Ugh, of course. He was probably a super nice guy if you didn't try to flirt with him. Now Aubrey felt like even more of an asshole.

He couldn't even enjoy that Jackson had called him *Donut*. "Great."

"So what the hell did you do?"

Aubrey sighed as he stabbed the button for the elevator. "I... may have implied that he needed to... loosen up some."

This time the pause held a note of definite horror. "Aubrey. What did you say?"

"I said he needed to get laid. On a hot mic with the whole production staff listening in."

"Jesus. You're lucky you didn't get fired."

Aubrey nodded glumly. The elevator began to climb. "Yeah. That's what Jess said too." He ran a hand through his hair, tugging at the ends in leftover frustration. "He just got under my skin. And in my defense, I mean, can I be honest, Jacks? The man is insanely hot. He should *not* be that uptight. Like, does this guy's husband have his legs glued together or—"

"You're not helping your case, here, buddy."

The elevator stopped at his floor, and Aubrey groaned and rubbed at his face as he stepped out. "I know. Anyway. I think the show itself went fine. It was just everything else that was godawful."

"That's something, at least. Hey—" Jackson's voice went indistinct for a handful of moments, and Aubrey could hear a few other people talking in the background.

"Nakamura, let's go! Fishy says you're buying!"

"—we're gonna go out to celebrate, but I'll hit you up tomorrow after I watch your debut?"

"At least I didn't fall on my ass doing a triple axel."

"If you'd done that, I'd be watching it tonight, I promise."

"Thanks for the support, asshole. Have a drink for me."

"With a fruity little umbrella."

That was Jackson's drink. Aubrey unlocked his apartment. "Go. I'm gonna shower and crash." Maybe by the time he poured himself into bed, he'd have forgiven himself enough to get some sleep.

NATE WOKE up determined that he'd make it an improvement on the day before. "Could hardly be worse," he muttered to himself as he stumbled bleary-eyed into the shower. Last night he'd been so hyped up over the divorce, the flight, the show, and not least, his maddening new cohost, that it had taken him ages to fall asleep.

On the upside, his apartment had a great bathroom with a huge shower and fantastic water pressure. Nate had thought more than once that he could spend an hour in it, especially if he had some handsome company.

Nate could hear the words again—*someone needs to get laid*—and he could imagine Aubrey's smirking mouth saying them. God, he'd like to wipe the smirk right off that pretty, petty face.

Something stirred in Nate's groin as he thought about Aubrey's face, and he froze before he could do anything he'd regret. Lust for his asshole coworker was the *last* thing he needed. He turned the temperature a bit cooler and hurried through the rest of his shower. Coffee. *Coffee* was what he needed. Coffee and some fresh air.

He knew the perfect location for coffee, and not just coffee now that he was past his PowerPowder and nutrition-plan days. As long as he could control himself enough that his suits fit, he could have an almond croissant or two. Or four.

The cafe was less than two blocks from the building, a totally pleasant walk when the weather was good, and today the sun was shining. A newsstand out front featured a spinner rack of trashy novels. Nate could spend the morning stuffing his face with carbs and his brain with spy stories and he'd feel better by lunchtime.

He accomplished the first two parts of his plan—pastry and coffee to go—without a hitch, but while he was choosing a book, he heard an irritatingly familiar voice.

"Good morning, Roger!"

"Aubrey! I have a new flavor today—cinnamon cappuccino! You want to try?"

"How could I not do the classic iced mocha?" Aubrey said, and Nate heard Aubrey walk down the aisle toward the refrigerator case. He held the copy of *Adventure in Andalusia* in front of his face as he ducked behind the newspaper display. He waited there like a coward—no, like someone healthily avoiding conflict before the first meal of the day— while Aubrey and Roger discussed the apparent virtues of cold canned coffees. Nate shuddered as he tried to sip his latte quietly.

After what seemed like a ridiculous amount of time, Aubrey left the shop. Nate dawdled a minute longer, then checked out so he could head back home. But when he turned the corner outside the shop, he stopped short.

Aubrey was a few yards in front of him, window-shopping and sipping from his can of "coffee." He looked back and met Nate's eyes before Nate could decide whether to turn around and walk the long way around the block to get back to his apartment. "Done hiding?" Aubrey asked, and Nate went from embarrassed to pissed off in half a second. Nate was almost impressed. Even his ex-husband usually needed more than two words to inspire that kind of turnaround.

"Done stalking me?" he sniped back, because if Aubrey knew he was there, he wasn't exactly innocent.

Aubrey absorbed this rebuttal with a neutral expression, then blinked, inhaled deeply, and rolled his shoulders. "Let me try that again, okay? Good morning, Nate."

Nate eyed him suspiciously. "Good morning." Though it hadn't been good so far, between his shower frustration and now this. And he still hadn't gotten to eat his pastries; they were cooling in the bag even now.

Aubrey dropped his gaze to the sidewalk and then looked up and met Nat's eyes. "Look, I just need to apologize. I was so out of line yesterday. It was unprofessional of me, and I'm sorry."

For a moment Nate couldn't think of anything to say. He hadn't expected an apology, much less a sincere one. "Okay," he finally said when he realized Aubrey was waiting for verbal confirmation that Nate had heard him.

"Okay," Aubrey repeated, some of the tension visibly melting out of him. "That's all I wanted to say. I know making comments about a coworker's sex life isn't okay, and it won't happen again. I promise I'm normally better at keeping my foot out of my mouth."

Nate felt his lips twitching in amusement despite his poor mood. "Yeah, isn't that a move figure skaters practice?"

Aubrey barked out a laugh, the smile transforming his face into something kind and almost magnetic. "So you do know who I am."

Aubrey was a two-time Olympian. Yeah, Nate knew who he was. "My mom used to love watching you skate." Nate didn't watch figure skating as a rule, but he couldn't say he'd exactly torn himself away from the screen when Aubrey skated either. He'd exuded some kind of forbidden allure in his flamboyant, sparkling costumes and glittery, overdramatic eye makeup.

By mutual unspoken agreement, they had begun to walk back toward Nate's apartment. "I could totally send her an autograph," Aubrey offered. "Token of goodwill."

Nate couldn't decide if that was sweet or narcissistic. Both? His mother would love it, though, and it might forestall some of her nagging about Nate's unpleasant on-air attitude. "I'll think about it." But he didn't want to soften up *too* much. He needed to keep this professional. Which, speaking of—he belatedly added, "Thanks."

"Seriously, it wouldn't be any trouble." Aubrey swung in a wide arc around a woman pushing a double-wide stroller. Nate increased his pace to catch up. "If you want to come up, I can—"

Oh no. "Come up?" Nate interrupted, his stomach dropping.

"Yeah." Aubrey gestured to the building behind him. "I've got a folder full of professional shots somewhere. You can pick one out and I'll personalize it. 'Dear Mrs. Nate's Mom, Sorry I made inappropriate sexual comments about your kid. Enjoy this glossy testament to self-centeredness.'"

Nate said, "You live here?"

"Yes?" Aubrey frowned. "If you don't want the picture, just say so. You're not going to hurt my feelings." He rubbed his left wrist and then amended, "Much."

No. Nate could not afford to let himself be charmed. It was one thing to make peace with a coworker and another to... just, no. "Since when?"

Now Aubrey was looking at him like he'd just said the Kings had a decent shot at the Cup this year. "Since when are you not going to hurt my feelings?"

"Since when have you lived here?" Nate corrected, exasperated, and tried desperately not to panic. Or smile. Fortunately the impulses almost canceled each other out. "I've never seen you in the elevator or anything."

Aubrey raised his eyebrows. "*You* live here? What floor?"

"Fifteenth."

"Huh." Aubrey shrugged. "I'm on seventeen. I wonder why we've never run into each other." They turned and went into the building, both waving at the doorman.

"Different schedules, probably."

Aubrey acknowledged this with a tilt of his head. "Well, that's changed. No wonder we're running into each other now." Then he quirked his lips. "So. You coming up for that autograph?"

Nate followed him into the elevator and pushed the button for his own floor. Was that an innuendo? Surely not. An autograph was just an autograph. Aubrey had just *apologized* for sexual harassment. He was hardly going to start again. "Ah, no. I think…." Crap, he needed an excuse. Right—he was still holding the bag of pastries with three fingers and his thumb. "Breakfast, and then I'm going to hit the gym." Old habits died hard. Pastries could be added to the diet plan, but he'd feel like lukewarm garbage if he skipped his workout.

With a shrug, Aubrey hit the button for his own floor—so high up he had to swipe his key card. Right, Nate remembered—he hadn't made his money, he'd been born into it. His parents owned a hotel chain or something. "Suit yourself."

The doors closed, and so did Aubrey's mouth. Nate kept quiet too, thinking that this was perhaps the longest elevator ride he'd been on in a while. Every second seemed to stretch endlessly as his sexual frustration ratcheted up along with the floor count.

But finally the doors slid open on his floor, and Nate was free. "See you later," he called over his shoulder.

The doors closed again before he could catch Aubrey's reply.

Inside his apartment, Nate dropped his keys, coffee, and pastries on the console table, left his shoes on the rack, and then crossed the entryway into the living room, where he lay down on the couch and pulled a throw pillow over his face. When screaming into it only half helped, he tossed it onto the floor.

He'd spent the last two years of his marriage convinced he and Marty had low libidos and that it was normal, that they were just getting older and it didn't mean anything. But clearly his dick wasn't as old as he thought it was if it thought getting to know his new cohost better was a good idea.

On the one hand, at least now he knew he wouldn't be walking into a potentially hostile work environment every Tuesday, Thursday, and Saturday. On the other hand, developing a sudden hard-on for his flamboyant coworker seemed like a recipe for disaster. In personality, Aubrey was as far removed from Marty as a gay man could probably get.

Maybe this was some kind of weird psychological divorce phenomenon. After all, Nate didn't exactly go out and meet people. Only rarely did he encounter available gay men in the wild, and his dick had just chosen the first one that had come along. Obviously Nate couldn't act on it. It'd probably go away in a few weeks, anyway.

He groaned and rolled over on the couch, pastries forgotten. "This is your fault," he said in the general direction of the ugly vase on the console table which always reminded him of Marty. They had bought it on their honeymoon in Murano, half drunk on wine, and had somehow managed to have it shipped home in one piece. Now it stood in Nate's living room as a monument to his failures, in case he ever forgot to be humble.

Finally he sighed and got off the couch. His appetite had deserted him, but the gym was still calling. Maybe he could make those pastries his reward for working out instead of jerking off to unwanted fantasies about his coworker.

CHAPTER FOUR

THEY DIDN'T have a show Thursday, preempted by some kind of network special on Michael Phelps or something; Aubrey didn't care enough to pay attention. Instead he took the time to grocery shop, catch up on his Twitter feed, and work out in the gym in his building. Jackson had texted him a blow-by-blow breakdown of the show when he watched yesterday, and Aubrey was pretending to give him the silent treatment for insinuating that Aubrey wanted to get in his cohost's pants. He did—Nate was, like, five-alarm-fire hot, with an absurd shoulder-to-waist ratio and the hockey ass and that carefully clean-cut image that made Aubrey want to mess him up—but Nate was married, and Aubrey was a grown-ass man, and he wasn't going to be a creep. But if he said that to Jackson, Jackson would say "methinks the boy doth protest too much," and then Aubrey would have to fly to Seattle and maim him.

He capped off the day with a trip to his therapist, who handed him a notebook and no-nonsense instructions. "You've got to stop believing everything is about you or has to be about you," she said, waving the book until he took it. "So next time you find yourself getting worked up because you think someone's ignoring you, I want you to write down what other things they might have on their mind. And every time someone spends time with you or does something considerate of you, you're going to write that down too."

Aubrey had thought graduating from high school meant the end of homework, but apparently not. He couldn't exactly say he didn't need to do this work either. He wanted to change, so he accepted the assignment with a mental note to get a really obnoxious sparkly plastic cover for the book.

Friday morning he got a text from a guy he used to train with—free ice time in exchange for a practiced eye and some feedback while he worked up a routine to audition for one of the on-ice Cirque shows in Vegas. In Chicago it wasn't so much about paying for ice time—Aubrey's trust fund handled that—but finding an open slot could be challenging. Besides, he hadn't seen Greg in ages.

Which was how he found himself standing at center ice in a rink that had seen better days, probably sometime in the sixties, judging by the hockey pennants hanging from the rafters. But beggars and choosers, et cetera. The ice was smooth. Aubrey didn't care about anything else.

"So, Cirque, eh?"

Greg barely nodded as he started a warm-up lap of long, elegant backward crossovers. Aubrey kept pace with him easily, neither of them pushing yet. "Too old to compete," Greg said, flicking his gaze at Aubrey and then toward the ceiling.

God, didn't Aubrey know how *that* felt. "Figure skating has completely ruined 'Pretty Young Thing' for me, I'll tell you that."

With a snort, Greg segued into a breezy one eighty, arms outstretched. "Let me shed a tear for you, white boy. Come on. No one's prettier than you," he teased.

"Sorry, I don't fuck straight guys," Aubrey laughed and put on a burst of speed. Three more long strides and he toe-picked into a casual single axel.

"Tuck your arms in, you're sloppy."

Aubrey flipped him the bird. "Do I look like I'm trying to impress you?" He had ice time a couple days a week to stay in shape. Now that he had retired, he got to skate because he *loved* it. Though it admittedly wasn't quite as much fun without thousands of people watching. "What kind of routine are you putting together, anyway?" He caught up to Greg and matched him stride for stride, holding his arms out at his sides to mimic his posture, the way pairs skaters might. "You wanna try some lifts? I might have to hit the gym first." Greg had an inch and probably ten pounds on him, which Aubrey might have been able to handle if he'd ever skated pairs.

"I was thinking something a little less...."

"Gay?" Aubrey offered dryly.

Greg pivoted and kept going backward. "You said it, not me. But I was thinking something Broadway style, maybe? Big gestures, overdrawn emotion, that sort of thing. Plenty to choose from that have two male parts. 'That Guy' from *Blood Brothers*. 'Consider Yourself' from *Oliver!* 'The Confrontation' from *Les Mis*."

Aubrey raised an eyebrow as Greg broke away for a lutz. Not much to critique there; he executed it perfectly. "You made the leap from 'less gay' right to show tunes, huh."

"Hey, no stereotyping."

They finished their warmup, which got competitive about five minutes in, and then took a quick break for water and to scroll through playlists on Greg's phone. Aubrey had a reasonable knowledge of musical theater, but he didn't recognize all the songs, so they cued up a few to listen to while they freestyled.

Before Aubrey knew it, their time ran out—the doors to the locker rooms kept banging open and closed as a hockey team trickled in.

"Cool-down?" Greg suggested. He skated over to his phone to change the playlist.

Aubrey nodded and reached for his water bottle, breathing hard. His muscles sang with exertion, and he imagined happy little exercise endorphins dancing through his veins. Skating didn't feel as good as sex, not by a long shot. But he hadn't exactly been tearing up the club scene lately, and the exertion loosened him up in the same way.

He grinned when Greg changed the playlist over to disco. "You're sure you're straight?" He paused. "Actually, scratch that. Are you sure you're not as old as the kids make you feel?"

Greg threw a sweaty towel at him. "You wanna go, tough guy?" He backed up, making a "bring it" gesture.

Aubrey snorted but put up his fists—all for show—and skated after him anyway. "Have you ever even been in a fight?"

"I was a straight black kid who was into figure skating," Greg said wryly.

"Fair point." Aubrey threw an easy faux punch in time to the beat of "Hot Stuff."

Greg faked taking a hit and went into a camel spin. "What about you?"

"I got in a hockey fight once. I was seven."

"Aww."

Since neither of them had much experience, their "fight" quickly evolved into a dance-off, with "Stayin' Alive" echoing from the speakers as they got increasingly ridiculous. Greg knew all the lyrics. Even Aubrey had to admit he was killing it.

He probably had to add this into the notebook.

When the last strains faded, hoots and applause echoed from the bench. Aubrey broke his dramatic disco pose and looked over to see a mixed group of hockey players tapping their sticks against the boards. He bowed flamboyantly, then motioned to Greg and began to applaud.

Someone whistled. Wait a second—Aubrey recognized that face. "Caley!" He ambled over for a fist bump. "Haven't seen you since PyeongChang." She'd played for Team Canada, so they'd seen each other around the Village. "How's retirement?"

"Eh." She grinned. "Ice time sucks, but the pregame show just got a lot better." She made eyes at Greg, which was hilarious, since Aubrey was pretty sure she was strictly into women.

Oh boy. "You should see us do 'It's Raining Men.'" Greg slid smoothly up next to Aubrey, grinning.

"Might have to take you boys up on that." She cut back to Aubrey and jerked a gloved hand over her shoulder. "We can't all get cushy retirement gigs like you and Donut over here."

Startled, Aubrey followed her gesture and met gazes with a wide-eyed Nate, who looked…. Aubrey took in the suddenly defensive posture, the way he broke Aubrey's gaze to stare over his left shoulder, the bright spots of color on his cheeks when he hadn't even touched the ice yet. He looked *guilty*. "Caught with his hand in the cookie jar" guilty.

Maybe Aubrey shouldn't have said what he said about Nate needing to get laid, but that didn't mean it wasn't true—not if a married man was looking at Aubrey like that.

"Didn't you go into sports medicine?" Aubrey said, mostly to cover that he didn't know what to say to Nate.

"I did, and you're gonna need it if you don't get off the ice and let the Zamboni do its job. Clock's ticking, twinkle toes."

"Hockey players. So bloodthirsty," he teased. But he was grateful for the out. He didn't want to examine how he felt about being the cookies when Nate was on a diet plan. Instead he just nodded to the group and made for the gate. "Guess I'll see you next week."

Mercifully, Greg didn't ask about it as they showered and changed back into street clothes. But Aubrey thought about it all the way back to his apartment, all the way up to his floor, all the way through sorting his laundry and ordering a late dinner and an episode of *Umbrella Academy*.

He was still thinking about it when the delivery guy left and he realized he had no idea what was happening on his show. He sighed and leaned back against the couch, tipping his head up to the ceiling. *Goddammit.*

NATE WAS used to traveling weekends to do an on-site show, but that weekend they stuck around to film an extra episode to make up for the one that was preempted. It gave him time to catch up on his Netflix shows—at least that was what he told himself—but by the time Thursday rolled around, he was so sick of his apartment and his own company he could've screamed. The vase on the console table had entered full-on "Yellow Wallpaper" territory. With its iridescent coloring and oddly irregular shape covered in bulbous protrusions, it reminded him of something a giant squid might have shat out.

He'd made a habit of showing up to set extra early ever since last Tuesday, as if he could somehow make up for previous lateness, and today was no exception. Only today, before he could make it as far as Makeup, Jess poked her head out of her office and beckoned him inside. "Nate! Can I have a minute?"

He followed her in and took the chair across from hers, his stomach sinking. The past few times he'd come in here, the news had not been good. Figuring she'd called him in to chew him out for his on-air animosity with Aubrey, he braced himself and asked, "What's up?"

"Ratings, actually."

Nate blinked in an attempt to mask his surprise. He and Aubrey barely managed a veneer of civility on the air. He'd figured viewers would find it juvenile. "That's good, right?"

"It's great." Jess leaned back in her chair and raised her ever-present coffee mug in a toast. "I can't believe you bit your tongue around John for three years and Aubrey Chase is the one who makes you lose it, but thank God you never got to be friends."

"People really enjoy us going after each other that much?"

Jess shrugged. "Guess so. Maybe they miss hockey fights and this is their replacement. I have to say, I personally prefer it to the blood." She set her coffee mug down and picked up her tablet, which she handed across the table. "Voila."

Nate looked down to see… a screenshot from the station's Twitter account. Nothing stuck out to him as being particularly noteworthy. "What's this?"

"*That* is a list of trending hashtags in Chicago last weekend. You booted the Bears right off the map. Which, considering how often and how vocally people complain about the Bears, is impressive."

Sure enough, in the right-hand column, #InsideEdge proclaimed in bold blue letters that yes, people were talking about them, though Nate still wondered why. "That's great, I guess."

"Oh, *you guess*. Yes, it's great. Swipe left, check out what the critics are saying."

@EndicottFleetman—If you thought the departure of John Plum meant there was nothing worth watching on hockey TV, check out this clip from The Inside Edge. These guys have it.

Below was a video. Nate tapped the icon to play it.

"First we have the Maple Leafs, who, despite a third-period push, weren't able to overcome the Sabres' defense—" That was Nate.

"Or the frankly terrible officiating." The camera panned over to Aubrey, who was rolling his eyes. Nate hadn't caught that before, but he had noticed Jess holding two thumbs up. Nate had rolled with that.

"An odd complaint, since Buffalo and Toronto each received three minors in the last frame." Nate smiled his most professional, confident smile at the camera.

"Buffalo—too many men, delay of game, and oh, a face-off violation in the O-zone, but nothing for cross-checking or slashing when Toronto got called for poltergeist activity." In contrast to Nate's demeanor, Aubrey was smirking. At the time it had been annoying, but now, seeing it like their audience, Nate had to admit it was engaging, even funny, with Aubrey playing the snarker and Nate the straight man.

"Poltergeist activity?"

"I'm not sure what else you call goaltender interference that isn't observable on this plane of existence. Maybe the ref has an e-meter?"

Nate had looked directly at the camera. "While my cohost auditions for *Ghost Hunters*, why don't the rest of us check out that no-goal. Roll the tape."

The video ended and Nate saw the number of likes and retweets. He couldn't remember any of his clips with John getting this kind of attention. He was still worried people were going to see this chemistry and assume they were sleeping together, but he couldn't do anything about that. He *could* continue doing what he was doing and maybe save the show.

Nate put the tablet back on the table. "So we're off the chopping block?"

"I—"

A rapid knock at the door interrupted, and a second later, Bob poked his head in. He flicked his gaze over Nate and then seemed to dismiss him. "Hey, boss. You got a minute? I have the breakdown for the new ad-space projections I need to go over."

Nate turned back toward Jess so he could safely roll his eyes. She met his gaze with a flat look and tilted her head. Nate guessed they wouldn't be getting anything else accomplished today, since Bob had a tendency to hijack meetings without regard for other people getting work done, specifically in situations that didn't include him.

"We'll finish up later?" Nate offered, trying to save Jess the trouble of trying to walk the line between being nice and telling Bob to take a hike. "I should get to Makeup anyway."

Jess's expression said she'd have preferred to tell Bob to take a hike, but they both knew he'd sulk for three days. "Go," she said. "Put a tack on Aubrey's chair or something. Or maybe pretend he put one on yours."

After seeing that eye roll, Nate wouldn't have to pretend to be annoyed. "See you on set."

CHAPTER FIVE

LIVING IN a single place rather than following a competition circuit might have felt weird if Aubrey didn't spend most weekends traveling for a game. A set work schedule that had him at the office at the same time two nights a week felt strange too; until recently he'd been training six days a week. Suddenly he had all this *time*—entire days he didn't have to be anywhere or do anything.

Part of him wanted to ask Nate how he handled it. He figured it must have been the same for him when he retired from playing. But then he reminded himself that it had taken an entire week to talk Nate into carpooling to work with him, so probably that was too personal a question.

At least the show seemed to be doing well.

Congrats, you're a meme! Jackson texted, along with a variety of fireworks emojis and a party hat. A GIF followed—first a clip of an opposing player catching up to a Bruin with the puck behind the net in Boston's defensive zone, picking his pocket, and scoring, then a cut to Aubrey: *At least one of these guys is gonna end up in the harbor.*

Aubrey snorted, amused. *Wow, now I've really made it.*

The phone rang a minute later. "Dude, like three different guys have made me promise they get to do the interview with you when we play Chicago next," Jackson told him over the phone, laughing. "Do you know how much these assholes hate talking to the media?"

Aubrey did not know, but when he asked Nate on the way to the studio one night, "Who would you rather have for a phone interview—Jean-Marc Poisson, Jordie Hamilton, or Nikita Namestnikov?" Nate looked at him like he was crazy.

"None of those guys is going to give us an interview."

So apparently Aubrey had an ace up his sleeve the next time they covered Seattle. Maybe he could talk Jess into doing a panel interview or something.

When he brought it up with her—his first time alone in her office since his royal chewing-out—she seemed interested in the idea but distracted. Aubrey wondered if their numbers were still struggling. He knew they wouldn't have dropped John and brought him on if the situation were anything but dire.

"That's not a bad idea, actually. You know, I always expected Nate would be the one using his contacts for ideas like this," Jess mused.

"Technically I think they're using me, this time around. I guess we have fans."

That got a smile, albeit one that didn't quite reach her eyes. He probably still had a way to go earning back her trust. "Wonders never cease."

Aubrey managed a weak smile back, but his curiosity got the better of him. "Look, I know my contract says you don't have to tell me anything about the show, but… is everything okay?"

She opened her mouth to answer—or maybe to tell him off for being nosy—but before she could say anything, her cell phone rang. The contact on the screen was Larry Melchor, the owner of the network. Aubrey wondered if that was an answer in and of itself.

"Sorry, he'll just call back six more times if I don't answer," Jess said, and she did actually sound apologetic.

"Sure." Aubrey backed toward the door, tamping down the impulse to feel sad. Jess wasn't ignoring him; she just had important things to do, and the show was still in trouble. "I'll see myself out." Maybe he'd stop at the coffee shop downstairs and grab pastries for the ride home. He could get his dose of appreciation from Nate instead.

But despite his occasional worries about his job, as the weeks passed, Aubrey fell into a comfortable routine—work, skating with Greg, skating by himself. On his off days, he checked out museums or went shopping or explored the city. If the weather sucked, he put his headphones in and went downstairs to the building's pool and swam laps until his legs felt like jelly. He went out clubbing a couple times, but he didn't connect with anyone, and the whole process just brought home to him that his friends had scattered across the globe, either still competing or working as coaches, and the closest thing he had to a gay friend in Chicago was Nate.

That thought didn't quite horrify him, but it didn't comfort him either. Maybe he shouldn't look too closely at his life.

Fortunately he still had Greg, even if he was tragically heterosexual.

"You are such a diva," Greg said fondly from the bench, where he was running a new set of laces through a skate after the old ones had snapped.

"I was a professional goddamn figure skater." Aubrey let that sink in as he scrolled through Greg's phone for a song he wanted—it'd take him a few minutes to gear back up, and Aubrey didn't waste ice time. "At the risk of making myself sound exactly as old as I actually am, duh."

And then he passed the perfect song and thought, *Yes*.

He took a lap around the ice as a typical cheesy eighties synth intro played, and then he caught Caley's eye as she came to the bench. She'd been coming earlier and earlier to watch the show, because her team somehow always had the time slot right after theirs, even though the league had four teams—and he swung by the bench and borrowed her stick.

"Diva!" Greg shouted.

Aubrey flipped him off and skated away with his makeshift microphone to go be ridiculous.

"Oh my God," Caley shouted when the lyrics started. "Is this from *The Cutting Edge*?"

Aubrey ignored her as he tried to work out how to do a lutz while holding a hockey stick. He managed not to fall, somehow, but didn't think he'd quite achieved *graceful*. Room for improvement. Greg and Caley catcalled and cheered anyway.

Truth told, while Aubrey had seen the movie a handful of times, he only half remembered the lyrics to the song. Fortunately it didn't much matter. A double axel later and he managed to knock the stick out of his own hands, sending it clattering to the ice, so he improvised thirty seconds' worth of program and then went down on one leg to shoot the duck, snagging the stick off the ice as he came up right at the chorus of "Feels Like Forever."

A crowd had gathered now, probably drawn by Greg and Caley's laughter. The sound of it made Aubrey grin, remembering what he loved about performing live. He loved doing the show with Nate, but it wasn't the same as entertaining people in person.

As much fun as he was having, though, the song didn't suit him as a skater—a little too slow, not enough energy. In the slower sections, Aubrey found himself bored and thought, well, what the hell. Suddenly, instead of figure skating, he shifted into a hockey stance, a little clumsy since he hadn't played a real game in almost two decades and Caley's stick was left-handed. He burned rubber for the imagined offensive zone, pulled the stick back—

—caught a blade and went down chest-first, sliding on his belly like a penguin.

"Toe pick!" someone shouted, and Aubrey knew without looking it had to be Nate. He wouldn't have thought he had enough air in his lungs to laugh, but he did anyway, raising his arm weakly to show he was okay and also to shoot Nate the finger. That fucker.

When he picked himself up off the ice, he got a mixed reception of applause and stick taps. But the thing that made his cheeks go pink was the way Nate looked at him, straight in the eyes for once, his face pulled into an expression of fond amusement.

He's married, Aubrey reminded himself, and the flush faded as he stepped off the ice.

"SO, YOU think this is the one?" Greg asked as they sat at a cafe after their skate one morning. Aubrey had offered to share his ice time now that they were really gearing up for the audition. Greg was poking at an enormous cobb salad. Sucked to be him. Aubrey had the best burger in the city.

"It has good energy, very dynamic." Aubrey dipped a fry in ketchup and gestured with it. "Once we nail the timing, I think it's the perfect program—dynamic and fun, technical without being stuffy."

Greg looked longingly at Aubrey's burger and speared a piece of boiled egg. He chewed, then put down his fork and said, "I agree. And since you bring up stuffy—"

Aubrey glanced at him, betrayed. "Who talked?"

"Freddie. He said you went out dancing with the crew but, and I quote, 'his head wasn't in the game.'" Greg methodically shoveled in a mouthful of lettuce. When he'd swallowed, he said, "Your head is literally always in the game, so naturally he thinks you're dying."

"Nice," Aubrey said dryly. Of course his… *friends* was too strong a word for the crew he went dancing with, since they only ever met to go hook up. Anyway, of course Freddie sold him out.

"So are you? Dying?"

Aubrey spitted him with a withering glare. "Eat your salad."

"See, I would, but I'm invested now. And anyway, isn't the phrase 'toss—'"

"You're hilarious." Aubrey picked up his burger and took an impossibly large bite, as much for an excuse to pause the conversation as because it was delicious.

"It's just not like you," Greg said, lifting a shoulder as he looked back down at his plate. "Forgive me for my concern if all of a sudden sex doesn't interest you." He stopped then, and Aubrey thought maybe he was going to stick in another mouthful of lettuce and let the subject drop, but when he looked over, Greg wasn't even holding his fork. "Or maybe...."

Oh boy. "Maybe what?" Aubrey asked in resignation.

"Maybe you're getting it somewhere else, and you don't need to go clubbing."

"I wish," Aubrey said reflexively, and then thought, *Oh damn.*

Greg's face lit up like a Christmas tree, and he pushed his salad away, perhaps with a little too much glee. "I knew it! You are screwing Nate Overton!"

"What!" Aubrey squawked. "He barely even likes me!"

"Come on, Aubrey. I watch the show the same as any other hockey fan. You're really gonna tell me there's nothing there?"

Fuck. Aubrey thought he'd had a better lid on his stupid crush than this. "He's *married*," he pointed out. "I know I'm not exactly Captain Discretion, but I'm not an adulterer." Ugh, that sounded so... biblical. "Adulter-ee? Accomplice to adultery?" Maybe he could distract Greg with semantics.

"Okay, so you're not fucking him," Greg said easily. Too easily, it turned out, because the next thing out of his mouth was "Doesn't mean you don't want to."

Aubrey mulishly swiped a few fries through his pile of ketchup and mowed them down. He wasn't owning up to that, not to Greg, anyway. "That's not...." He wiped his greasy fingers on a napkin. "It just doesn't...."

Greg waited him out. *Asshole.*

Fine. "I want more than just a hookup, okay?" Aubrey bit out, and then found himself shocked into silence.

He'd intended it to be a lie. He didn't want to talk about Nate, and he'd have said anything to get Greg to back off. Only it turned out he'd stumbled onto an inconvenient truth, and now he was having trouble catching his breath.

Because he did want more than a hookup. Not necessarily with Nate, though Nate was hot and fun to talk to when he could be coerced to remember Aubrey existed outside of work. But in general—he wanted someone to share his life, someone who'd pay attention to him even when he wasn't his best, someone he could show off for and spoil.

Aubrey pushed his plate away too.

Greg looked from Aubrey's face, which felt like it must have gone a bit gray, to his plate, and grimaced in sympathy. "Sorry, man. I should've waited till you finished your burger."

"Just for that, you can pick up the tab," Aubrey said, injecting as much levity as he could.

Greg didn't push further.

THAT WEEK took them to Houston. To his surprise, Nate was actually looking forward to it. Now that he was able to associate the city with just work and hockey instead of home and Marty, he felt much better about it. Given a late schedule change, the network gave *The Inside Edge* an extra half hour before the game.

"Okay, let's take a few to figure out what we're going to do with this." Jess had them crammed into a tiny conference room in the arena. Next to her were Bob from marketing and her boss, Larry, who never looked completely pleased even when Jess was giving him good numbers. He'd always been nice enough to Nate, but there was something squirrelly about him that Nate didn't like.

Bob immediately produced something from his jacket pocket with a flourish. He held up a small tube. "As it happens, Crotchguard is co-sponsoring a ball-hockey tournament in Houston next week, and as they are one of our largest advertisers, I think a short segment would be in order."

Nate noticed Aubrey's jaw drop slightly before he regained his usual composure. Nate wondered if Aubrey was wondering the same thing Nate was: did Bob carry samples of all their sponsors' products on his person or did he just need—no, better not go there.

Aubrey shot him a sideways glance and raised an eyebrow as if reading Nate's mind.

"Great idea," Jess said. "We'll send Dev or Kelly, but that'll take no more than five. What else we got?"

"How about a segment on grading the last expansion draft?" Nate suggested.

Aubrey nodded. "Sure. We could call it 'And Yet More Mistakes by Edmonton.'"

"I was going to go with 'New Horizons in Fuck-uppery,' but yours is more professional." Nate grinned at him and then looked back at Jess with a bland smile.

"On the other hand, Dallas—"

"Totally fleeced them by making an overaged Russian with a bad hip look like—"

"Pavel Datsyuk?"

Unbelievable.

Despite their trading barbs on-air, a lot—most, maybe—of their opinions actually aligned. Nate could admit that he'd been playing it up a bit, at first because Aubrey irritated him, then because the audience loved it. But more recently Nate had to admit it was just *fun.*

Aubrey knew his shit, and he was clever, willing to make a hit, but he seemed to delight in taking them almost as much. Nate hadn't had this much fun at work since he was playing professional hockey. If he had to pretend not to enjoy getting into it with Aubrey for an audience that was eating up their fake dichotomy, so be it.

After the game, when they'd wrapped the postgame comments, Nate took off his headset and checked his phone. As promised, Bonesy had texted him—twice. The first was what he was expecting:

Meet us at O'Malleys?

But the next one definitely wasn't:

Big G says bring Aubrey. Thinks he's hilarious.

Fuck. It wasn't like Nate could say no to one of his favorite former teammates. Or, well, he could, but he didn't want to lie. Bones had a very sensitive bullshit detector.

I'll tell him. Meet you there. Looking fwd to seeing everyone.

Nate hoped they'd have a good crowd so on the off chance Aubrey wanted to come along, he and Nate could each do their own thing.

Aubrey did come, but their large group spilled almost the length of the bar. Nate sat beside Bonesy at one end, while Aubrey took the far corner between a recently acquired winger Nate didn't know well and

Kaden, a young D-man who was living up to the promise he'd shown when Nate was with the team. Kaden and Aubrey were talking, so Nate should have been able to forget Aubrey was there, but he couldn't resist checking to make sure Aubrey wasn't being obnoxious or inappropriate. Only the next time he looked down the bar, it was Kaden talking animatedly, gesturing with his hands, and Aubrey listening attentively, head tilted toward him. Apparently Aubrey could be an engaged listener when he was motivated. Nate frowned and tried to focus on his own conversation.

"Anyway, so Amy said a two-seater wasn't practical," Bonesy said. Nate nodded in apparent agreement about a car (probably) while he wondered what a young defenseman from North Dakota could possibly have to say that engaged Aubrey so much.

While Bonesy went on, Nate couldn't help trying to keep up with Kaden and Aubrey. Out of the corner of his eye he saw Kaden's body language shift. He was leaning in toward Aubrey like a sunflower trying to find the light, as if Aubrey were something radiant.

Aubrey wasn't bad-looking. At all. And he was certainly turning on the charm—head tilted, fingers tapping on Kaden's forearm as he made a point about something. He had Kaden enraptured. When Nate caught him flashing a smile, he was reminded of a big bad wolf. It was a little sexy. Nate didn't like it.

"Earth to Nate? Nate, this is Houston, come in." Bonesy waved his hand in front of Nate's face.

"Uh, sorry. Anyway, you were going to buy the Mercedes—"

Bonesy huffed. "Oh no, we're done talking about car shopping, and we've moved on to you and your new coworker."

"What about him?" Nate turned his head as if looking at the conversation down the bar for the first time. He didn't think Bonesy was fooled.

"Well, I don't think Kaden's your type—"

Nate snorted.

"So I gotta go with you're a little preoccupied with slim, dark, and handsome down there."

Nate shook his head. "He's not so handsome," he lied.

"Dude, *I* can tell he's handsome. I'm straight, but I haven't been concussed *that* many times."

"He has a big enough head already."

"Yeah, well, I've met your ex. I know that's not exactly a turn-off for you."

Nate's ears went hot, and he reached for his beer to give himself time to think of a comeback.

He didn't want to sleep with Aubrey really, right? Finding someone attractive wasn't the same as wanting to spend time with him naked.

Plus, there was the show. Jess said their dynamic worked, had brought their numbers up. Nate didn't want to fuck with that. He and Aubrey would be fine if they got canceled, but what about the rest of the crew? He wouldn't jeopardize their livelihood just to get his dick wet.

"It's not like that," Nate protested, but it sounded weak even to his own ears.

Bones raised his eyebrows. "Uh-huh." He leaned his elbows on the table and put his head in his hands, eyes glinting with mischief. He looked like a teenager at a sleepover. "Why don't you tell me what it *is* like."

Nate could tell him to butt out. He probably *should* tell him to butt out. But sitting there at the bar, surrounded by old friends, glancing down the table at where Aubrey had taken the lead in the conversation again and was diagramming something on the table using lowball glasses and stir sticks, he couldn't help himself. He wanted someone to talk to about everything that had happened, and his former captain was as good a therapist as anyone, probably.

"I haven't been single in almost ten years."

He might as well start at the beginning.

Without changing his expression, Bonesy lifted a hand to signal for another round. Nate knew he could count on him. "I get the feeling we're going to need that."

Nate acknowledged it with a tilt of his head. "And even when I was younger, it wasn't… I never got into the whole pickup culture, you know? I never really dated. And then I met Marty, and that was it."

"Uh-huh," Bonesy repeated. The server brought the next round of drinks, and he raised his to his lips but paused before taking a sip. "And now that's over." He sounded sympathetic, but he was also clearly inviting Nate to elaborate.

"Yes!" Nate said, a little too loudly, and he glanced down at his glass and wondered if maybe he shouldn't slow his own pace of drinking, because he'd drawn a bit of attention with that. Even Aubrey had stopped at the end of the table, in the middle of saying something that had his eyes wide and his mouth parted in surprise. Nate quickly looked away again.

When he didn't say anything for a few long moments, Bonesy leaned forward, pitched his voice so it wouldn't carry, and said, "Are you telling me you can't figure out how to fuck someone without any strings?"

"Not exactly. Okay, yes. But that's only part of it." He swirled the ice in his glass as though it would help him order his thoughts. "I never wanted those things before. Or maybe I did but I wouldn't admit it to myself. And now I feel... cheated? But I'm also not sure how to tell if...." He glanced toward Aubrey again. An attractive flush had spread across his face, but he wasn't looking at Kaden anymore; he was staring at his own hands.

Nate took a long drink.

"Let me get this straight." Nate shot Bonesy a look. "Shut up. It's a figure of speech. You want to know if that guy wants to fuck you as much as you want to fuck him. Do you talk to him in person like you do on the air?"

Nate snorted, using his thumb to draw a sad face in the condensation on the glass. "No. I kind of avoid him." He inhaled deeply and made himself hold it for a few seconds before letting it out slowly. "We got off on the wrong foot."

"Never would've guessed," Bones said, dry. "But here's a thought— if you want to know if he's DTF, try it. Your show is a master class of sexual tension."

Nate winced, wondering how to explain that was part of the problem. Once he and Aubrey slept together, that tension would disappear, right? "The thing is, I sort of have instructions, uh, not to make friends."

Bones blinked at him over the top of his glass. "What?"

"My boss, okay, ratings were... suffering with John, and with Aubrey they're not, and she said, and I quote, 'Don't. Change. Anything.'" He smeared the sad face. "What if I screw it up and the show gets canceled?"

Carefully, Bones put his glass down. Then he said, in a clear, slow voice, as though Nate were being particularly obtuse, "Nate. I know your ego is as out of control as any other professional hockey player's. But if the show gets canceled, it's not going to be because you and Mr. Bedroom Eyes gave in to your hormones and got your poles waxed."

Nate didn't have time to respond to this allegation before Bones continued, "You're making excuses because moving on from divorce is hard and you're chickenshit."

Nate's shoulders seemed to recognize the truth of it ahead of his brain, because he felt them slump even before he admitted to himself that Bones had a point. He sighed, spun his glass around on the table, and finally raised his eyes again, looking down the table almost automatically, as though Aubrey really were magnetic—only to find Aubrey looking back at him.

A second later Aubrey looked away, returning his focus to Kaden, but it seemed to Nate as though his heart wasn't really in it.

None of this gave him the slightest idea what to do next. "I hate you," Nate mumbled. "Why couldn't you just tell me to forget about it and move on?"

"Hey, you get what you pay for. You want your head shrunk, get a therapist."

Nate was screwing up his face in a grimace, reaching for something cutting to say, when a wadded-up napkin flew through the air, hit Bonesy in the face, and fell into his glass. The rookies in the center of the table erupted in cheers, and Nate ended up smothering a laugh with one hand lest he inadvertently encourage them.

"Just for that you're picking up our tab," Bones threatened, shaking his head. "And get me another drink."

NATE HAD obviously not expected Aubrey to accept the invitation to drinks with him and his former teammates. Even Aubrey was a little surprised at himself. He'd fucked a couple hockey players, but aside from a few carefully curated outings with Jackson, he didn't spend time with them en masse—too much aggressive heteronormativity. But something about the possibility of seeing Nate in his natural habitat called to him irresistibly. So here he was.

Having, it must be said, a surprisingly pleasant time.

"I don't know, man, call me a weirdo if you want, but there's something about folding your socks and putting them in a drawer to look all nice that's soothing, okay?"

"No, I actually agree," Aubrey said, wondering how the hell he'd gotten into a conversation about Marie Kondo with an NHL defenseman. "It must've taken me an hour to get folding a T-shirt right, though."

"Trial and error," Kaden said, reaching for his mojito. "Hey, you got a picture of your closet?"

They swapped pictures for a few minutes. When Aubrey swiped past a photo of his last trip to the Caymans, Kaden slapped his hand down over Aubrey's.

"Hey, go back to that." He tilted his head toward the phone, which let him look up at Aubrey from under long lashes. Aubrey wondered if Kaden knew how flirtatious that seemed.

"What? I thought we were sharing home organization pics. Me at Seven Mile Beach is a lot less interesting."

"I'll be the judge of that." Kaden flashed a little half-smile, head still tilted coquettishly. "Can I see?

Yeah, that's flirting, consciously or not.

Aubrey pulled up the gallery from the trip and handed his phone to Kaden. Aubrey had gone with two other skaters from Team Canada, so Bianca and Marie-Laure were featured prominently in the pictures. He was curious at what Kaden would have to say about the two beautiful, scantily clad women in the photos.

Turned out, not much.

"Wow, you get really tan!" Kaden stopped and squinted at a photo of a sun-kissed Aubrey in bright yellow swim briefs. "Looks good on you. I mean, not that you look bad without."

Definitely consciously. That was flattering as well as unexpected. It would be easy to respond in kind. Aubrey liked when handsome guys flirted with him, and he liked flirting back. He also liked when he could sense how easy it would be to whisper, *Want to get out of here?* and get a smile and a nod in return.

It was almost as if Kaden had a blinking sign over his head that said *I'll say yes.*

For a moment Aubrey considered it. Kaden was hot and willing, and not giving any sign that he was going to get hung up about hooking up with another guy.

Add to that, the only action Aubrey had been getting lately was his own right hand. Or his left, when he wanted to change it up a little. He looked down at said hands.

Kaden passed the phone back, but his smile had changed. He'd noticed Aubrey's hesitation in flirting back, but he didn't seem disappointed. "Maybe I'll head out that way at the All-Star Break. You can give me tips on where to go."

Where to hook up with other guys, Aubrey heard, and smiled. "Yeah, for sure."

From there the conversation drifted to the show—how Aubrey had ended up subbing in at the last minute, his charged first meeting with Nate, the ups and downs of it since then. Then the server swung by to ask about the next round and the conversation lulled.

"How's he doing, anyway?" Kaden asked, and Aubrey belatedly realized he'd been staring at Nate down the table as he and Bones talked. Had to be interesting, whatever it was, to get Nate looking like that, like he was squirming.

Aubrey would like to make him squirm like that.

Aubrey had apparently had enough alcohol tonight. Maybe he should've told the server he wanted to pay his tab. "I'm sorry?" he said, trying to get his head back in his conversation with Kaden.

"Nate," Kaden said. "I remember what it was like when he and Marty first separated. He was like a zombie, man. He seems a lot better now that the paperwork's all signed, but... you see him every day. What do you think?"

"What do I think?" Aubrey echoed as Kaden's words reverberated in his seemingly empty skull.

"Yeah. I mean, he looks happier now than he did for a long time even before he and Marty split."

Before he and Marty split.

Nate was divorced.

Nate was *divorced*?

"Thank fucking God," Aubrey said. Then he realized he'd said it out loud and glanced sidelong at Kaden. "I mean, it seems like it was a long time coming, but yeah. He's come a long way in the time I've known him." Totally true. Oh *shit*, no wonder Nate got so pissed when Aubrey said he needed to get laid—could Aubrey have said something more insensitive?

"I'm glad." Kaden flicked his gaze down the table, and Aubrey's stomach tightened uncomfortably. Oh no. "Do you know if he's seeing anyone?"

Fuck Aubrey's entire life. "No idea," he managed. "We don't really socialize outside of work." Nate had kept things between them professional most of the time. But he'd slipped on enough occasions that Aubrey wondered, and he'd seen the way Nate looked at him sometimes. Maybe he should push his luck. Sure, he'd more or less just admitted to himself that he wanted something more lasting than a roll in the sheets... but he could put that on hold long enough to satisfy a mutual curiosity.

Right?

CHAPTER SIX

"ANYWAY, THANKS for coming in," Jess said, reaching out to shake Jackson's hand. "It'll be a good segment to run during the game coverage tomorrow."

Jackson smiled back at her. "Sure, it was fun." He elbowed Aubrey in the side, lowering his voice to a tease. "The guys'll be jealous I got to watch part of the show in person."

"You *were* part of the show," Aubrey pointed out, rolling his eyes. With the Kraken in town to play the Hawks, they'd taken the opportunity to have Jackson come in to pretape an interview with him and Nate.

Jackson turned a facetiously patient smile on him. "I was a prop to use in your ongoing banter war," he corrected, "but that's all right. I had a good time, and I think I even helped Donut take you down a peg or two."

"*You* try fighting a battle on multiple fronts," Aubrey faux grumbled.

Jess laughed and waved them off as she disappeared down the hall.

"But seriously," Jackson said once she'd gone out of earshot, "is it always like that between the two of you? Because you give off enough sexual tension to power a small country."

Aubrey twitched and automatically checked over his shoulder. Kelly had snagged Nate the second the interview was over, and Aubrey didn't want him overhearing anything. "Shut up," he hissed. Then: "How would that even work?"

Jackson opened his mouth to reply, but as they passed a conference room, a high-pitched giggle cut him off. He raised an eyebrow at Aubrey, who shrugged.

Together they peered into the conference room, where Nate was sitting—still in his suit—next to a dark-eyed toddler who had two hands over his mouth.

"I don't believe it," Nate said. He had one of the old-style interview mics they never used anymore and was using it as a prop, Aubrey guessed, to interview the kid. "Tell me really. What's your mom's favorite sport to watch on TV?"

"Pillow fights!" the kid exclaimed through his giggles.

"That's not a sport!" Nate protested.

"Yes!" said the kid, nodding emphatically now. Apparently he didn't like to be called a liar. "Her favorite is Shady Godiva."

Shady Godiva. Aubrey watched Nate mouth the words and come to the obvious conclusion that the kid hadn't made that up.

"I have obviously been watching the wrong sports all my life," Jackson murmured.

Aubrey stepped on his foot. "Don't be such a horndog."

In truth, he was impressed he managed to say anything. His brain was still stuck on how *cute* this was.

"What about you?" Nate finally asked, recovering from his shock. He didn't seem to have noticed Aubrey and Jackson yet. "Do you have a favorite pillow fighter?"

More emphatic nodding. "Lynn Somnia."

Jackson had his phone out. "I don't know whether I should be recording this or googling 'pillow fight league.'"

Actually, recording it probably wasn't a terrible idea—they could save it for a show with an unexpected break… assuming they could get this kid's parents to sign off on it. The problem, of course, was that in order for Aubrey to suggest that, he'd have to reveal himself to Nate, and….

Jackson looked up from his phone, glanced at Aubrey, and winced. "Dude. Literal heart eyes right now. Take it down a notch, you're at work."

"I can't *help it*," Aubrey hissed furiously, very tempted to clutch his face.

"Lynn Somnia, of course," Nate repeated, completely engrossed in this fictional interview. Aubrey wanted to die. "She sounds pretty great. Do you have any pillow-fighting tips?" He held the mic to the kid's face.

Before the kid could respond, a voice from behind Aubrey made him jump about three feet in the air. "Oh, hey, Aubrey, have you seen Nate—"

Aubrey whirled around, his finger instinctively to his lips. Kelly was behind him, wearing a bemused expression.

"What?" she said quietly.

Aubrey jerked his thumb toward the door.

Kelly peered around it, smiled, and retreated. "My kid's a natural, huh? Takes after me. Born to be on camera."

That explained where he'd come from. "That's Carter?" Aubrey asked. "He's cute."

"He's a charmer," Kelly confirmed. "He sure has Uncle Nate wrapped around his finger too."

"Uncle Nate," Aubrey repeated aloud, completely without meaning to. That just fucking figured. His crush had been bad enough before *Uncle Nate* turned out to be a natural dad type. Aubrey had never been into that in his life.

This personal-growth shit was for the birds.

"Mama!" Carter exclaimed, and whoops, time to put on his game face. Aubrey schooled his features as Nate looked up and smiled at them.

"Thanks for looking after him," Kelly said, swinging Carter up into her arms and then smacking a wet kiss to his cheek. "I take it everything was fine?"

"Of course. We're looking forward to our next guys' night, right, Carter?"

Guys' night, Aubrey thought, dying a little inside. He wondered if Nate babysat when Kelly and Caley needed an adult break.

"Yeah," Carter said, but he looked pretty content in Mom's arms too.

Kelly and Carter said their goodbyes, leaving Aubrey, Jackson, and Nate without an obvious conversational direction. *Shit.*

Floundering, he said, "So... dinner?"

Only after the words were out of his mouth did he realize that he'd have to include Nate or else risk being unforgivably rude. He forced his face into a smile and raised his eyebrows in question.

"I've been wanting to try that place you talked about—what's it called again? Sharky's?"

Nate looked at his watch and shook his head. "Not without a reservation."

Jackson blanched. "Even on a Wednesday?"

"Two-for-one appetizers," Aubrey and Nate chorused.

Aubrey's ears went hot.

"They do takeout, though," Nate offered before the silence could get too awkward. "My place?"

"Hell yes." Jackson grinned. "Just don't tell my nutritionist."

IF SOMEONE had told him after their first meeting that he would willingly invite Aubrey into his apartment for dinner, he would have laughed in their face. Yet here he was, unlocking the door for his guests, feeling only the slight hint of butterflies because he was an idiot who wanted to sleep with his coworker.

Honestly. He hardly recognized himself.

Both Aubrey and Jackson took their shoes off by the door—most of Nate's Canadian teammates had habitually done the same—and followed him into the apartment.

Jackson whistled. "Nice view."

Nate had a clear line of sight to Lake Michigan, with the Shedd Aquarium and the Fields Museum in the background. "Thanks."

Aubrey, on the other hand, presumably had a similar view, so his attention focused… elsewhere. "Oh my God," he said, staring at the vase on Nate's living room table.

Ah. Well, Nate couldn't blame him for taking issue with that. Though he wished he'd realized they might come back here. He'd have hidden the damn thing if he'd known he was going to have to explain it.

Aubrey walked closer to stand next to the sculpture. "I know it's a stereotype that we homos all got the interior-decorating gene," he said seriously. "But this"—he gestured expansively—"is not the way to fight the stereotype, Nate."

Two weeks ago Nate wouldn't have been able to laugh at that either. It was uncomfortable—nobody liked bringing up their ex to people they were sexually interested in—but he made himself behave normally. He decided to have a little fun. "Marty and I bought it on our honeymoon," he said coolly.

Gratifyingly, the color went out of Aubrey's face, and Jackson made a poorly concealed noise of amusement at his friend's misstep as Aubrey opened his mouth to backpedal. "Uh, I mean… taste is so personal," he offered pathetically. "Just because something's not really my style…."

Nate finally grinned, shark-sharp, putting him out of his misery.

Aubrey sagged. "Oh, you asshole. You had me going. Seriously, why do you have this?"

That *was* a fair question, actually. "I don't know. Haven't gotten around to buying something else. Plus I don't know if you can just recycle something that big."

"I don't think Goodwill would take it," said Jackson.

Nate rolled his eyes for real this time and raised the bag of takeout. "Are we going to critique my interior-design choices or are we going to eat while the food's hot?"

It turned into a nice evening. Jackson made a good buffer, keeping dinner from feeling like work or its opposite, a date. With the pressure off, Nate could relax.

But relaxing became a problem of its own when, on his third glass of wine, he found himself unable to tear his eyes from the smudge of sauce at the corner of Aubrey's mouth. Aubrey had a nice mouth, plush pink lips that perpetually hid the hint of a smirk. It shouldn't have been attractive, but then again, Nate's libido had just woken up after a long nap, apparently.

Nate should tell him about the sauce, probably. But then he'd be admitting he was looking at Aubrey's mouth. Out loud. He didn't want to do that.

"You've got a little something," Jackson said for him, motioning.

Nate expected Aubrey to reach for his napkin. He'd never shown anything less than perfect table manners, whatever other trespasses he committed.

But maybe the wine had loosened him up too, because he swiped at it with his thumb and then sucked it off.

A strangled noise attempted to escape Nate's throat. He covered it with a cough and reached for his wineglass to wash down a phantom tickle.

Jackson glanced at him sidelong. "Are you okay?"

"Fine," Nate rasped, blinking rapidly so he could pretend his eyes were watering.

WHEN THE wheels touched down in Winnipeg, the sky had already taken on a foreboding iron-blue hue. Aubrey shivered as the driver put his carry-on in the back of the SUV next to Nate's. Winter here seemed to be a few strides ahead of Chicago.

"Hope you brought your snow boots," the driver commented as he pulled into traffic. "Forecast calls for six inches by tomorrow morning."

Aubrey automatically opened his mouth to make a joke, then second-guessed himself. He'd already crossed the line with Nate before, and that had gone badly.

On the other hand, if that didn't call for a dick joke. And he didn't *have* to make it about Nate. "Well, maybe we'll get lucky."

A *subtle* dick joke. Nate probably wouldn't even get it.

Maybe he did, though—and maybe he was starting to relax, because he raised a hand to his mouth and stifled a fake-sounding cough.

So he *wasn't* made of stone. At least when the cameras weren't rolling. But before Aubrey could prod him further, Nate dropped his hand, and just like that, he was all business. "We should look over the notes Jess sent. We've got points to cover for our interviews."

Aubrey sighed a long-suffering drawn-out huff. "All work and no play makes Nate a dull boy. But fine. Hit me with it. Who're the targets this time?"

Nate had stopped trying to avoid Aubrey and focused, at least when they were working. They finished their show prep in Aubrey's hotel room, Nate sitting at the small table and taking notes on his tablet, Aubrey on the bed, spitballing as he stared up at the ceiling. He was in the middle of a breakdown of everything that was wrong with the New York Rangers' defense when Nate made a surprised noise at the table.

Aubrey looked over. "What, you don't agree? Wow, I'm so surprised."

Nate spitted him with a look. "First of all, quality D-men don't grow on trees. There's nothing wrong with farming out the labor to Syracuse via trades from Tampa Bay—"

"It's cute that you think that's what's happening."

"—but *actually* I was looking at the weather report." He held up his phone. "Weather system's delayed. Maybe no snow. Or maybe we'll get nailed tomorrow morning instead."

"If only," Aubrey murmured. "Uh, the Senators flew in today, right? We're not going to end up with a canceled game?"

"This morning, I think. They're on their Western Canada road trip. So we're good there." Nate's face held an actual expression—was that amusement? The man should let himself smile more. Then again, Aubrey barely had a handle on his professionalism as it was. Who knew what would happen to his self-restraint if Nate started smiling regularly. "Although it's almost too bad. A friend of mine recommended a small-plates restaurant downtown that I've been meaning to try out, but they're closed for a private event tonight."

"Oh, Chez Sono?" Aubrey perked up, then deflated again, because damn. He'd have liked to try it too. "My cousin loves that place. Although she's more into the cocktails."

Nate lifted an eyebrow.

Aubrey felt judged. "What?"

He lifted the other eyebrow.

Aubrey got it. "Oh, everything's an innuendo with you. *Cocktails.* That's what it takes? You weren't going to jump on *expecting six inches,* but cocktails—that gets you?"

Nate lifted one shoulder. "I'm gonna blame low blood sugar. It's past dinnertime."

Startled, Aubrey glanced at the bedside clock and found it had ticked over to past eight. Their shooting schedule meant he usually ate early. Nate probably did too. "Huh. Room service?"

For a second he thought Nate was going to agree, and he had a fleeting hot flash of what could happen afterward if he did. If Nate finally let Aubrey close to him. If he brushed the chip off his shoulder and just went with the flow. Aubrey knew they could get along—at the very least outside the bedroom, but maybe in bed too. Nate would be a demanding lover, he thought, but Aubrey could rise to that challenge. Hell, Aubrey would thrive on it.

And then Aloof Nate slipped back into place, and he shook his head. "Thanks, but I think I'm just going to eat in my room."

Aubrey fought off a sigh. "Sure," he said. "Hey, pass me the room service menu on your way out?" If he was going to wallow, he would do it in bed as God intended.

The door clicked softly open. Aubrey made a point not to watch Nate leave.

THE SNOW started coming down halfway through the first period, and Nate's long experience of winter road trips told him not to count on timely air travel.

By the time he and Aubrey wrapped up the postgame interviews, he had three text messages on his phone. *Flight delayed. Flight delayed. Flight canceled.*

Nate called the hotel and managed to reserve a king room—apparently the last one the hotel had available, as the storm had knocked out power and heat in more than one neighborhood and all outbound flights were canceled.

Then, on a whim, he called Chez Sono, but even leveraging his "mildly famous, especially in Canada" name, they didn't take reservations.

Getting a cab seemed unlikely, given the forecast, but the restaurant was only a few blocks from the hotel. Maybe he could walk it.

By some miracle he did manage to get a cab back to the hotel. He'd just finished checking in again, and was turning to take his suitcase up to the room when he saw Aubrey at the desk two down from him.

A bellhop took Aubrey's suitcase, and Aubrey turned toward the hotel bar but stopped when he saw Nate.

"You get the same message I did?" Nate asked.

"Yeah, no flight and now no hotel room. At least they'll hold my bag, and I think I can buy enough overpriced cocktails down here that they'll let me stretch out on a couch all night."

"Probably," Nate agreed. He had to bite his tongue because he nearly caught himself offering to share his room. Sometimes he had to squash his inborn Midwestern politeness before it caused him to do something stupid.

The bellhop passed, and Nate flagged him down to have his suitcase brought up. Maybe he wouldn't go whole-hog crazy, but he could at least be friendly. "I was going to brave the snow and check out Chez Sono. They're open but no reservations. You want to tag along?"

Aubrey paused, looked toward the hotel lobby, then looked outside. Snow beat fiercely against the windowpanes, swirling so thick Nate could barely make out the glow of streetlights. They'd had a matinee, so it was only six. "You think we can get a cab?"

A car drove slowly by, braked, kept going, and bumped gently into a parked vehicle.

Nate looked from the blinking lights and blaring alarms back to Aubrey. "Actually, I'm thinking about walking."

"I'm game." Aubrey grinned. "Maybe with our combined charm we can wrangle a table. Or maybe we'll look so pathetic by then they'll take pity."

"Whatever gets us fed." Nate held the door open for him, feeling something akin to camaraderie. Or maybe he was just that hungry.

They didn't talk on the walk, between being bundled up and hustling along the sidewalk. Aubrey held his phone up, and the map app glowed like a beacon.

When they arrived, Chez Sono was bustling—Winnipeg wasn't going to shut down over a little snow. The hostess gave them a ridiculous wait time before suggesting that they try for a spot at the bar. Aubrey took off as soon as she said that, leaving Nate to mutter, "Thanks" before following in his wake.

He had to admit it gave him a pretty good view. Aubrey's suit was tailored to flatter his lean frame, showing off a slender waist and strong shoulders. He wasn't the only one who noticed either. A high-top table of women turned their heads almost in unison as he passed.

"I can't believe they're slammed in this weather," Aubrey commented, shaking his head. "This better be some restaurant."

The cocktail menu was eight pages, leather-bound, with prices to match. When the bartender managed to stop mixing drinks long enough to take their order, Nate asked for a Negroni and Aubrey an Aviation, and then Nate asked for a plate of the bacon-wrapped dates to start.

Aubrey raised an eyebrow.

"Hardly anyone has food right now," Nate pointed out. "It's early. Kitchen's just getting started. We're going to be here a while."

"Yeah, I know. The eyebrow was for your selection."

Oh, were they going to give each other a hard time at dinner too? Fine by Nate. He rolled his eyes gamely. "Hey, you don't have to have any."

"Let's not be hasty. I'll try anything once." Aubrey batted his eyelashes.

"Now why doesn't that surprise me."

Aubrey flashed a sly smile. "Can't just do the same thing over and over. What fun would that be?"

Just then a raucous crowd of thirtysomething guys behind Aubrey laughed uproariously, making him flinch. He leaned forward, a tactical error as the loud group took it as an opportunity to invade their space. Aubrey spared them one annoyed glance before hitching his stool closer.

If that group spread out any more, they'd push Aubrey into Nate's lap.

That would be awkward.

"If you wanted to fight them for it, you think you could take them?" Nate meant it as a joke, but hearing himself, it sounded weirdly like innuendo.

Aubrey pursed his lips, as if considering. "Maybe the big one in the blue shirt, but I've had better."

Nate's eyes widened. "I meant—"

"Aviation and Negroni," the bartender interrupted.

"Thank you!" Aubrey chirped. "Hey, can I put in an order for those truffle-oil fries with the banana ketchup? I'm intrigued."

"Sure thing."

"Banana ketchup," Nate repeated. "That sounds...."

"Both disgusting and kind of dirty?" He grinned and hooked his feet around the bar rail. "I know, that's why I ordered it." For a second, Nate thought he'd escaped their previous conversation, and he couldn't decide whether he was relieved or disappointed. But then Aubrey went on as if they'd never been interrupted, "What about you?"

Nate's throat went dry, so he picked up his drink. Even in his shock he could tell it was expertly made, the perfect balance of sweet and bitter. Strong too. He licked his lips afterward and cleared his throat. Still dry. "What about me, what?"

Aubrey gestured at the party behind them. "You had better than blue-shirt guy?"

Damn it. Nate's ears went hot. Fortunately the restaurant kept the lighting dim. Aubrey probably couldn't tell. "I've never had blue-shirt guy. How do I know what he's like in bed?"

"Oh come on." Aubrey bumped his shoulder. "Guy like that? You can definitely tell. He probably shaved again tonight before coming out to dinner. His shoes are gleaming, even though there's six inches of snow on the ground. He's eating french fries delicately. With a fork. Completely avoiding the banana ketchup, I might add."

"Maybe he's allergic," Nate said, half in defense, half amusement.

"Maybe he's a priss who doesn't like getting his hands sticky."

"Sounds like he's not your type." Nate was pretty sure Aubrey would tell him what his type was, and Nate wasn't quite comfortable with why he wanted to know.

"He's in good shape—the type who treats his body like a temple." Aubrey rolled his eyes. "I'm with Tony Bourdain. Your body isn't a temple. It's an amusement park; enjoy the ride. I mean, I like to look good, and I appreciate a guy who puts in the effort. But I also like a man who knows when to cut loose and have a good time. But maybe he's your speed?"

What? Aubrey thought he'd be into loud and big and obnoxious in public, not to mention apparently bad in bed?

"How do you figure?" Nate snapped.

"Well, big and dumb is probably pretty plentiful in the NHL, and I guess there were a few that would let you tap it in, so to speak."

Boy was Aubrey wrong on so many levels. Nate couldn't resist a derisive chuckle. "You have no fucking idea what I like or what I've done." *Or what I haven't done*, Nate mentally added.

Aubrey raised his hands defensively. "All right, you're right. Sorry." His eyes had widened in surprise, and they were still wide, but now they held something else too, something shrewd. Calculating. "Big and dumb has historically been *my* type, not yours. Sorry for projecting." He gave a slight grin, somehow inviting Nate to envision him with a mildly tarnished halo.

Nate took another sip of his cocktail and let himself be mollified. He was in a nice restaurant with a fabulous drink, and the weather was, at least for now, something he didn't need to worry about. He was going to enjoy this unexpected downtime. And that meant he had to give Aubrey *something*. "I don't know that I have a type." In juniors he'd fooled around with guys who could be discreet. By his sophomore year of college, he felt confident enough about his future to come out, but between hockey and homework, he didn't have a lot of time to meet anyone.

"What about your ex?"

"Marty's a decent guy. We had a good partnership for a long time. I wish him the best."

"Whew." Aubrey finished his drink in one long swallow—Nate watched his throat—and then gestured to the bartender for another. "That is some Stanley Cup Final quality shade."

Nate looked at him, wide-eyed.

"Come on, tell me your ex is a 'nice guy' when I ask who you like to fuck—" Aubrey paused, squinted at Nate as if trying to focus on something, then flicked his tongue to moisten his lips before continuing. "—or who you like to fuck you?" he finished, making it a question.

Nate reflexively tightened his fingers on his glass, then decided he might be better off drinking the stuff and letting the alcohol deal with the sudden tension in his shoulders. He knocked back the rest and made sure the bartender noticed him too. He'd planned to order something different, just to try, but expediency seemed more prudent. "He *is* a nice guy," he said, expecting to come across as defensive. Instead it sounded defeated, so he figured he might as well add, "That was part of the problem."

Aubrey had been taking a sip from his water glass, and at this, he sputtered and nearly sprayed the bar top. Fortunately he managed to grab a napkin in time to avoid that level of attention-calling mishap. "Oh wow. Uh. I don't know what to say to that."

With a shrug, Nate picked up a bar napkin of his own and absently tore off a corner. "I mean, the part where he fell in love with someone else while we were still married and then left me for him, that was definitely the main issue. So. I can't blame it all on the… on the sex."

Look at him, a grown man at a bar having a mature conversation about his sex life. Like a real hockey player! He felt like he'd slipped into another dimension.

At this, Aubrey nodded slowly, mercifully keeping his gaze fixed on his water glass. Nate appreciated the privacy as he tried to school his body's reactions. Sex wasn't anything to be embarrassed about. And it wasn't even the state of his sex life with Marty that made him blush. For some reason Aubrey had assumed Nate regularly took men home, had sex with them, then lost their numbers and went on with his life. That kind of casual relationship with sex had never interested Nate—or he'd told himself it hadn't. Now… well, now that things with Marty were over, he wished he at least had the experience to go out and hook up and scratch an itch he hadn't scratched properly in years. But he didn't know where to start. And that… okay, *that* embarrassed him.

Finally Aubrey cleared his throat just as the bartender came around with their drinks and, wonder of wonders, the dates Nate had ordered. They thanked him, and then Aubrey said, "Well, you know what the best revenge is, right?"

Nate nodded, unaccountably disappointed. "Yeah, yeah. Living well. Blah, blah."

"Living well?" Aubrey scoffed. "Hell no. Going out and having lots of filthy, no-strings-attached sex with the hottest guys you can find— *that's* revenge."

"That's a bit out of my wheelhouse." Nate watched Aubrey's jaw drop. He could practically hear the record-scratch sound as Aubrey went completely still, a forked date halfway to his mouth.

Aubrey's eyebrows were the first to move, rising in two evenly matched, perfectly formed arches. "Well that's a fucking shame for the men of Chicago." He glanced around, then whispered conspiratorially, "And Winnipeg. Can't imagine there's not a few guys here who'd take home a big slab of All-American beef." He paused for a sip of his cocktail. "Some of them might even know what to do with you."

A plate of fries with a pot of sauce was placed in front of them. Aubrey immediately plucked one, then dunked it daintily, raised it up, and gave it a tentative lick.

"Oh. Oh. That's *good*." Aubrey proceeded to slip the fry into his mouth like a straw and suck the sauce off of it. "You have got to try this." He swallowed and grinned at Nate. "And act fast because I could eat the whole thing."

Nate would have liked to pick up a fry, except the only parts of his body that could communicate with his brain at the moment were located below the belt, and he didn't think he could manage it with his dick. What was happening to him? He'd never had trouble keeping a lid on his physical reactions—at least not since before he met Marty. Finally he realized he was staring stupidly and managed, "So you're a fan of the banana ketchup, huh."

"In all its forms, apparently," Aubrey said salaciously. He picked up another fry. "Seriously. These are amazing."

The glue binding Nate in place eventually gave, and he reached for a fry of his own. The hot oil on the surface stung his fingers, but it did smell incredible. The ketchup was an ugly sort of yellow-brown, but Nate dunked anyway, surprised to find it did taste similar to traditional ketchup, but sweeter and a little spicy. "Mmm," he agreed, licking at a spot of sauce that had dripped down his thumb. "Okay, I admit these are better than the dates."

Aubrey was staring at his thumb. The heat of it burned Nate's skin, made his neck tingle. His dick jerked in his pants when Aubrey licked his lips. Nate bit the inside of his cheek hard to distract himself.

"Told you," Aubrey said. "Sometimes you've gotta get your hands dirty."

"Getting your hands dirty? Is that how you do it?" Nate blurted.

There was a brief pause as Aubrey flicked his gaze from Nate's thumb to his lips to his eyes. He seemed to decide something, because he finally said, "Do you want me to tell you or would you like me to show you?"

Nate swallowed hard. He'd been wondering if maybe they might get there, but Aubrey had just cut to the chase, cool and confident. That did something for Nate. He pulled his wallet out and shoved enough bills on the bar to cover a nice tip.

"I know you're a show-off," Nate quipped. "But can you put your money where your mouth is?"

This time when Aubrey smiled, it was that slow, teasing, burning one that made Nate's pants feel tight. "Wouldn't you rather know if I'll put my mouth where the money is?" For just a second, he put his hand over Nate's, and the contact sent an unfamiliar thrill up Nate's spine. "C'mon, let's get out of here."

CHAPTER SEVEN

THE WEATHER—AND it was shitty, with big, wet flakes of snow and a wind to blow them sideways—at least kept them decent on the way back to the hotel. Aubrey started on his coat buttons as soon as they were in the lobby, and Nate was already fumbling for the key card when they got into the elevator.

Were his hands shaking? Aubrey thought so as Nate tapped the card, opened the door, and immediately looked for somewhere to put his coat.

That wouldn't do, giving himself a chance to get jittery. "Hey," Aubrey called out as the door closed behind him. Nate turned around, and Aubrey crooked a finger.

Nate took two steps toward Aubrey, smooth and fast like he was being pulled on a string. That was a response to file away for later. In the meantime, though, Aubrey needed them to be touching. He hauled Nate in by his lapels. "That's better."

It *was* better—Nate was somehow already radiating warmth, his chest firm under Aubrey's hands. Aubrey couldn't tell if his cheeks had reddened from the wind or something else, but his eyes, those he could read. He wanted this just as much as he had at the restaurant, but nerves were getting the better of him.

"I," Nate began, and Aubrey kissed him.

He reached up one hand to Nate's cheek, traced his thumb over Nate's jaw as he coaxed him to turn and angle just so as Aubrey parted his lips against Nate's to deepen the kiss. Aubrey was aiming for *slow, sweet* before he worked up to *sexy, devastating* in order to give Nate a few minutes to relax and make sure he was comfortable. Aubrey was already getting hard, and fuck if he hadn't been thinking about this for weeks. But if Nate wasn't good with this, Aubrey wanted to give him an easy out. Better to spend the night on a lobby couch than to seduce someone less than enthusiastic into a no-strings hookup.

Aubrey planned to start slow and sweet, but the moment Aubrey grazed Nate's side with his hand, Nate made a low, hungry sound. *He* made the kiss deeper and harder and walked Aubrey backward until his ass hit the closed door.

Out of practice or not, Nate kissed absolutely filthy. He curled his fingers into the fabric at the waist of Aubrey's shirt, tightly enough that it almost pinched, and when he swept his tongue through Aubrey's mouth, he followed by scoring his teeth over Aubrey's lower lip. Aubrey gasped in encouragement, widening his stance as Nate pushed closer between his legs. Nate's dick was hard against his hip, and Aubrey relished the pressure of Nate's thigh against his own erection.

Apparently Nate had two settings—slow and *now*. While Aubrey was still trying to convince his fingers away from Nate's chest to remove his clothing, Nate was way ahead of him, nimbly unfastening Aubrey's belt. Nate's stubble rasped over the skin around Aubrey's mouth as they kissed, and the raw, sensual prickle left him wondering how much better it would feel on the insides of his thighs.

He couldn't wait to find out.

Nate might have read his mind, because a moment later, he broke the kiss, lips swollen, eyes dark. "I want to try something."

Aubrey waved his hand in a helplessly turned-on gesture of acquiescence. "The floor is yours."

"That's the idea." Nate slid his hand to Aubrey's fly and dropped to his knees as he unfastened Aubrey's trousers.

"Fuck," Aubrey muttered, letting the back of his head thud against the door as he dropped his shoulders. He hadn't realized how tense he was, taut and ready like a bow string. Nate was taking advantage of that, pushing Aubrey's trousers down, thumbing the placket of his briefs out of the way. He felt a warm puff of air against his cock. It almost tickled, and if Nate was going to start teasing now, Aubrey was going to have an aneurism.

Then Nate let out a soft, *hungry* sound, and Aubrey's stomach swooped. He didn't even have time to brace himself before Nate opened his mouth and took him inside.

Aubrey's brain shorted out. He almost didn't want to look, afraid of what it might do to his stamina, but he couldn't help himself. Nate had his eyes closed, his mouth soft and wet and gentle on Aubrey's dick. As Aubrey watched, he made another desperate sound and pulled back to lick around the head.

"Fuck," Aubrey whispered again. The word seemed to send a shiver through Nate, and Aubrey belatedly remembered *he* was the one with the hookup experience. It didn't seem fair to make Nate do all the heavy lifting, so he raised his hand and traced his thumb down the side of Nate's cheek and rubbed the corner of his mouth. "Baby. You like that, huh?"

Nate's eyes flicked open, went to Aubrey's face, and flickered closed on another satisfied moan.

God. "How long have you been waiting for this, babe?"

Nate's answer was muffled because *Aubrey's dick was in his mouth.* It was amazing, but Nate followed up by sucking harder, pushing himself down farther on Aubrey's cock. Aubrey could work with that. It didn't take a genius to figure out Nate's answer.

"I can't believe no one else has seen you like this." The idea made him feel possessive—but he didn't have that right, not when they'd agreed on casual. Nate hummed in agreement, quiet but desperate, and the vibrations went right to the base of Aubrey's skull and buzzed there, setting his whole body on fire. Nate looked incredible and felt *better*, flicking his tongue over the head of Aubrey's cock before taking him deep enough Aubrey could feel his throat muscles working. His stomach clenched; it had been a while since someone made him feel this good. "You're incredible. Gorgeous." He let his thumb trace the outline of his cock through Nate's cheek, and they both shuddered.

Just like that, Aubrey rocketed to the edge. Nate doubled his efforts, stroking with his tongue even as he tightened his mouth and sucked.

"I can't believe this is your first time having slutty casual sex. You're a natural." Nate sucked cock like it was the only thing he cared about. Aubrey bit his lip half bloody with the effort of not thrusting into his throat. And failed, cursing briefly as Nate choked. "Sorry, sorry. God, you're good at that."

Nate wiped moisture from the corner of one eye. "It's fine," he said, voice rasping. "I like it. Keep going."

Aubrey didn't ask if he was sure. His brain had forgotten how to make his mouth work. But the rest of his body operated fine on autopilot. He pulled Nate's face back onto his dick and started to thrust.

Nate didn't choke again. His eyes watered and his mouth stayed hot and slick and perfect, driving Aubrey to the edge.

Aubrey wasn't going to last much longer. Not with Nate working him like this, like this was the best thing he'd ever done. He took his hand from Nate's hair and warned him, but Nate only gave him a dirty look, like he was offended Aubrey thought he might want to pull off.

"Fuck, have it your way," Aubrey said, and he might have felt embarrassed at how quickly he came after that, but the night was young, and the sooner he got his, the sooner he could have his hands on Nate's dick.

That thought pushed him over, and he spilled in Nate's mouth while Nate watched with smug satisfaction in his heavy-lidded eyes.

He wanted to give himself a moment to recover. His brain felt utterly blank, as though any intelligent thought it might have offered had been sucked right out. But somewhere in some part of his mind, some shred of personal pride remained, and he called on that to haul Nate up off his knees and back him toward the bed.

Nate's mouth opened under his as Aubrey pushed him back, back, until his head hit the padded headboard. And then Aubrey lay down beside him and splayed his hand on Nate's abdomen, the muscles there just as firm and defined as he'd imagined.

"Fuck, you're gorgeous," Aubrey muttered as he ran his hand over and lower, to where Nate's trousers were unbuttoned, the fly tented by his cock.

"You can do more than look." Nate's voice was a little rough, used sounding. *Because he'd just sucked Aubrey's brain out through his dick.*

Aubrey could do that. He definitely could do that. He grinned at Nate as lasciviously as he could, keeping eye contact as he pulled the zipper down, trying not to be too grabby when all he wanted was to take a big handful of—

"Come *on*." Nate bucked up into Aubrey's hand. "I won't break. Didn't you say you'd done this before?"

Aubrey's eyes widened with the sting of the remark, but when Nate's eyes twinkled in challenge, he let himself chuckle before turning his head to capture Nate's mouth with his.

"You bastard," he laughed between kisses as he tugged at Nate's trousers. Nate raised his hips and wriggled to help Aubrey shimmy them down so Nate was left in a pair of pale gray briefs. When Aubrey smeared his thumb over the wet spot, Nate shuddered.

Aubrey wondered how long it had been since anyone touched Nate like this. Too long, obviously. And even when he was married, it seemed like he hadn't—

And that train of thought suddenly made him surge with jealousy. How could anyone have been married to Nate for so long and failed to see this side of him? If this was the only night they'd have, Aubrey was going to make sure Nate jerked off to it for the rest of his life. And for that... he needed a better angle.

And unobstructed access to Nate's dick.

Aubrey teased his fingers under Nate's waistband, scratching his nails lightly over the soft skin. "Help me out here, babe. You want to take these off?"

"Yeah—yeah." Nate's hands flew to his waist to shove down his briefs and slide them off. He kicked them away and then toed off his socks. It should have been awkward—Aubrey was vaguely aware that objectively, this was never terribly sexy—but Nate just looked so good. Fit, strong, pale, and flushed. Aubrey wanted to devour him. He shucked off the rest of his own clothes as quickly as he could and tossed them carelessly toward the corner so he could get back to Nate.

He bent his head to kiss Nate's neck and suck lightly at the place where it met his shoulder, then moved lower, his intention to return the favor clear.

Nate's hand found his hair and tugged. "Your hands. Please." He pulled Aubrey in for another filthy kiss.

Fuck, Aubrey could do that.

He brought a hand up to Nate's hungry mouth.

"Lick," he instructed. Nate compiled without hesitation, getting Aubrey's palm wet and slick.

"That's a good boy," Aubrey said without meaning to or thinking of the implication of the words, but Nate flushed scarlet and closed his eyes.

Aubrey wrapped his fingers around Nate's cock, feeling the weight of it, heavy and hard, and then slid his fist up, cupping, barely squeezing. He swiped his thumb over the head, and damn, he hadn't needed Nate's spit at all, because he was positively dripping.

Nate had a nice cock, hard and eager in Aubrey's hand, the skin smooth and hot and slick. And he looked incredible spread out like that—like he was Aubrey's for the taking. But looking couldn't satisfy him, and like this he hardly got to touch everything he wanted.

Aubrey smeared his thumb over the tip of Nate's dick again, slowly this time, a filthy circle. Then he lowered himself to the bed, cataloging Nate's brief noise of protest.

"Shh," he soothed, curling his body around Nate's as he urged him onto his side. "What, you think I'm going to leave you hanging? I have a reputation to uphold."

He nuzzled the back of Nate's neck, the skin below his ear, and wrapped his hand around his cock again. "Besides, I want to know what it takes to get you to lose your composure." He stroked once, slowly, twisted his fingers at the top before moving them down again. "Going to let me see that?"

"Show me what you can do," Nate gasped as Aubrey jacked him slowly, but he still managed to make it a challenge.

"Show you, huh?" Aubrey nudged his thigh forward, teasing it between Nate's legs until it brushed the curve of his ass. "I think I can do that." He kept the words a gentle susurration against the shell of Nate's ear.

Nate shuddered, and his cock blurted precome in Aubrey's hand. "Yeah," he whispered, thrusting into Aubrey's grip—and then, better, grinding back against his leg like he needed it, like he couldn't wait for Aubrey to fuck him. "Yeah, fuck, show me."

Aubrey pressed his open mouth to the skin of Nate's neck, tasting the salt of his sweat. "Maybe I can do one better, hmm?" He rocked his thigh in time with Nate's hips as if he were fucking him, and Nate gasped again. Not just the actions, Aubrey thought—the words. He was getting off on Aubrey talking to him.

"I mean." Nate's hips bucked forward again. "You're doing great so far."

"Mmm," Aubrey murmured. "I do respond well to positive feedback." He sucked Nate's earlobe into his mouth and then released it. "You know what you respond to?"

"Fuck." Nate panted as Aubrey twisted his wrist, moving his hand incrementally faster, still a deliberate, slow stroke. "Having my—having my dick touched, for one thing."

"Yeah," Aubrey agreed. "And it's been so long since someone touched you like this, hasn't it, babe? Since someone gave it to you like you so obviously need it. But that's not what I meant." He unwrapped his fingers from Nate's cock long enough to gather the fluid at the head again and slick his hand with it.

Nate shook with tension, and he arched his back, pressing his neck and ass against Aubrey. God, he was easy for it, and Aubrey was going to give it to him.

"So easy for it, sweetheart," Aubrey breathed, making Nate shudder again. Aubrey stilled his hand, just cupping Nate's cock before he whispered, "Letting me know how much you need it."

Nate whined in response. As much as Aubrey had wanted to return the favor, to get his mouth around Nate's cock, having it here where he could talk and Nate could listen was probably doing it for him as much as Aubrey sucking him off would. More, maybe.

Aubrey grinned against Nate's neck, then kissed and nipped at the spot. Aubrey could definitely oblige him; he was finding it harder to shut up than to keep talking.

He moved his hand again, jerking Nate a little firmer but not much faster while he rocked forward. Aubrey's cock gave a twinge of interest that he'd be up for another round, but he still needed to get Nate there.

"Going to show me?" He circled his thumb under the crown of Nate's dick, pressing lightly. "Going to come for me like this?"

Nate nodded, and every muscle in his back, his legs, his neck went tense. He was right there, hovering on the edge, waiting for that last push. Aubrey slowed down. Nate had waited a long time for someone to fuck him like he needed. It would be a shame to let it end so soon.

"Please," Nate whispered. He worked himself back against Aubrey's thigh with jerky, uncoordinated movements.

"I know what you need, babe. You want me to fuck you, right?" Nate's whole body was trembling, and Aubrey's dick had taken notice. He was better than halfway hard now, and his blood burned in his veins. "If you weren't so good with your mouth, I'd be inside you right now, giving you what you need."

"God, fuck," Nate whispered, the words barely audible over the slick sounds of Aubrey's hand on his cock.

Aubrey worked his left hand between Nate's asscheeks, skimming lightly over the skin, more intimate than the press of his leg. He took the soft part of Nate's ear between his teeth, tugging gently, until Nate froze, as though he couldn't decide whether to move forward or back. Or maybe his brain had just stopped sending signals altogether.

"That's it," he murmured, circling the crown of Nate's dick again as he teased his left hand closer to Nate's hole. "Let go for me, sweetheart."

Nate's hand went to his mouth, smothering the moan that Aubrey so desperately wanted to hear even though he recognized the neighbors in the next room would not. Another time he'd hopefully get a chance, but now all he was getting was the muffled gasps as Nate tensed and then shuddered, back bowing as he came and spilled over Aubrey's fist in a hot, slippery mess.

"So good, baby," Aubrey said hoarsely, gentling his touch as Nate tried to catch his breath, the hand at his mouth dropping down to cover Aubrey's. He managed a gentle squeeze.

"Oh." It was only a little more than a sigh before Nate repeated, "Oh."

Aubrey was overcome with the need to kiss him, and he could reach the corner of Nate's mouth, so he did. Nate turned his head to meet him for a kiss that was a little uncoordinated and sloppy, but grateful. His body was warm in Aubrey's arms, the tension bled out of it.

"Feel better?" Aubrey inquired softly.

"Mm, a little." Nate chuckled and then stretched, rolled his shoulders, and squirmed away from Aubrey's embrace.

A *little*?

Aubrey regretfully pulled back. He might be used to no-strings-attached sex, but he still enjoyed a bit of afterglow. Apparently Nate didn't, at least not with Aubrey.

He shouldn't be disappointed. After all, he was the one who'd told Nate to get his revenge by having dirty hookups with as many hot guys as he could. He didn't get to be upset Nate was treating him like one.

This was probably a bad idea.

THIS WAS an incredible idea.

Nate couldn't remember the last time he'd come like that, if he ever had. He couldn't remember ever feeling so desirable.

He *could* remember the last time he'd had more than one orgasm in a night, because it had only happened a handful of times in his six years with Marty. But he was pretty sure it was going to happen again tonight.

Aubrey was still lying on his side, breathing hard, when Nate got up and pulled out the toiletry bag in his suitcase. For once in his life he was daring to be optimistic about sex, and he was damned if he wasn't going to follow through on his original plan. He retrieved the lube and condoms—items he'd carried with him on road trips since the divorce out of formless hope—before turning back around and basically thrusting them at Aubrey.

"Um—" Aubrey looked like he had something to say, possibly about the fact that… yeah, there was no way he was going to get a condom open with that much come on his hands.

No problem. Nate could do that part. "Fuck me," he said, taking the condom himself. Aubrey was half-hard again. Nate had faith in him and, for once, in his own desirability.

Aubrey blinked, dazed but clearly not unwilling. "*Now*? Won't it be too…."

"Normally, yeah." Nate actually didn't have a lot of data on his feelings about being fucked post-orgasm, but Aubrey knew enough about his sex life already. "But tonight I'm having a slutty no-strings hookup to get back at my ex-husband, or something. I want the full experience. For science."

Meaning he wanted Aubrey's cock, long and fat and as gorgeous as the rest of him, and he wanted it bad enough he hadn't gone soft.

Aubrey didn't argue, for once. Stop the presses. "Well, as your guide to the world of slutty hookups, it's my solemn duty to provide." He sank his teeth into Nate's shoulder, right near his neck, just hard enough to make Nate shudder. "I'm gonna get a washcloth first, though. Don't go anywhere."

As if. But Nate *did* shift in the bed to watch him move. Aubrey had a tight, lithe, compact body, and he moved like he had every step choreographed. Right now those steps were designed for seduction, a swinging gait that made his ass bounce.

Maybe if Nate could talk him into another no-strings hookup, he could get to know it better.

Aubrey returned with clean hands and a stack of linens, which he dropped next to Nate before crawling up his body like an apex predator. Nate watched him with lidded eyes, waiting. But Aubrey paused halfway to his face and dropped his mouth to Nate's hip, tonguing the skin as he coaxed Nate's legs apart.

"What—" Nate started, but the stroke of the washcloth on his abs cut him off.

"Don't get me wrong; dried come has its place in the slutty hookup." Aubrey gently worked Nate's thighs and stomach and then eased the rough cloth over his cock and balls. "But since we're going for round two, I want a clean slate." He looked up and quirked an eyebrow. "No glue-come handicap."

"That seems… fair," Nate said, biting back a hiss as Aubrey swirled the cloth over the head of his dick. It was still too sensitive to feel good, exactly, but some part of his body hadn't gotten the memo, because his hips bucked up into it anyway.

Aubrey snorted. "I hope we can do better than 'fair.'" Then he had Nate's oversensitive dick in his mouth, hot and wet and gentle.

It felt like his whole body was inverting. Aubrey knew exactly what he was doing. The room felt close and dark, full of the slick wet noise of Aubrey's mouth and Nate's ragged breathing.

The moment Nate gave himself over to the pleasure and stopped bracing himself against it, Aubrey coaxed his thighs apart and went in with two fingers, smooth as anything, like he knew Nate's body could take what it craved.

Nate submitted to thirty seconds of necessary stretching only because he'd been up close with Aubrey's dick and he had to sit still on a plane tomorrow, but before he could even nudge Aubrey to move on with it, he was curling his fingers up instead, making Nate swear and fist the sheets.

"You should," Nate began, but Aubrey was already withdrawing his fingers and making an impatient motion for Nate to turn over.

"I'm gonna," he promised, arranging Nate's hips.

Nate almost laughed. They'd spent four weeks sniping at each other, and all it took to get them agreeing on everything was—

"Now would be good," Nate prompted, but the last word came out strangled because Aubrey slid in deep, one smooth thrust that Nate felt in his *tonsils*.

Okay, yes. Hookup sex. That was a thing.

"Jesus Christ," said Aubrey, sounding exactly like Nate felt. "Your ass is criminally undersexed."

This time Nate *did* laugh, and Aubrey made a sound like he was dying and dug his fingers hard into Nate's hips to hold him still. "What're you gonna do?" he asked, biting down on a moan as Aubrey pulled out. "Arrest—*fuck*—arrest it?"

"Nnnnno." Aubrey grunted in apparent dissatisfaction and then leaned over his back and shoved Nate's shoulders toward the mattress.

Nate's breath hitched as Aubrey nailed the angle to hit his prostate just right. "I think… it can be… rehabilitated."

Nate could only nod in agreement.

Together they set a punishing rhythm. Nate spared half a thought for the room's neighbors, but then Aubrey laced their fingers together and guided Nate's hand to his own cock, and that killed any misguided civic-mindedness.

Aubrey didn't ask if he was okay or draw it out or attempt anything fancy. He seemed happy to fuck Nate until his teeth rattled, chasing the high of orgasm until a particularly brutal thrust sent Nate cursing over the edge, coming over his hand in spasms that felt like they were wringing his whole body dry. Aubrey fucked in another handful of times, and then his hips stuttered as his fingers clenched bruisingly tight on Nate's skin.

The world took several moments to right itself. Nate realized he'd collapsed into the wet spot and honestly couldn't give a fuck. Aubrey pulled out and flopped beside him on the bed, gasping up at the ceiling.

Nate's freshly Zamboni'd brain was blissfully, completely silent.

"So filthy, no-strings-attached sex, huh?" he said after a moment, half muffled by the pillow. With great effort, he turned his head. "Who knew."

Aubrey held up a finger without otherwise moving. "Don't forget the 'hottest guy you can find' part."

Nate's mouth made a noise that might have been agreement if it could've found a brain cell capable of conveying it.

After a moment Aubrey groaned, pulled off the condom, and snagged another of the washcloths from the bed. Nate grabbed one too, wondering if he couldn't ameliorate some of the damage. He felt bad for the hotel cleaning staff.

"I think traditionally this is the part where I kick you out." Nate fought the urge to giggle into the pillow, but a snicker sneaked out. "But considering the conditions, I'm okay with breaking protocol for one night."

"And my mom said my philandering would never get me anywhere." Aubrey flung a cloth toward the washroom.

"I reserve the right to kick you out of bed for snoring, though." With effort, Nate dragged himself into the bathroom. Just a quick shower, and then he could crash. But when he returned, suddenly self-conscious enough that he'd put on the track pants he brought for working out, Aubrey was sitting up in bed watching *Sports Night* with a room service tray.

"I worked up an appetite," he said sheepishly. "My treat. Got you the salmon, but if you'd rather the tenderloin, I'll trade."

Nate's stomach growled on cue. Apparently a few dates and fries hadn't been enough for him either. "Salmon sounds great."

It was odd to eat dinner in bed next to a guy who'd just fucked his brains out... at first. It felt like a date gone backward. Then Aubrey said something stupid about the show and that feeling disappeared—and Nate realized that the tension he'd been carrying in his shoulders for God knew how long had left too.

Maybe there was something to this hookup thing after all.

CHAPTER EIGHT

AUBREY WASN'T the last person on the plane—the gate agent was still sorting out the stand-bys when he dashed down the jetway—but most everyone was seated by the time he slid into his aisle seat, almost directly across from Nate.

Nate, who'd sneaked out of the room that morning while Aubrey showered.

Aubrey had spent the intervening time trying to decide what he'd say to Nate when he saw him—something flirty and witty, hopefully—and also what the hell he was going to do about sleeping with a coworker who, it turned out, was his perfect match in every way and definitely wasn't looking for a relationship.

He didn't get the chance to say boo to Nate, though, because while Aubrey was stowing his bag under the seat in front of him, Kelly appeared at Nate's side.

"Check this out." Kelly leaned over to show Nate something on her phone. "Do you remember him from the wedding? I told him about you."

Aubrey caught himself before he leaned forward like a creeper, but he adjusted his toque so he could overhear more easily.

"He's a doctor," Kelly wheedled. "And a cutie. Single. Nice guy. Looking for someone nice, stable. Sound like anyone you know? Anyway, maybe have coffee with him?"

"Um."

Aubrey held his breath, waiting for Nate's response.

"He sounds great," Nate said.

Something in Aubrey's gut lurched. It wasn't like he hadn't known this was coming ever since he realized Nate was actually single. Nate was hot and kind and had a good job. He was never going to stay single for long. Even if he did, he'd just expressed his interest in pickup culture—an interest Aubrey had very much used to his advantage last night.

He had no right to feel disappointed, let alone… whatever else he was feeling that he didn't want to name… because Nate was looking to expand his repertoire beyond just Aubrey.

"I'll let him know," Kelly said brightly. Then she ruffled Nate's hair. "Oh, hi, Aubrey," she added as she headed back to her seat. The gesture made Aubrey feel like an afterthought. Definitely one for the notebook.

At least he knew where he stood with Nate. Clearly he wasn't relationship material. He'd been foolish to even entertain the idea.

He wondered if Nate would come sniffing around for another go if Dr. Nice Guy had more in the bank than in the tank.

If he did, Aubrey would—he would—

Aubrey wanted to believe that he'd tell Nate where to stick it, but if he were being honest with himself, the problem was Aubrey knew exactly where he wanted to stick it, and if Nate gave him another opening, Aubrey would take it.

At least he had something new to work on in therapy.

NATE GRIMACED at the grinning model on the cover of the in-flight magazine as if it were her fault Kelly was getting all up in his business when he was still feeling the effects of one *specific* coworker getting all up in his business.

Nate shifted in his seat. He definitely could still feel that, and frankly, if it weren't for the fact that he might embarrass himself, he'd much rather reminisce about last night than contemplate meeting Kelly's cousin for coffee.

If he hadn't spent almost an hour lamenting the state of his love life to her and Caley two weeks ago, he would've just told her he wasn't interested in dating right now. But after that conversation, what was he supposed to say? *Sorry, but I've decided to sleep my way through this country's gay population, beginning with my cohost?* She'd probably try to stage an intervention.

His cell phone chirped as the crew started the safety video, and he spared it a brief glance. Earlier in the day, he'd gotten a message from Jess about rescheduling a meeting. Maybe she was canceling that? But no—it was his mother texting him flight details. *Can't wait to see you this Thanksgiving!*

So that was one weekend he wouldn't be exploring his new approach to life, but he could probably take a four-day break from casual sex to spend some time with his parents. He added the details to his calendar and turned his phone to flight mode.

It was only then that he noticed Aubrey in the aisle seat across from him, apparently engrossed in the safety demonstration.

Maybe he was a nervous flier.

IF AUBREY was worried at all about how sleeping with Nate would affect their working relationship, he didn't need to be. Their first show back after Winnipeg was the smoothest yet. Aubrey spent the commercial breaks drafting the most ridiculous yet still relevant phrasings he could come up with to get Nate to crack. Nate stared long-sufferingly at the camera to let the viewers know in no uncertain terms that he didn't get paid enough to put up with Aubrey's nonsense, and Bob in Advertising walked around like he'd personally given the show license to print money. Of course their demographic had shifted enough that he didn't know who to sell ad space to, but that wasn't Aubrey's problem.

Aubrey had plenty of other things to worry about.

"You're underrotating on the triple," he told Greg at their practice on Friday.

"Do you think any of the Cirque people are going to notice if I land on the wrong edge?" Greg asked testily, and okay, maybe Aubrey had been a little extra critical today. Most Olympic judges would've needed a slow-motion replay to catch that.

"Uh," Aubrey said, scrambling with whether to word an apology or an excuse.

"Speaking of edges, you've been on one since you got back from your trip to Winnipeg. Did something happen at work?"

"Uh," Aubrey repeated. Without thinking about it, he started to skate backward, away from Greg. Some primal part of his brain had engaged the fight-or-flight response. Aubrey was a lover, not a fighter. Flight it was.

Greg narrowed his eyes, obviously scenting blood in the water. "Did something happen with—"

Somewhere in the rink, someone laughed, and a locker room door banged open into solid concrete, fortunately reminding Greg that not only were they not alone, but Nate's group had the ice after them.

Aubrey's skates bumped slowly into the boards and he let out a breath, figuring he was caught anyway. "Come on," he said firmly. "We still have five minutes. Then I'll let you interrogate me over beer."

Greg lifted a shoulder easily, unperturbed. "Sure. But after this week? You're buying."

Considering his propensity for gossip, Greg behaved himself admirably, waiting until they were ensconced in a booth in a down-market neighborhood place not far from the arena before he prompted, "All right, tell me everything."

Aubrey scrubbed his hands over his face. A server stopped by for their drink orders, offering him a few seconds' reprieve, but in the end, he didn't have to say much. As soon as he met Greg's gaze, Greg knew.

"Holy shit."

Aubrey groaned and fought the urge to bang his head against the table.

Greg lowered his voice and hunched forward. "So? Are the two of you a thing now?"

"Uh. Not exactly."

"What do you mean, not exactly? This isn't a question with a lot of gray area. You said you were looking for something long-term. So…?"

There was nothing for it. "Does twice in one night count?"

Greg sputtered into a cough. "Not in most people's books, although congratulations, I guess." Then he turned serious. "I'm assuming that rather than approach the idea of having a relationship with him, you just charmed his pants off and hoped for the best?"

Aubrey had plenty of empirical evidence about how good he was in bed; he didn't need to hope—but that wasn't totally inaccurate either. He flashed the server a smile as she deposited their drinks and then immediately pulled his toward himself and took a swig.

"So, yes."

"It was really good?" he offered feebly. He sounded miserable about it. Because he was, apparently. That just went to show how messed up everything had gotten, if Aubrey could be depressed about how great the sex was.

"So what's the problem, exactly?"

"He basically asked me to help him figure out how to hook up with people."

"And you decided a live demonstration was the way to go."

"Would it make it any better if I pointed out that the hotel didn't have any more rooms free, there was a blizzard, and I needed a place to sleep?"

Greg put down his drink without taking a sip. "No, you dumbass, that makes it worse."

Yeah. Aubrey thought so too. "Anyway, now he knows," he said. "So he's free to take that knowledge and...." He waved his hand broadly to indicate, vaguely, *offer himself to the Chicago meat market.* "And *I* am going to respect his decision to explore what being hot, out, and single is like, because this is probably karma or something."

"You're being suspiciously mature about this."

Aubrey managed a pathetic smile. "Don't worry, it's temporary." He just needed to go out and get it out of his system.

"That's very reassuring." Greg shook his head and raised his glass. "Good luck."

CHAPTER NINE

DR. DEVON Bailey was a thirty-six-year-old anesthesiologist with perfect hair, perfect cheekbones, and perfect teeth. He had two hairless cats because he liked pets but was allergic to dander, he was training for a triathlon, and he'd just become an uncle for the first time.

Nate learned all of this within the first five minutes of their date at Ciao, an exclusive steakhouse in a trendy neighborhood.

Devon was handsome, all right. And Nate could be reasonably sure he wasn't after his money. He was nice. Nate had never cared for cats and thought the hairless ones looked like Roswell gray aliens only scarier, but pet owners in general were kind people.

Devon was handsome and nice and family-oriented, and he wore a suit really well.

He bored Nate to tears.

At first he thought he was having trouble because it had been so long since he went on a date. Maybe it wasn't Devon. Maybe the niceties of small talk just didn't interest Nate anymore because he'd become a misanthropic cave dweller who only cared about himself.

But no. The server came by to take their orders, and Nate cheerfully detoured into a stimulating discussion of the wine list, as it turned out she had once lived next door to one of the vineyards, which happened to be near where Nate grew up. They reminisced about their mutual favorite drive-in ice cream diner until Devon set his water glass down and clinked it against the plate and Nate realized he was being rude and ordered a bottle of pinot.

Thank God he'd taken a Lyft.

"It's just so hard to meet people at our age," Devon said as Nate nodded along, hoping his phone would magically come off silent mode and ring with an urgent telemarketing call. "I can't get into the club scene at all. I just don't see the appeal of meaningless sex."

You've obviously never met Aubrey Chase, Nate thought, but he inclined his head like he was supposed to. Was this what he used to sound like, judging people for their choices? Feeling alive, wanted, desirable wasn't *meaningless*. God, he was such a douchebag. "It's a meat market," he responded automatically. That was the party line, wasn't it?

"Exactly!" Devon said brightly, nearly sloshing his water out of the glass. He'd informed Nate at the beginning of their date that he didn't drink more than one glass of wine, ever. This was the most animated he'd been all night. "Exactly."

Maybe they could still salvage this, Nate thought. Maybe he could just stop answering Devon with what he wanted to hear and have a discussion, a conversation, instead of a call-and-response session. It felt like a weird sermon. Maybe they'd find common ground on a subject that actually mattered and Nate would suddenly find Devon sexually appealing and, if nothing else, go back to his place for sex. Or maybe their food would come quickly and end Nate's suffering before he started contemplating stabbing his own thigh with his steak knife to escape.

Devon would probably insist on driving him to the hospital, but Nate would at least have a good excuse for feigning unconsciousness.

He didn't have luck on any count. Devon mostly kept the conversational topics safe—weather, traffic, the proposed site of a hospital expansion. Nate sat on his left hand and pinched his thigh at intervals in an effort to stay engaged. Devon probably didn't even need drugs to put patients to sleep.

The restaurant was the type of establishment to pride itself on a dining *experience*. In Nate's estimation that mostly meant they took long enough delivering the food that people ordered twice as much alcohol. He didn't think it would reflect well on him if he finished more than one bottle by himself, so numbing his brain was not an option.

The last time he'd gone out to a nice dinner, he'd been with Aubrey. He'd never felt the least bit pressured to say something Aubrey would agree with. Even in bed—

No. He wasn't going to go there now, because apparently that was all it took for his dick to go from "medically induced coma" to "sentry duty."

"Nate?" Devon frowned. "Are you okay?"

Nate snapped himself out of it. "Fine," he made himself say and turned to the server. "Ah, no dessert for me tonight, thanks."

Devon looked like he approved. Maybe he wanted to run screaming away from this date as bad as Nate did.

But Nate's luck persisted. Devon paid the check and then gallantly offered Nate a ride home without even making it sound like an innuendo.

Nate couldn't find a good reason to decline and had to subject himself to an even more boring version of the car-buying spiel Bones had gone through the other night, only this time starring the safety features of a high-end Volvo SUV.

"It's all part of the IntelliSafe system," Devon said of the electric seat belts, which would retract if the car sensed an imminent collision but would then revert to normal if the collision were avoided. "There's even an inflatable curtain in the roof in the event of a rollover accident. I wanted something family-friendly."

Nate wanted kids too, but this was enough to have him debating opening the door and taking his chances. "Modern technology is amazing," he offered instead.

"Oh yeah. And if you saw the things I see in the OR—safety is so important." He shook his head as he signaled well in advance of the left turn his GPS was telling him to take. "I can't believe you played hockey professionally. Talk about a dangerous sport."

"Ah, well," Nate said. Because hockey was dangerous, but it was also fun, and he loved it, and he couldn't stomach the idea of agreeing with someone who seemed to be saying he shouldn't have played. Apparently he had limits. "Sometimes when you love something that much, the risks are worth it. I have a few scars, but I wouldn't change them."

Devon didn't look at him, but then again, he wouldn't. He had to keep his eyes on the road. "Really?" He sounded surprised, but not in a horrified way. "Hmm. I suppose everyone's different."

Wonders never ceased—a real moment of communication, tame as it was. Maybe Nate wasn't completely hopeless.

Maybe he could invite Devon up to his apartment. His dick had never completely forgotten the way he'd reminisced about his night with Aubrey, and now it was ready for action. He could make this thing work with Devon well enough for one night, couldn't he? He had faith in his own hotness.

He could do this.

"Well, here we are," Devon said, pulling into the circle in front of Nate's building.

Oh my God, who says that. "Ah, thanks." Shit, now what? How did Nate ask him up? Was it even fair to do that? What if he thought Nate was interested in him for more than just blowing off steam?

"Thank you for the ride," Nate said automatically and couldn't make it come out sounding like a double entendre. "And for dinner."

Devon smiled *sincerely*. "It was my pleasure. I had a wonderful time."

Before Nate could think of anything to say to that that wouldn't come out sounding sarcastic as fuck, Devon leaned across the car and kissed. His. Cheek.

"Me too," Nate said on autopilot, over the horror track playing on max volume in his brain.

Somehow he managed to say goodbye. He did not have a breakdown in the elevator. He didn't scream when the apartment door closed behind him.

He did drop his clothes just inside the door and walk naked to the bathroom, where he stepped under the hot spray of the shower and leaned his head against the wall.

Was this just the type of guy he attracted? The kind of guy who'd kiss you goodbye on the cheek after a first date and say they had a nice time? The kind of guy who thought sex was cheap? The kind of guy who thought having sex in the missionary position once a week made for a satisfying sex life?

Nate was not going to date Marty again. Not for anything.

He just hoped Kelly didn't take it too hard.

THE SECOND week after Winnipeg, work was hell.

The next road game they covered was in Ottawa. Aubrey didn't understand why they couldn't cover winter road games in warmer climes. The game and the show itself went off smoothly until midway through the third period, when one of the visiting players had some kind of heart problem on the ice. The medical team brought out the defibrillator. Canadian Tire Centre went completely silent, and the rest of the game was called.

Aubrey and Nate ended up at the hotel bar, not speaking, just sitting with their shoulders touching and drinking very expensive scotch very slowly until the news came through that the player was stable.

Nate slumped on his stool. Aubrey paid their tab and poured him into the elevator, then into his hotel room. Then he went back to his own room and hyperventilated for a few minutes. He'd never meant to sign on for nearly watching someone die during competition.

For the rest of the week, sleep was elusive. Aubrey could tell Nate wasn't sleeping much either. They both spent a long time in the makeup chair, having the dark circles under their eyes airbrushed away. Jess must have been feeling the strain too, because she was short with everyone, even though their numbers were up more than ever. Nate mentioned that she actually knew the player who'd had the heart attack, but it didn't make the work environment any more pleasant.

By the time Friday came around, Aubrey needed to unwind. His shoulders were tense, his jaw hurt from grinding his teeth, and he couldn't remember the last time he'd had a good night's sleep. He went to practice with Greg, but his head wasn't in it.

"Tough week?" Greg asked sympathetically.

"I don't want to talk about it," Aubrey said and performed a viciously ugly triple axel.

He went straight home afterward and marched his ass into the shower, where he went through his full primping routine before giving himself a pep talk in the mirror. "This is just a temporary setback. You are hot." He smoothed moisturizer onto his face and neck. "You are rich." A quick but deft application of sixty-dollar mousse to his hair. He reached for the blow dryer. "And you really need to get laid and get it out of your system."

Still, he only had the energy for so much effort. He squeezed into an exorbitantly priced and very flattering pair of jeans, paired them with a black polo shot through with silver thread, and grabbed his fall jacket from the hall closet. He needed to get laid, but he didn't need to get fancy about it. He didn't have the drive to go clubbing, but he knew his neighborhood. The bar down the street would do fine.

It wasn't even ten yet when he arrived, but the bar was full—always a good sign. Aubrey ordered his usual from the bartender, slid onto one of the last available stools, and glanced around to get his bearings.

Everyone else seemed glued to the television screens, which were all playing the same show. Aubrey ransacked his brain, trying to come up with the name. *Love Vote* or something like that? Some sort of train-wreck-like mashup of *Survivor* and *The Bachelor*, with too many barely clothed straight people and not enough brain cells.

The bartender deposited Aubrey's beer, and Aubrey caught his eye with a tilt of his head. "What's up with the screen zombies?"

The bartender rolled his eyes. "It's bingo night."

Before Aubrey could fathom a response, the TV program went to commercial. Someone yelled, "Artificially cutting off a sentence to manufacture suspense!" and three other people yelled, "Bingo!"

Aubrey tore his eyes from the screen and realized that nearly everyone had a piece of paper in front of them. He looked back at the bartender. "I want you to know that a piece of me just died."

"You want a shot to numb the pain?"

Aubrey laughed. "Yeah, sure." Why not.

If everyone here was too busy playing bingo to notice Aubrey was hot and looking for company, his chances of getting laid had just gone out the window. But maybe someone here had gotten dragged along and wasn't in it for bad reality-TV bingo on a Friday night. He just had to find the right target.

Aubrey took the shot.

A couple guys seemed to be present without bingo cards, so there was *some* hope, at least. Though if they were anything like Aubrey, they might give up and leave if bingo went on for long enough.

"Show's over at ten," the bartender told him.

All right. Aubrey could wait that long. Meanwhile he nursed his beer, watching the patrons for people who weren't watching the TV. Wedding band, wedding band, terminal heterosexuality… hm. That one had potential.

Aubrey couldn't see much. The guy was standing at a high top on the other side of the room. The woman next to him was blocking his face, but he was standing in a classic "come and get it" pose, elbows on the table, ass out. It was a good ass too, high and round and interestingly not marred with any kind of underwear line. Jeans that tight, there was a better than average chance the guy was into men. Target acquired.

Now Aubrey just needed to choose his moment.

The show came back on, and the majority of the patrons returned their attention to the screens, leaving Aubrey's path to Maximus Gluteus clear. Unfortunately for Aubrey, before he could make his move, Mr. World Squats Champion 2019 left his table and went to the restroom.

Well, fine. Aubrey could intercept, but he didn't want to be creepy. He gave it sixty seconds and then gave pursuit.

Aubrey lived in a nice neighborhood. The bar was likewise a nice establishment. Even the bathroom had mood lightning.

Captain America's butt double was the only other person in the room, and he was washing his hands, which was a nice affirmation of Aubrey's choices. He had his head ducked, so Aubrey still couldn't see his face, but the rest of him was nice—broad shoulders showed off under a lavender cotton T-shirt that clung lovingly to every muscle. And there were many. Aubrey helped himself to an eyeful, leaning back against the door in a way he knew would show himself off just as well.

"Not into the whole bingo theme, eh?"

The guy's head came up.

Oh shit, Aubrey knew that haircut.

"Don't tell me *you're* here for *Love Vote*."

"To tell you the truth, I was looking for something a little more temporary."

Nate raised his eyebrows. "This place is kind of low-key for you, isn't it?"

Aubrey felt judged. "I can't do Lycra and glitter and thirty-dollar cocktails every night." The conversation was getting away from him. "What are you doing here?"

Nate's brows went up farther and he looked down at himself, expression pointed. Aubrey could see his nipples. Yeah, it was a stupid question. "Picking the wrong night to try this whole hookup thing, apparently."

On the other hand, this gave Aubrey the opportunity to ask a question that had been nagging at him all week. "I take it things didn't go well with Kelly's cousin."

Nate's face shuttered like a seaside villa in a hurricane. "He's an anesthetist who's very good at his job."

Yikes. "My condolences," Aubrey said, torn. On the one hand, maybe that guy's loss would be his gain. On the other hand, Aubrey had enough feelings already, and getting them more tangled up in his cohost seemed like a bad idea.

Aubrey only had two hands, so it would've been a tie, but when his dick weighed in, the balance tipped pretty obviously in one direction.

"So I was thinking," he started, just as Nate said, "Do you want to get out of here?"

They both stopped. A flush was creeping up Nate's cheeks. He flexed his fingers as though he was trying not to fidget.

Aubrey shoved his hands in his pockets to quell the same impulse. This was stupid. He was smooth, God damn it. He didn't fidget. He didn't stammer. He did not have trouble getting hot men to go home with him for sex.

Before he could think of what to say next, Nate raised his arm and rubbed at the back of his neck. Aubrey followed the movement with his eyes, tracing the underside of Nate's arm, the way the fabric pulled against his chest. "I mean," Nate said, "we obviously came here with the same thing in mind. I know hooking up with someone you've already had sex with is sort of the opposite of the point, but on the other hand, that's twenty minutes I don't have to spend pretending to give a fuck about some spray-tanned brats in an ugly house."

Fuck it. If this was all Aubrey was going to get, he was going to take it with both hands and be grateful. "You had me at 'Do you want to get out of here,'" he said. "Let me pay my tab."

CHAPTER TEN

NATE WOKE up five minutes before his alarm more well-rested than he had any right to be, given the activities of the night before. He made himself a breakfast smoothie, took a quick trip down to the gym to run a few miles, then hit the shower and grabbed his go bag from the hall closet.

Aubrey was waiting for their car in front of the building, sipping his abominable canned coffee, but even the thought of that couldn't dim Nate's mood. "Morning."

Aubrey gave him a once-over that made the back of Nate's neck feel hot. "Good morning. You look relaxed." He passed Nate a coffee from the kiosk. "Good night last night?"

Oh, is that how we're playing it? Nate took a sip and wasn't even surprised when it turned out to be his usual order. He didn't know whether Aubrey had memorized it or if he'd asked the kiosk guy. "It was all right," he said casually. "Yours?"

Aubrey's mouth curved up in a smug smile. "Best night's sleep I've had in weeks."

They made small talk on the way to the airport. They had next weekend off for Thanksgiving, and Nate's parents were coming to town. Aubrey, being of the (wrong) opinion that Thanksgiving was an October holiday, was considering spending five days in Hawaii.

Nate wondered if he'd find someone to enjoy it with.

That took some of the fun out of his morning. Nate didn't like to think of himself as selfish, but if Aubrey was going to have sex, he should have it with Nate, who had years of near chastity to make up for.

"Maybe I'll go visit my parents at Christmas," Aubrey said with a shrug, sounding like he'd rather rip out his fingernails with pliers.

That derailed Nate's jealousy spiral. "You really don't get along with them, huh?"

"It's less that we don't get along and more that we're locked in a continuous cycle of mutual disappointment." He turned away from the window and put his empty coffee can in the trash bag on the back of the seat. "They wanted a son who would take over the business, or at least one who'd have a family they could leave the business to. I wanted parents who cared about me more than building their empire."

Suddenly so many things about Aubrey made sense. "I'm sorry."

"Don't be. I mean, I'm lucky. My parents love me. They're not homophobic. I never went to bed hungry or whatever. They supported me when I wanted to be a figure skater. I had every advantage in life."

Not every one, Nate thought, reminiscing on his own childhood. He'd always felt close with his family. "I had a typical hockey mom," he offered, feeling the need to reciprocate somehow. "She used to get a part-time job whenever school was in to pay for all the hockey sticks, 'cause I kept breaking them. She never said that was why she did it, but I knew."

Aubrey looked away from the window and favored him with a soft smile. "She must be proud of you."

Nate swallowed. "I think so." Then he shook his head as another memory hit him. "Tell you what, though, it wasn't all smooth sailing. I thought she was going to hit the roof the day she caught me with my hand down Danny's pants."

Aubrey raised an eyebrow, that soft expression sharpening into amusement. "Oh?"

"I was fourteen. I wasn't out. I mean, I wasn't actively hiding it— at least not very well—"

Aubrey laughed, and Nate did too. Nate's idea of not actively hiding it and Aubrey's were probably a little different.

"—but I hadn't told my parents. Mom was… surprised. Good, though. I think it would've been worse if I was caught with a girl. At least with Danny, neither of us could get pregnant."

"Can't jeopardize that budding NHL career." Aubrey shook his head. "Though I guess being gay is its own kind of jeopardy. Probably not as much as a baby at fourteen."

"That would've been a real nightmare." Nate leaned his head back against the seat and closed his eyes. There was traffic on the way to O'Hare. Well, it was Chicago; there was always traffic.

"Did you want kids?" Aubrey asked suddenly, and Nate's eyes snapped open again. "Or I mean, maybe you still do. Still don't?"

Aubrey could really put his foot in his mouth when he put his mind to it. Among other things. "I always did. Marty and I planned on it, you know, in that vague 'after retirement' way."

"Not just because it's what hockey players do?"

"No. I like kids." Admitting it felt bittersweet now, since God knew when or if he'd ever have any. "What about you?" he asked, half joking, half to deflect attention.

Aubrey opened his mouth as though to give a prepared answer, then paused. Nate watched his shoulders creep toward his ears and then back down again as he fought some kind of instinctive reaction. Then he said, "I, uh, I never thought I did. I had all those wild oats, and it's not like I had great parenting role models. But uh, therapy, right? A lot of the hang-ups I've had in the past were just excuses to keep evading my own issues. I'm overcoming my compulsive need to be the center of attention. And kids… maybe. I like them, but that's not the same as wanting my own. Is it weird if I say I've never really thought about it?"

"Not weird," Nate decided. Given Aubrey's relationship with his family, it made sense. Sad, maybe, but he didn't say that out loud. "It makes you think, though."

"Hmm?"

"I spent my whole life doing what people expected, regardless of whether it was what I wanted. And you spent your whole life doing whatever you wanted no matter what people expected. But here we are."

Aubrey tilted his head.

"Are you happy?" Nate blurted.

Aubrey's mouth dropped open. Then he looked at his watch. "Nate. It's not even ten a.m."

"You can wait until after cocktail hour to answer if you want." Maybe he'd overstepped.

But maybe not. "Are you?" Aubrey countered after a moment.

"I'm not *unhappy*." He had a good life—a good job, a nice place to live, fairly few worries, a few good friends, a loving family. "But I think if I'd made different decisions—if I'd really thought about what I wanted instead of what other people wanted for me—I don't know. Maybe I'd be happier." Now for the uncomfortably honest part. "You seem like you've done the opposite. I was just wondering if you thought it was better—if it made you happier in the long run."

"I think there's a saying about this," Aubrey mused without answering the question. "Something about—happiness is appreciating what you have, rather than having everything you want."

Nate sipped his coffee and looked out the window. "Maybe you should get me the number for your therapist."

Aubrey laughed. "Therapy's not that simple. I read that on a fortune cookie."

Nate's stomach rumbled. "I wonder if there's a good Chinese place in Tampa."

They pulled up to the airport, and Aubrey tipped the driver while Nate got their bags. When Aubrey slipped off after Security to indulge in his weird airport pulp fiction fetish, Nate grabbed breakfast pastries and staked out a couple chairs in the lounge.

Before he could get more than a bite into his croissant, Kelly sat down in the chair across from him.

Nate wouldn't say he *panicked*. Nate would not say he shat his metaphorical pants. Nate would not say those things, but they were still true.

"So," Kelly said. Nate's balls tried to crawl back up into his body. "You've been kind of hard to pin down the past couple weeks."

Fuuuuuck.

"Uh, sorry," Nate said, knowing it sounded feeble. Before Aubrey, he'd spent a lot of time with Kelly on breaks in filming. He'd always had lunches with her too. But he had a feeling she was talking about more than the fact that she was eating alone. "It's just been a really busy few weeks, you know? Trying to get ready for the holiday and everything."

Kelly crossed her legs and raised an eyebrow. "Wow. Good thing you're a sports announcer and not an actor."

Nate winced but didn't bother trying to defend himself.

"I don't get it," Kelly said. "Devon said your date went well. But you haven't returned his calls. You ghosted him. That's pretty shitty."

"Yeah." Well, it was. Nate had managed to reply to one text, but it was a trite *it's not you, sorry* that he still cringed even thinking about. "I know. I...."

"I mean, either you're going to call him and do a *lot* of groveling, or...." She sighed. "Maybe this was a dumb idea. I should've stayed out of it."

She sounded like she meant it. She looked like it too, which made it that much worse—especially since Nate was the one who'd introduced her to Caley. He knew she wanted to return the favor.

"No, it's not your fault. When we talked the first time, I really did think I wanted to start dating again, I just...."

Aubrey came into the lounge, nose already buried in the paperback. One of these days he was going to run into something, or someone.

"I'm not looking for anything serious right now," Nate forced himself to say. There. The honest truth. Not that he'd consider Devon either way, but Devon didn't have to know that. "I thought I was, but I'm not."

It wasn't until Kelly softened and the tension eased from her face and posture that Nate realized he'd made her believe he wasn't over the divorce. "Oh. Nate, I'm sorry too. It's really none of my business, but I want you to be happy, you know?"

"I do, and I appreciate that."

Nate was saved from having to elaborate further when Aubrey took the chair across from Kelly, barely looking up from his book. Nate nudged the pastry bag at him, and he took it without looking.

"But I'm actually pretty happy being single," Nate finished, which was also weirdly true. He hadn't had one of those moments of self-pity in weeks.

She shrugged. "If you say so."

Fortunately their flight was called for boarding before anyone could choose a more awkward conversation topic. Saved by the buzzer.

They did their pregame meeting in one of Amalie Arena's conference rooms, throwing around ideas of how to fill the dead air.

"First guy to mention Alex Killorn went to Harvard buys dinner," Aubrey suggested with a smirk.

Nate cracked up. "You're on."

"While I have you here," Jess interrupted, "there's something we should talk about."

Aubrey and Nate locked eyes, then turned to her. Nate knew her serious business voice, and this wasn't it, not exactly. This was stress, anxiety… maybe something else too.

Kelly straightened in her chair. "What's going on, boss?"

Jess leaned back and stared up at the ceiling for a moment, drumming her fingers on the armrests. "The thing is, I don't know." She lifted her head and regarded each of them in turn. "I'm not going to lie to you—our decision to fire John Plum didn't go over well with our usual audience. You all know ratings in our traditional market suffered in the wake of that, even though I stand by that decision."

That sounded ominous. "I thought things were going better," Nate prompted. Twitter loved them, or at least loved to talk about them, which was almost the same thing.

"They are. We're actually up a couple points over where we were last year. That's why I'm cautiously optimistic about the meeting the director of the board called me to. It's the second week in December."

Kelly leaned forward over the table. "Any idea what it's about? Like, did you get a feeling, positive or negative…?"

"I got a notification from our calendar app." Jess shook her head. "His assistant set it up. She doesn't know anything either."

"It might not be bad news." Aubrey sat forward too. His gaze sharpened from lazy amusement into something focused and intent. "It could be they're thinking of a time-slot change—more episodes, different format. What's the guy like?"

Jess sighed. "He's the kind of guy who takes weeks to make up his mind, but once he does, he'll never change it."

"There we go, then," Aubrey said. "We have two and a half weeks to show him why the network should keep us."

"So, no pressure," Kelly deadpanned.

Nate looked at Aubrey, looked at Jess, then shrugged. "We're professional athletes. Working under pressure is kind of our thing."

NATE AND Aubrey did, in fact, work best under pressure. That night's show in Tampa, they found another level to the back-and-forth that had made them a surprise hit on the internet, even if all Aubrey's goading couldn't coerce Nate to say the word *Harvard*. Instead he managed to needle Nate about official NHL height statistics during intermission while Kelly was setting up to interview one of the Lightning players in the tunnel.

"I'm just saying, NHL height statistics are a little like"—*don't say Grindr, don't say Grindr*—"online dating profiles. Look, here's yours. It says you're five eleven."

Nate gave him a long-suffering look—he was *maybe* five ten if Aubrey were being generous—but Aubrey could see the amusement playing behind his eyes. "And that's our cue to go to Kelly outside the Bolts' locker room, where she'll be interviewing Tyler Johnson about the penalty kill, big saves from Vasilevskiy, and his power-play goal."

The interview was smooth enough—typical hockey talk, full of buzzwords and rehearsed answers, signifying nothing—but when the video cut back to the two of them in the booth, Aubrey looked at Nate and said flatly, "If that man is five nine, I'm Evgeni Plushenko."

This time Nate responded without missing a beat. "Maybe the NHL let a Russian judge take his measurements."

Before Aubrey could recover from Nate making a figure-skating joke live on air, Nate went on, "And now for score updates from around the league," and he had to scramble to keep up.

He was pretty sure it was a meme before they even left the arena.

The show staff had rooms for the night at the Marriott Waterside, but Aubrey still had that hankering for American Chinese food. He and Nate caught a cab after the game and ended up at Ming Garden, where Aubrey ate his weight in the house special lo mein while Nate put away a respectable amount of barbecue pork, both of them bickering good-naturedly the whole time.

When the server brought the check, they looked at each other blankly. Neither of them had won the bet, but usually restaurants back home asked them if they wanted to split it. Apparently they weren't recognized as work colleagues here, but that was fine. Right? Aubrey was determined it should be fine, so he shrugged and reached for his wallet. "You can get it next time."

It was stupid. Because until that moment of blank panic, it had felt kind of like a date. Or like Aubrey imagined a date would feel, since he'd never really been on any. The conversation came easily, he felt comfortable, the evening held that undercurrent of attraction that made it feel like anything could happen. The night held *possibilities*.

Except, of course, that Nate wasn't looking to date anyone. He was happy being single. Aubrey had forced himself to forget about that remark while they were working, but it had sneaked up on him again during dinner, and now it threatened to spoil his evening.

He couldn't afford to get maudlin. Nate would notice, for one thing.

Nate cracked open his fortune cookie while Aubrey was signing the check. "What's yours say?"

Aubrey bit off a chunk of crunchy moon-shaped goodness and glanced down at the paper he pulled away. When he'd swallowed, he read aloud, "Work with your destiny. Stop trying to outrun it." Maybe a little too on the nose, and considering Nate's recent announcement, it stung. He wasn't trying to outrun anything anymore. "Yours?"

"Follow the middle path," Nate recited dutifully. "Neither extreme will make you happy." He shook his head. "That's almost creepy, considering our conversation this morning."

And Aubrey thought his had been too insightful. "Don't know why I spend all that money on therapy when I could eat fortune cookies instead."

Though it was late November, the air was pleasant and warm. "You want to walk back?" Aubrey suggested, and then immediately realized how date-like that sounded and had to wipe suddenly sweaty palms on his pants. Nate was pretty oblivious. He'd probably pass it off as an innocent suggestion that they get some exercise. "We're not gonna get weather like this in Chicago for a while."

"Yeah, not a bad idea after that."

The restaurant was in a pseudo industrial area, which kept the walk from feeling romantic, but Aubrey couldn't help thinking of what it could be like. It was nice, going out to dinner with Nate. Riding in cars with Nate. Even waiting around in airports with Nate was superior to traveling alone, and not just because Nate bought him pastries.

What if he could have that all the time?

"You're quiet tonight," Nate commented as they reached the shinier, cleaned-up Channelside.

"Just thinking," Aubrey answered. Just thinking, *Why does my timing suck so bad? Why couldn't I have met you when you were actually looking for a relationship? What can I do to convince you to give this a shot?*

Not that it would matter if he did, probably, because the bigger question was still *Who do I think I'm kidding?*

Normally Aubrey would've expected his comment to earn him a smart remark. Tonight Nate only cocked his head and glanced at him sidelong. "All right. You want to talk about it?"

Yes. But he couldn't make himself say the words. "Maybe some other time."

CHAPTER ELEVEN

THE TRIP home from Tampa was a shitshow.

The first flight got canceled when the aircraft experienced difficulties with its landing gear, leaving the crew stranded in the airport for four hours until the next flight to O'Hare… which was delayed several more hours due to a freak blizzard that had blown in off Lake Michigan.

Even the private lounge couldn't keep them entertained. Nate broke two hours into the second delay and went for a walk. By the time he returned, Aubrey was slouched on a sofa with a posture that suggested his spine had slithered out his ass and crawled away to die. His paperback, which he'd finished before Nate left, lay discarded on the table.

Nate dropped a new one on the couch next to Aubrey and picked up his castoff. "This any good?"

Aubrey looked down at the book—it was the next in the series he was reading—and then at Nate. "It beats staring at the wall for two more hours."

He had a point there.

When they finally landed in Chicago, it was close to midnight, the ground was covered in a layer of white, and Nate was wiped. "I'm getting a cab, if you're going straight back," he offered as they slogged through the airport.

Aubrey shot him a quizzical and also very tired look, which was fair. Where exactly did Nate think he was going to go after eleven on a Sunday night? Especially when they were supposed to have been home twelve hours ago.

"Stupid question?" Nate asked.

Aubrey waved that off. "I'll cut you some slack this time since today sucked so bad."

Nate snorted. "I appreciate it. I'm beginning to think I left my brain in Tampa."

"At least it won't get frostbite."

Just as Nate opened his mouth to reply, a harried-looking woman pushing a tandem stroller knocked into his leg.

"Oh God, I'm so sorry!" She had dark circles under her eyes, and the baby was fussing. "I'm just, I'm exhausted, I'm supposed to be flying to my parents' for Thanksgiving and then the snowstorm and—I'm so sorry, I wasn't looking where I was going."

"It's fine," Nate promised her, and was about to move on when he noticed Aubrey kneeling next to the stroller.

"Dropped something," Aubrey explained, holding up a stuffed lamb with a visible coating of baby slime on its ear. "I don't know, do these things have to be disinfected before they go back in the baby's mouth?"

"Not if I don't want everyone in Chicago to hate me."

Aubrey conceded the point with a tilt of his head and wiped the stuffed animal on his trousers before offering it to the baby, who paused mid fuss and reached out a chubby fist. Beside the infant, a curly-haired toddler slept peacefully.

Aubrey glanced at Nate, brows raised in an implicit question. Nate wanted to say no, but this woman could probably use the help. Sleep would wait another ten minutes. He nodded imperceptibly, and Aubrey asked, "Can we offer you a hand getting to your gate?"

By the time they climbed into the car, Nate's legs were throbbing and his eyes kept falling closed.

Aubrey seemed to agree, if the way he leaned his head against the window and sighed were any indication. "God. I cannot wait for a hot shower and a warm bed."

A warm bed *did* sound nice. Especially one that potentially had Aubrey in it, not that Nate had the energy to do much with him tonight. It would be convenient to stash him there until morning, though.

For the life of him, Nate couldn't figure out how to ask. *Hey, I know you're leaving for Hawaii tomorrow afternoon, but want to spend the night so we can get laid first thing tomorrow morning?* Aubrey probably had plenty of willing bodies lined up for him in Hawaii anyway, or he would as soon as he landed. Nate had no doubt he'd find as much company as he wanted.

They rode back in sleepy silence. Nate wasn't expecting anything more than a muttered good night, but then their phones chimed simultaneously as they waited for the elevator.

"The fuck?" Nate griped as they reached in their pockets in unison. "I swear, if this is Jess telling us the show's canceled, I will do a murder. I need sleep. Whatever it is can wait until tomorrow."

"Not Jess." Aubrey seemed to have gotten the message first, and he didn't look happy.

Nate soon found out why: They'd received a text from building management apologizing to residents of the top four floors for the lack of heat and water due to "unforeseen circumstances beyond our control." A second text promised that residents who submitted receipts for hotels would be reimbursed up to $250. Nate guessed the message had been delayed by his phone's habitual reluctance to come out of flight mode all at once instead of in stages.

"Oh, fuck *me*," Aubrey muttered.

Nate could relate. He couldn't imagine summoning the energy to pack up a fresh bag and head out into the cold, only to have to pack again tomorrow.

"Well, that's one good thing about being a peon on an unfashionable floor," Nate quipped. "Warm air and hot water."

Obviously Aubrey could stay with him. But now he was torn. First he hadn't known how to ask Aubrey to come over for sex. Now he didn't know how to say, "Come over, but we're only sleeping. I can't even get my eyelids above half-mast; my dick is a lost cause."

Aubrey huffed. "Not funny, Nate."

The elevator doors opened, and Aubrey cut Nate off to get in. He jabbed at the Close Door button, obviously in no mood to be teased.

Damn it. He might as well give it a shot. Nate stuck his arm out before stepping in beside Aubrey.

The doors closed.

"Didn't mean it to be," he said, mentally fortifying himself. Although really, what was he worried about? What was Aubrey going to do, turn down a warm place to sleep that didn't involve trekking all over the city? "Come stay at mine. I would've asked earlier, but I'm kind of beat. I didn't want my mouth to write checks my body couldn't cash."

Aubrey stared at him for a second, expression unreadable. Then he sighed and his shoulders relaxed. "Thanks. Got the guest room made up?"

Nate rolled his eyes. "Maybe not *that* beat." He pressed the button for his own floor, then Aubrey's. "Get whatever you need. I'll leave the door unlocked."

CHAPTER TWELVE

THE DOOR was unlocked when Aubrey got down to Nate's apartment, which was a good thing, since Nate was sacked out and snoring softly when Aubrey padded into his bedroom and then through to the bathroom. He shut the door gently behind him so he could shower without waking Nate.

And wasn't that a trip? From unprofessionalism to grudging professionalism, to a friendly fake rivalry with hot sex, a romantic walk, and now here Aubrey was, being *domestic*, and so thoroughly exhausted he couldn't even properly freak out about it.

At least Nate had a really nice shower with great water pressure for Aubrey to not freak out in.

It took five minutes or so to soothe enough of the tension from his body that he could stomach the idea of sliding into bed with Nate. He couldn't remember the last time he'd shared a bed with someone with sex off the table. At a sleepover with Jackson his first year of high school, maybe. It felt like a lifetime ago.

Feeling a very strange urge to be modest, he slipped on a clean pair of boxers and crawled into bed. Nate didn't move; his breathing was deep and even now, with no trace of that wheezy snore. He was throwing off enough heat to make the whole bed feel cozy and welcoming, which was impressive considering he kept his apartment basically sub-zero when he wasn't home.

Aubrey closed his eyes. The window was oriented differently than the one in his bedroom, which gave him a start a few times when he began to drift off, only to jerk awake wondering where he was. Then Nate let out a gusty sigh in his sleep and rolled over, flinging his arm around Aubrey's waist as he did so.

Aubrey's fight-or-flight instinct said, *Fuck this, I'm out.* Nate was warm and he smelled nice, and the steady rise and fall of his chest against Aubrey's shoulder sealed it. Between one moment and the next, Aubrey fell asleep.

Waking up again happened decidedly more gradually.

Sometime in the night Aubrey had shifted onto his side, facing the window. The lightness behind his eyelids coaxed him to consciousness. He must have flailed around a little while he slept, because now only the sheet covered him, and that only halfway up his chest.

But he was warm. *Really* warm. Especially along his back and across his stomach. A few more breaths into wakefulness, he realized that Nate had crept closer in the night and was now pressed up against him, his stubble scratching at the back of Aubrey's shoulder.

Aubrey wasn't sure if Nate was entirely awake, but parts of him definitely were, and they were getting intimately acquainted with Aubrey's ass.

He was just taking a deep breath to fortify himself to move out of Nate's embrace when Nate rumbled and rubbed his scruff against the back of Aubrey's neck. Aubrey's dick went from *Good morning, I guess* to *Hello, sailor.*

"Hey," Nate said in a register an octave and a half lower than his normal speaking voice. His thumb was making small concentric circles on the sensitive skin of Aubrey's abdomen.

Aubrey's body was on a low simmer now, all systems coming online at once. "Hey," he rasped back, shuddering as Nate nosed against his ear.

"How, ah…." The nuzzling paused. "How do you feel about morning sex?"

Aubrey had never stayed the night with anyone, but this didn't feel like the right time to mention that. "Strongly in favor."

Nate kissed the juncture of his shoulder, hot and wet with a scrape of teeth. "Happy to hear that."

Happy was one word for it. Aubrey's dick jerked hard enough against his stomach that Nate probably felt the vibration. He swallowed, hot in a way that had nothing to do with body heat. When Aubrey inhaled, Nate's hand slid lower on his abdomen, his fingertips just shy of Aubrey's boxers. Aubrey sucked in another breath through his teeth and tried not to buck too obviously into the touch. "You seem like you have a plan in mind."

Nate nipped his ear and nudged his hips closer. "Maybe. You good if I take the lead?"

Aubrey could not lead his way out of a wet paper bag right then. Every sense was on overload. "Good," he agreed. Good. Great. Absolutely incredible.

"Good," Nate repeated, dragging the prickle of his scruff over the side of Aubrey's neck. He slid his hand around Aubrey's side, sneaking under the waistband of his boxers. Aubrey wriggled, intent on being helpful in freeing himself, but Nate sank his teeth gently into Aubrey's earlobe. "Uh-uh. Like this."

Like this—with his boxers pushed down around his upper thighs and no farther, exposing his ass and his erection without leaving him room to move.

Aubrey took a deep breath, but it felt like inhaling molasses. The air smelled thick with sex already. He swallowed, licked his lips. His tongue felt too big for his mouth, and his cock was drooling. "I, ah. With you so far."

"Mm-hmm, I can tell." Nate cupped his balls, then trailed his fingers up to the head of Aubrey's dick, a featherlight touch that was hardly even a tease. Then his hand disappeared and a familiar click told Aubrey Nate had been optimistic when preparing for bed last night. A second later Nate's hand nudged between his asscheeks.

Aubrey's pulse thundered in his ears. It had been a while since someone fucked him, but he wanted it now, bad enough that his brain was lining up words like *please* and *I want*.

Nate didn't even try to push inside him. Instead he slicked Aubrey's cheeks, sparing only the filthiest flirting caress for Aubrey's hole.

Then he lined up and slid the head of his cock between Aubrey's thighs.

Oh fuck.

Aubrey took a shaky breath, biting back a moan. A couple weeks ago he'd fucked Nate six ways from Sunday the filthiest way he knew how, and now Nate was dismantling him with a little casual frottage. His whole chest hitched, and his breathing stuttered when Nate pulled back too far and his cock slid between Aubrey's asscheeks on the next thrust. It reminded him viscerally that Nate wasn't fucking him, but he *could*. Nate exhaled quietly next to Aubrey's ear and adjusted his dick between Aubrey's thighs again. The heat seeped into his brain, into his being.

Aubrey parted his lips, hoping to cool himself, but his whole body was burning. Nate's deliberate, unhurried thrusts had him struggling to stay quiet, afraid any noise might break the spell. The rasp of Nate's beard on his neck and shoulders and next to his ear set every synapse firing, creating a molten sea of sensation. When Nate pushed forward, his cock nudged Aubrey's balls and the base of his dick. It was a hot wave that crashed and receded, and Aubrey was adrift on it, was drowning.

When Nate's hand, still slick with lube, slid lower and wrapped around his cock, Aubrey gave in to it. The pleasure of that firm, slow, knowing touch brought him to the edge and held him there. All he could do was pull the pillow close enough to his face to bite into it, stifling the noises that begged to be released.

Without conscious thought, Aubrey was moving too, clenching his ass and thighs, pushing back against Nate, rolling forward into the grip of his hand. His body was strung to the limits of its tension, vibrating on a precipice, waiting for the slightest change to topple him over. He couldn't move his hand to curl it around Nate's and force it tighter, faster. He could barely do more than breathe and hold on.

But even Nate must have had limits, because suddenly he groaned, and his thrusts came quicker, harder. Aubrey pressed his open mouth against the pillow in a silent scream, moisture leaking from the corners of his eyes. He was so close. Just a little more.

Nate sucked his earlobe into his mouth and thumbed the head of his cock, and that was enough. Aubrey came without a sound, half holding his breath, half convinced this was an incredible dream. His orgasm went on and on as Nate rocked between his thighs, teasing out every last drop with his hand, until finally he broke too, his mouth a wet brand on the side of Aubrey's neck as he came, spurting over the insides of his thighs, his balls, his hole. Aubrey's cock jerked again in sympathy, producing another pathetic dribble that felt like it was wrung out of him.

Holy fuck.

Holy *fuck*.

"Mmm," Nate said, mouthing Aubrey's skin in what even Aubrey's addled brain could tell was lazy satisfaction.

All Aubrey could come up with was *hnnngh*, which seemed stupid and obvious and dangerous. He didn't say anything.

"That was nice," Nate murmured, rubbing his beard on Aubrey's neck again like he was a cat and Aubrey was his scratching post.

Nice. *Nice*. He'd just taken everything Aubrey thought he knew about sex and turned it upside-down, and he thought it was *nice*? He'd taken a sex act Aubrey had considered foreplay until twenty minutes ago and turned it into possibly the hottest sex of his *life*.

Nice?

Aubrey was gathering himself to voice this protest when Nate snuffled happily and then… relaxed.

Aubrey's protest died on his lips the same as his pleas, this time out of shock rather than self-defense. Had he really—*really*?

He turned to glance over his shoulder. Sure enough, Nate had fallen asleep.

I cannot believe this. Fuck my life.

But at least this gave Aubrey the chance to fall apart in private. On shaky, reluctant legs, he stood from the bed and wobbled toward the en suite.

On second thought, if he was going to have a full-on breakdown, he wanted to do it far enough away that Nate wouldn't hear him if he managed to get his mouth to say actual things out loud, like "What the fuck" and "No, seriously, what the *fuck*."

This was, he reflected as he walked very awkwardly to the guest bathroom on the other side of the apartment, the sort of situation that people paid their therapists for. But so far, words had not even returned, so Aubrey was—Aubrey was so fucked.

First sex, then romance, and now domesticity. And it turned out domestic sex, at least with Nate, was so blisteringly hot, it broke Aubrey's entire brain into component parts that couldn't even speak to each other. He stared at the knobs in the shower for thirty seconds before remembering he should get in. He stared at the little guest shampoo and soap lined up neatly on the shower shelf.

He stared at the water pooling in the drain as a gob of come unstuck from the back of his thigh and landed next to his foot.

That, at least, jolted him out of his stupor. He cupped his hands and scrubbed his face, washing away the salt of sweat. He needed to get clean. Somehow they'd managed to sleep until—Aubrey didn't actually know, but his internal clock was telling him it was closer to lunch than breakfast time. His flight left from O'Hare at two and he hadn't packed.

The trouble was, he kept slipping back into thoughts of Nate. Nate's charm, good humor, and smile, and the way he always seemed to think of Aubrey even if he wasn't directly talking to him. The stupid notebook was full of examples by now.

His whole life, Aubrey had waited for someone to put him first. He knew that was part of what had kept him from dating anyone seriously—no one had ever done it, and he equally feared finding out no one ever would and having it and then losing it again.

Nate didn't put him first. Aubrey wasn't going to romanticize their whatever it was *that* much. Nate made him feel like he *didn't actually need that*. He just needed someone to be considerate.

It was far more dangerous.

I need to make an appointment with my therapist, Aubrey thought grimly as he reached for the shampoo.

He made it through his shower on autopilot, washing his hair, working come out of undignified places. In a few hours, he'd be on a plane and he wouldn't have to think about Nate again for a whole week. He'd have ample opportunity to find someone in Hawaii with an ass that could compete with Nate's. It probably existed. If not, maybe Jackson could hook him up later. Either way, he'd be fine. He just needed some perspective.

Clean now, Aubrey shut off the water, realizing belatedly that he'd forgotten to grab a towel. He ran both hands through his hair, shaking out as much water as he could, then squeezing out a little more. There was a linen closet in the hallway. He wouldn't have to drip for too far.

Aubrey used the bathroom hand towel to dry himself as much as he could, not wanting to damage the nice floors. He carried it with him into the hallway to drop in the laundry once he was done with it. Nobody needed to dry their hands on it now.

Nate had a nice collection of home linens, which amused Aubrey because he didn't have any other decorating sense to speak of. Look at that deep blue. Aubrey could tell just from looking at it that it would be soft and fluffy. He reached out to grab it and had just closed his hand around an actual absorbent cloud when there was a soft click, and then—

"Surprise, Nate! We changed our flight—"

Instinctively, Aubrey turned around and met wide eyes with a woman in her sixties who, from her sharp nose and high cheekbones, was immediately recognizable as Nate's mother.

The towel dropped from Aubrey's suddenly nerveless fingers.

Nate's mother raised her hand to her mouth. "Oh my God! Oh my God, I'm so sorry—" and she fled the apartment, closing the door behind her.

Aubrey stared at the door. He stared at the tiny hand towel on the floor between his feet. Then back to the door again, which he'd have to leave through in order to escape this waking nightmare. At least, unless he wanted to fling himself out Nate's fifteenth-story window. He'd never had to meet any of his conquests' parents before, and now, when he actually wanted to make a good impression, one of them walked in on him *naked in her son's apartment*.

"Fuck my actual life," he sighed, wrapping the towel around his waist, and went to wake up Nate.

CHAPTER THIRTEEN

"NATE. NATE, wake up."

"Mnnn," Nate grumbled, pulling his pillow closer. There was a reason he didn't often sleep in, and that was that the longer he did, the less he wanted to get out of bed. That went double after morning sex.

"Nate," Aubrey hissed again, urgently enough that this time, Nate opened his eyes. Aubrey's eyes were wild and his cheeks were pale. "Get your ass out of bed *right now*. Your parents are here."

Nate's brain went from warm and fuzzy to cold, almost painful clarity. "They're not supposed to be here until Wednesday!"

"They got an earlier flight," Aubrey bit out, scrambling around for the clothes he must've brought the night before. "They wanted it to be a surprise. Well, *I'm surprised*!"

It occurred to Nate as Aubrey frantically tugged on his underwear that he was *very* naked. "How surprised?" he asked, reaching for clean clothes of his own.

"Fully frontal surprised, Nathan!"

Nate winced. Okay, so that was bad. "Fuck."

"You might say that!"

At least she seemed to have walked in after Aubrey showered, rather than before. Though considering Aubrey's mood right now, Nate kept that thought to himself. "All right," he said, thinking out loud as he hopped into a pair of sweatpants. "This is okay. We can fix this."

"Fix *what*?" Aubrey said, throwing a venomous look over his shoulder as he struggled into a cashmere sweater that probably cost half a month's rent. "I'm pretty sure we can't go into your mom's brain and *remove the image of my dick*!"

"Okay, yes, that's awkwardness we're just going to have to live with—"

"We?" Aubrey asked. "*We*?"

"—but it's not like they have to know we're, I don't know, casually fucking or whatever."

This gave Aubrey pause. "You want to just pretend I was staying here because of the broken heat upstairs?" His voice came down half a register.

"Oh no, they definitely won't buy that. They've been hinting that they think there's something going on for weeks. I've just pretended not to notice. But we could tell them we're dating."

"*What!*"

But the plan was coming together now, and the pitch of Aubrey's indignant squawk couldn't derail Nate's train of thought. "It's perfect. The timing is right. They've been bugging me to move on. I've been stalling them, but that could just as easily be because I wanted to keep the whole dating a coworker thing quiet."

"Nate—"

Nate loved his parents, and he knew they loved him. But they had certain expectations of their son, and casual hookups with a coworker didn't fit them. He might be ready to adjust his expectations of himself, but he didn't know if he was ready for his parents to see him differently.

"Please," he said. "Hear me out."

To his surprise, Aubrey sat on the bed and folded his hands in his lap. He looked uncomfortable, and his shoulders were hunched, but he was listening.

"Just for the week," he pleaded. "If I tell them the truth, they're going to think I'm having a midlife crisis a few years ahead of schedule."

"Aren't you?" He let that hang in the air for a moment and then continued, "Anyway, we work together, remember? You were there when Jess demanded not to change anything."

"So we tell my parents it has to be a secret!" That was just obvious. "They had a gay son who played hockey. I wasn't always out. They understand."

Aubrey spitted him with a flat stare. "You want to have a secret fake relationship. You do know this isn't a Hallmark Channel Original Movie, right? Besides, I'm supposed to be on a plane to Hawaii in three hours. How do we explain your beloved boyfriend jetting off to a tropical island paradise without you?"

Shit. "Cancel it! I will pay you whatever it cost, okay, just…." He couldn't articulate why this was so important. "Please."

Aubrey stared at him, calculating. Nate was wearing him down. He could see it. Finally.

"All right," he said. "All right! This is the craziest thing I've ever done. I've never met anyone's parents. They're going to hate me or think I'm a gold-digger or—"

Nate exhaled a long breath as relief flooded his system. "No, you're good. Mom followed your skating career. She knows you have more money than I do."

"—and we have to get rid of your fugly vase, okay? You can't be shacking up with a boyfriend when you still have your horrible honeymoon trophy on display."

That was a fair point. "*Thank you*," Nate said.

Aubrey sighed. "I can't believe I'm doing this. Come on. Let's go hide the evidence so we can let your parents in. I can't believe your mom saw me naked."

"If you thought that was awkward," Nate said grimly, "wait till she tries to give me a high-five."

IN POINT of fact, it turned out to be a fist bump.

A few moments after they finished hiding the ugly vase in the master bathroom, there was an actual knock on the door, and Nate and Aubrey went together to open it.

Aubrey wanted to die. He was making his own bed and he knew it. The problem was he was going to be lying in it alone after this week was over.

Nate cleared his throat. "Hi, Mom. Dad. You're early."

Nate's father gave his son a look that Aubrey interpreted clearly as *this was all your mother's idea*. "Nathan. We're sorry to drop by unannounced."

"So, so sorry," his mother chimed in, stepping inside. Aubrey believed her—her mortified reaction hadn't been fake—but she was beaming with a lot more than embarrassment. She flung herself into Nate's arms and squeezed.

Aubrey watched with a mounting sense of dread, but he still wasn't prepared for the speed at which she released her son and fell upon him, taking both of Aubrey's hands. "You must be Aubrey. Oh, we've heard so much about you. I should have suspected...."

Aubrey attempted a smile. "It's nice to meet you, Mrs. Overton."

"Oh, no, no. It's Diane, please."

Nate's father, Elliot, was more reserved, and within seconds, it was obvious where Nate got his sense of humor. While Aubrey was shaking his hand, Nate's mother turned to Nate, mouthed, "Oh my God," and held out her fist.

Aubrey had the pleasure of watching from six feet back as Nate went scarlet from his nape to the tips of his ears. He did the fist-bump, though.

Nate's dad watched Aubrey watch this, his own amusement evident, and said, "On the plus side, it's not like things can get any more awkward."

"Bite your tongue," Aubrey said automatically, then immediately regretted saying something so rude.

But Elliot laughed like Aubrey was hilarious and clapped him on the shoulder. "Come on, you can help me with the bags. She's going to talk his ear off for at least the next fifteen minutes, and I swear she brought three outfits for every day."

If Aubrey was expecting a shovel speech, he was disappointed. He almost felt indignant on Nate's behalf. But he couldn't really fault them. It was obvious the Overtons were warm, open people—a close-knit unit. No wonder Nate had never really thought much about hooking up. If Aubrey had grown up in a family like this, he would have been looking to build his own too.

He managed to make his escape after about an hour, citing a lunchtime social commitment. In actuality, he went upstairs to his frigid apartment, canceled his Hawaii trip, scheduled an emergency session with his therapist, and ate a sleeve of Oreos.

Then, feeling sorry for himself, he took out his phone and scrolled through the contacts.

Mom.

He left the name highlighted for a few seconds, deliberating. Did he really want to put himself through this? He almost always ended up hanging up feeling worse, irritated, even if the conversation had been fine.

He hit Dial before he could talk himself out of it, but the line rang three times and then went to voicemail.

Probably for the best.

Aubrey couldn't have said what made him leave a message. Maybe it was the happy-families scene going on downstairs. "Hey, Mom. It's me." Wow, original. "Uh, I just wanted to let you know there was a change of plan and I'm sticking around Chicago this week. Anyway, I was just… calling to say hi." For the first time ever. "Maybe I'll try you again later."

Click.

Well, that went well. Aubrey sighed at his phone and winced when his breath fogged in the cold air.

Now what?

WITH AUBREY technically on vacation for the week, Nate spent Tuesday filming with Paul Mitchell, a guest star they'd had booked since the preseason.

Nate liked Paul. They'd never played together—Paul had retired a few years earlier than Nate, and they'd never been on the same team—but they'd met several times over the years, and he was easygoing and personable enough to run a successful web series of his own.

Maybe Nate had gotten spoiled filming with Aubrey, because it took him and Paul the first half of the show to find their rhythm, and even then, it felt lacking. Nate would leave the airspace open for a quip, line it up perfectly for Aubrey, but Paul would miss it entirely or go in a direction so unexpected it left Nate floundering.

But it was the last show he had to do until Saturday. Thursday Kelly was hosting a combination clip show and commentary with Caley while Nate spent the whole holiday with his family. He hadn't been able to do that in years.

Of course, this year would be a little different.

By the time he returned from the studio, his stomach was growling. He waved to the concierge and got into the elevator, vaguely hoping there was something left in the fridge. If not, maybe he could sneak upstairs and raid Aubrey's cupboards.

But when he pushed open the door, he found the apartment rather more occupied than he expected.

Before he could do much more than say hello, Aubrey got up from the couch, leaving Nate's parents alone in the living room, and tilted his head toward the master bedroom. Nate followed, bemused. "What's going on?" he asked. "I thought they fixed the heat at your place this morning."

"Yeah, they did." Aubrey looked wild around the eyes. "I ran into your parents in the lobby when they were on their way back from the Art Institute. They insisted on inviting me up for dinner and a show. *Our* show, except without me."

That sounded even more awkward than Nate's evening. He winced. "Sorry."

But Aubrey shook his head, some of the manic brightness receding from his face. "It was mostly fine. Well, no, your mom wanted to make your 'favorite' for dinner, but I convinced her you'd mentioned a craving for sushi this morning, so we ordered takeout. Your spicy tuna roll and whatnot is in the fridge."

Nate's stomach growled on cue. "*Thank* you." He'd loved his mother's spaghetti growing up, but now the idea of white pasta in a sauce that was mostly ketchup made him consider a hunger strike. "How was the show? From the outside, I mean. It felt like a train wreck from where I was sitting."

"Eh." Aubrey waggled his hand back and forth. "It wasn't the best, but it wasn't bad. I could tell Paul missed a lot of the cues you were feeding him, but it went smoother when you both just stuck to the teleprompter." He scratched at his nape, looking sheepish. "Your mom kept commenting on how much better we are together."

"Well, she's not wrong about that, even if she is wrong about why." Nate wondered if the change of pace would have an impact on whether they got canceled. It didn't seem fair, but that probably wouldn't matter to the execs.

Then again, a more serious, less banter-driven show might have appeal with the market they'd alienated when John got fired. It could go either way.

"Anyway, I'm starving," Nate said, which Aubrey would know because Nate was always hungry after a show. "So I'm going to eat. You want to stick around? Four's the right number for a game of euchre."

"God, I haven't played since high school." Aubrey grinned as though reminiscing on a fond memory, but then he cut his gaze back to the living room, where Nate's parents were studiously ignoring a commercial break via their cell phones. "You're sure you don't want me to get lost? I don't want to, I don't know… crash your family time."

"My parents literally invited you to family time without me," Nate said wryly. "They like you fine."

Aubrey's grin dimmed a little at that, and he shook his head like he couldn't quite believe it. But then he said, "I guess I understand. I mean, I never brought a boyfriend home. Mom would probably cry tears of joy. She was always trying to pair me off with a society boy. You'd do in a pinch." He raised a hand and traced a faint scar on Nate's cheek, a remnant from a stray Zdeno Chara slap shot. "You're a little rougher around the edges than those guys, but you clean up nice and respectable."

Nate fought not to shiver at the unexpectedly intimate touch, not to mention the level of personal sharing. Aubrey didn't talk about his family much. "You say that like it's an insult."

The moment broke as Aubrey shook himself and winked. "Well, I do prefer you disheveled and debauched."

That, Nate decided, did not require a response. "So, are you in or what? We always play at Thanksgiving, but Emily's visiting Jurgen's people this year, so we're stuck without you."

And anyway, in the quick glimpse he'd caught when he first came in, Aubrey seemed to be enjoying himself, sitting opposite Nate's dad on the sofa, engaged with his mom in a discussion of something that had them both smiling. Aubrey was certainly more than capable of turning Nate's parents down when they asked him to come for dinner. Maybe he was getting something out of this.

Maybe he was just humoring Nate.

"All right." Aubrey lifted a shoulder in a shrug. "Where are the cards?"

CHAPTER FOURTEEN

TUESDAY NIGHT Aubrey lay awake in bed for two hours, staring at the ceiling. It was a weird inverse repeat of the night before, when he'd gone to bed with Nate without the obvious pretext of having sex with him, because his apartment was a deep freeze.

He expected it to be awkward, but instead, he'd closed his eyes, was assaulted by Nate's body heat, and fell asleep within thirty seconds.

Tuesday Aubrey sneaked out of bed before Nate could open his eyes.

Ignoring the consequences of his own bad decisions was a lot easier when he was with Nate, but that was mostly because he kept forgetting the whole thing was fake.

By the time he dropped off to sleep, alone in his own bed, it was technically Wednesday morning.

He woke up after a half-remembered dream that he immediately wanted to purge completely. He needed to get out of his apartment—out of the whole building, preferably to do something that wouldn't permit any distraction.

When his cell phone beeped an appointment reminder, he smiled. *Perfect.*

There were seven cars in the arena parking lot when he pulled in. Aubrey picked up the stuffed dog and yellow roses from the passenger seat, snagged his skate bag from the trunk, and hightailed it to the locker room.

Greg groaned when he saw him. "What is this? Aren't you supposed to be in Hawaii? I don't need someone documenting my failures."

"Obviously I should've brought vodka for the kiss and cry," Aubrey said wryly. Greg always got like this before a big skate, and he was always fine. "Come on, suit up. I'll warm up with you. Take your mind off it."

"You're a terrible man and I hate you."

Aubrey clapped him on the shoulder. "Love you too, buddy. Let's go break a leg, okay?"

"Don't think you're getting out of telling me why you're not three mai tais deep right now."

"It's, like, six in the morning in Oahu."

Greg had the ice for twenty minutes of warm-up time before his Cirque audition was scheduled. They spent ten minutes stretching and skating, and then Greg's jitters got so bad Aubrey gently checked him into the boards and called up their playlist on his phone.

"Change of plan. You need to loosen up." Aubrey's portable speakers pumped out the opening bars of "Hot Stuff." "You remember how it goes, right?"

For a few seconds, he thought Greg might really balk. He skated backward away from Aubrey a half meter or so, shaking his head.

Then he shot him the finger and launched into their routine. For three minutes and forty-seven seconds, Greg and Aubrey dance-fought to Donna Summer. Greg kept his part simple to conserve his energy, but Aubrey lost himself in the rhythm and the pure athleticism, reveling in the stretch of his body, pushing his limits. He nailed every landing and couldn't keep from grinning as he mentally awarded himself top marks.

When the song wound to a close, Aubrey caught sight of a man and a woman dressed in business suits making their way into the stands. He clapped Greg's shoulder again. "You got this." Then he skated over to the visitor's bench.

He was right too—Greg nailed the routine, putting on a very entertaining program for the Cirque officials. Aubrey watched them when he wasn't watching Greg, and though they didn't give much away, he thought they were impressed.

At the end of the program, they came down to the ice and shook Greg's hand, and Aubrey could tell from the mutual smiles that Greg was in.

He grinned and collected the flowers and stuffed animal and skated over to deliver them. "I guess we can skip the crying this time?"

Greg snorted but accepted the gifts. "Yeah. I still want my kiss, though."

"Smartass." Aubrey gave him another gentle bump and then a loud smack on the cheek.

"Mr. Chase!" The male Cirque rep extended his hand. "Pleased to meet you. I'm Lucien Bastille, and this is my colleague, Sharice Kim."

"Pleasure's mine. But please call me Aubrey." He shook with both of them.

Sharice palmed a card and slid it to him. "We know you have commitments in Chicago. Greg's been very forthcoming about that." Oh, *had* he? "But if you ever find yourself in need of a diversion or a change of scenery and you think you might like to spend some time in Las Vegas, please don't hesitate to give us a call. You're obviously in competition shape, and your choreography would be a good fit for us."

Aubrey blinked and looked sideways at Greg. It had never occurred to him that he might end up with a job offer at the end of this, but judging from Greg's tiny smirk, he wasn't surprised. "Thanks," he said, taking the card. "I'll keep that in mind."

He held on to his questions until Lucien and Sharice left and they were packing up in the locker room, but they came rapid-fire after that. "What just happened? You looked like you knew something was up, but I thought I was going to be in Hawaii for this until two days ago."

Greg shrugged. "I knew they were looking for more talent. Your name came up when we arranged the audition."

"I didn't book my vacation until last week," Aubrey realized. "You sneaky bastard."

"Don't get me wrong, you were never going to get the gig instead of me, but I know you miss performing with your whole body and not just your face."

Ooh. That one landed hard enough that Aubrey winced as he wiped down his skate blade.

"Oh, uh-oh, back up, speaking of your face, what's it doing right now? Aubrey? What did you do?" Greg snapped a skate guard on and shoved it in his bag. Realization dawned, and his eyebrows shook hands with his hairline. "Did you sleep with Nate again?"

"No!" Aubrey said, because that wasn't the problem. Then, in the interest of honesty: "Well, yes, twice, but that's… okay, that is how I got into this mess. I—"

His phone buzzed on the bench beside him. The call display lit up. *Mom.*

Well, saved by the bell, sort of.

"Sorry, I have to take this."

Greg rolled his eyes, and Aubrey walked out into the hallway to answer.

"Hi, Mom."

"Hi, Aubrey, sweetheart. Is everything okay?"

Apparently all of his poor decisions were coming back to haunt him today—though he couldn't decide if the decision in question was limiting contact with his mother or picking up the phone again to call her.

"Everything's fine, Mom. I just wanted to…." *I just wanted to see if maybe we could have a better relationship, since one of the most important ones in my life is in danger of disintegrating at any moment.* "I just wanted to check in. I haven't talked to you and Dad since…."

"Thanksgiving," his mother supplied. "In October."

Aubrey winced. "Right. Sorry, I know… I know we don't talk much."

But instead of the response he expected, his mother just said, "Oh, honey. I didn't call you either. But I wanted to."

For a moment all Aubrey could do was flap his mouth soundlessly. He'd been expecting accusations, veiled rancor. This hurt in a different way. "Why?" he finally managed. "I mean, not why do you want to talk to me—I'm delightful and you love me—but why didn't you call? If you wanted to."

His mother exhaled a long, slow breath. "Honestly, Aubrey? Even my therapist can't work that out."

Aubrey's brain did a record scratch. "Wait, you're in *therapy*?"

"You don't have to say it like that." Ah, there was the mother he knew. "There's nothing wrong with getting the help you need."

Bizarrely, Aubrey found himself smiling. "No, that's not what I meant. I mean, I'm also in therapy." Was that rude to say to your mother? Did that imply some kind of judgment on her parenting skills? "I was just surprised."

His mother huffed. "Well. Perhaps going forward, we can spend a little time talking to each other instead of talking to our therapists."

"Is yours terrible?" Aubrey asked. "Who gave these people license to be right about everything?"

She laughed, and Aubrey felt the power of it zing through him. For years he'd craved his mother's attention and approval while she was busy pursuing other things. But now, making her laugh—genuinely laugh—was enough.

Therapy. Who knew.

"They're the worst," his mother said. "Although I think they do actually have a licensing body, so your question isn't as rhetorical as you think."

"Yeah, yeah." He shook his head. "So, what're you in for, Mom? You may have guessed my main issues are attention-seeking behavior and poor coping mechanisms."

"Ah, well, that's a personal question, Aubrey." He could almost see her deliberating, tapping her perfectly manicured nails on whatever was nearest—a table, an armrest, a steering wheel. "The usual suspects for a woman my age. Guilt, regret, nostalgia." She said all these flippantly enough that Aubrey could guess none of them was the real issue, but she was right, it was a personal question. She didn't have to tell him, especially not when their relationship was just starting to find its first solid footing in years.

A month ago he'd have snarked at her. Today, though, he just agreed. "The usual."

Greg poked his head out of the locker room, one skate bag slung over each shoulder, and Aubrey realized he was holding him up. "Look, Mom, we're obviously not going to solve our multiple issues in one phone call, but I'm willing to work on them if you are."

"That…." For the first time he could remember, his mom's voice grew tight, almost to breaking. "That would be really nice. I'd like that."

Aubrey found himself blinking back tears of his own. "Okay. Well. Then let's keep the lines of communication open, yeah? Meanwhile I've got to go, because I'm being terribly rude to a friend who needs to celebrate a successful audition."

"All right. I love you, sweetheart. I'm glad you called."

"Yeah," Aubrey agreed, his throat too thick to squeeze out what he wanted to say. "Me too."

He pulled his phone from his ear as Greg handed over his bag. "Hey. Sorry about interrupting."

"No, no, it's fine. I've done enough character development for one day."

"Good. Because I just lined up a job for you, so I think you owe me a drink."

"It's not even noon on a Wednesday." Aubrey was no stranger to a champagne brunch, but he was thirty now. He saved that stuff for weekends. "How about we start with lunch?"

THE RESTAURANT they chose was quiet. Aubrey figured half the city was knocking off work early for the holiday, rather than going out to lunch. That suited him fine. The longer he spent away from his apartment building, the more likely he could forget what was happening with Nate and how much it was great and sucked at the same time.

Greg let him off the hook until he'd eaten half his weight in fish tacos. Then he said, "So, you're sleeping with Nate. That's an exciting new level of stupidity and reckless disregard for your emotional health."

Aubrey looked forlornly at the last half of a fish taco, but no, the moment was gone. "Yeah, well. The second time was an accident, sort of."

"Sort of?"

"I went to a bar to pick up. He went to the *same* bar to pick up. We just… went home together."

"Uh-huh." Greg sipped his mimosa. "And the third time?"

"Yeah, the third time was the problem." He blew out a breath. "So you know how the heat in my apartment building went out a couple nights ago? We'd just gotten back from Tampa after a day of flight delays. Nate offered to let me crash with him. I was too weak to say no. The next morning, one thing led to another…."

"Say no more." Greg stole one of Aubrey's fries.

"Oh, I'd love if the story stopped there, believe me."

"Wait, the stupidity extends past sleepy domestic morning sex?" Greg gave up the pretense that he wasn't going to consume the rest of Aubrey's fries and pulled the whole plate toward himself.

Aubrey felt a headache coming on. He closed his eyes and rubbed at the bridge of his nose, only half so he didn't have to look at Greg while he said, "I got up and took a shower, and while I was looking for a towel, Nate's parents showed up."

Greg inhaled on a fry and spent a few seconds coughing into a napkin. He reached for his water glass and took a deep gulp. Then he managed, "That was awkward, I assume."

"Not as awkward as the fist-bump she gave Nate after."

"Yikes."

"Yeah."

"So that's it? You made a bad decision—three bad decisions—and then your crush's mom saw you naked?" He dunked a fry in ketchup.

Aubrey knocked back the rest of his beer. "No. Then Nate asked me to pretend to be his boyfriend so his parents wouldn't think he was having a midlife crisis."

Greg stared at him, speechless.

Aubrey didn't have much to say for himself either, but the buzz of his phone with an incoming text saved him yet again.

Well, sort of.

He looked at the screen and groaned.

"What?"

"It's Nate," he said. "He needs me to pick up butter and sage for Thanksgiving dinner."

Chapter Fifteen

Nate had made one major miscalculation about Thanksgiving dinner: how long it would take one person to prepare it.

His mom had always done everything when he was growing up. Now he wanted her to be able to relax, enjoy the sights in Chicago, and come back to a nice dinner. But at this rate, the dinner he'd scheduled for five was going to be more like eight.

Fortunately Aubrey picked up on the first ring.

"Please don't tell me you need me to go to the grocery store."

"I don't need you to go to the grocery store," Nate said obediently. Then something occurred to him. "Although… you don't happen to have any wine?"

He could practically hear Aubrey's eye roll. "Red, white, rosé, or sparkling?"

Yeah, that was a stupid question. "Yes," Nate answered. "Actually, are you busy?"

"I'm watching the 2019 World Championships in my underwear and eating cereal out of the box."

Now there was an image. "What kind of cereal?"

"Corn Pops."

"Nice. Good choice."

Aubrey crunched on some Corn Pops. "So, what's up?"

Clearing his throat, Nate surveyed the carnage of his kitchen. A bag of unpeeled potatoes. A similar mound of yams. Unstemmed green beans. A can of pumpkin filling, a bag of flour, powdered sugar, mace and cloves. He'd managed to get the stuffed turkey in the oven, but that was it. Time to swallow his pride. "I kind of need a sous chef."

"Oh?" The laugh in his voice was obvious. "Parents can't be trusted in the kitchen?"

"I kicked them out to go sightseeing and enjoy their holiday, but I think I bit off more than I can chew. Or will be able to chew. No chewing will be happening for a long time unless I get some help, is what I'm saying."

"Mm-hmm," Aubrey said, crunching a little more.

He was really going to make Nate ask. Fine. "If you're not too busy, would you mind putting on some pants and helping me out?"

Aubrey let himself in ten minutes later, in a purple T-shirt and sweatpants that said PINK in glitter across the ass. He'd brought his own apron too—a black one with a giant sausage and the legend Size Matters.

"Classy," Nate said.

"Beggars and choosers, Nate." Aubrey plunked two bottles of wine on the counter and cracked one open.

Nate coughed. "Feeling a little parched after those Corn Pops?"

"I love cooking with wine," Aubrey said seriously, taking down a pair of glasses. "Sometimes I even put it in the food." He poured and then handed Nate a glass. "Cheers. Now, what do you need me to do?"

Nate held up a potato peeler and the can of pumpkin. "Choose your weapon."

Aubrey selected the peeler—wise choice—and Nate turned on the radio to play in the background as he flicked through his tablet for directions on how to make a pumpkin pie.

"I always preferred apple." Aubrey had amassed a pile of potato peels the size of a dinner plate.

"What!" Nate turned so sharply he got sugar all over the counter. Oh well, the kitchen was a total loss anyway. "Shit. That seems like the sort of thing a boyfriend should know."

Aubrey's brows furrowed. "Yeah, but they probably find out at their first joint Thanksgiving. I don't think our cover's blown."

True, but it didn't make Nate feel any better. Actually he felt kind of... ill. Maybe he should've eaten lunch. He dusted his hand off on his pants and grabbed his phone to send a quick text.

"Hey." Aubrey bumped Nate's arm, still frowning. "Look, it's fine. It's not like this would've come up in casual conversation. We can always say we were too busy having sex to talk pie."

Jesus. Nate laughed despite himself. "Stop trying to make me feel better, please."

"Is it working?"

"No comment."

Aubrey grinned.

With the two of them working and the oven on, it didn't take long for the kitchen to heat up. Nate ditched his sweater over one of the breakfast-bar stools before he mixed together the pie filling.

"Exactly how many potatoes do you think four people can eat?" Aubrey asked finally, reaching for one of the final spuds. Then: "It is just the four of us, right? You aren't springing more surprise family members on me?"

Nate eyed the pile. What was the rule? Two per person, two for the pot? So ten potatoes? Aubrey had peeled fourteen. "What? No, Emily and her husband brought the baby to visit his family in Vancouver. It's just the four of us." He paused and did some calculations. Even in his prime hockey days, he'd have had trouble putting away more than two potatoes that size. Oops. "You can probably stop now."

"Oh, you think?" Aubrey laughed. "You're gonna be making potato pancakes for a week."

Nate's stomach growled. "I can live with that."

With the pie done, Nate turned his attention to the green beans, stemming away next to Aubrey at the counter while Aubrey hummed along with eighties dance pop. "So this is your first time making Thanksgiving dinner, eh?"

"Was it the potatoes that gave me away?"

"The fact that you didn't realize how much help you were going to need, honestly."

Nate shrugged and tossed another handful of beans into the colander. "Mom always insisted on doing Thanksgiving dinner, just her and Dad. Though now that I think about it, she started the day before with the prep work and the baking. She used to say my sister and I got underfoot. Marty…."

Aubrey bumped his hip. "You don't have to tell me."

"No, it's fine. He was just kind of a control freak in the kitchen. He's a professionally trained chef."

"Ah." Aubrey put down the last sweet potato. "That'll do it."

"He didn't even work in a restaurant anymore when we met—he owned a catering company." Nate had felt judged every time he so much as reheated leftovers. Which was maybe Nate's problem as much as Marty's, in retrospect.

But this Nate liked. Aubrey was easy to work around, maybe because they were used to working together in a different context, maybe because Aubrey was also a professional athlete. Maybe because they were sleeping together.

"Can I ask you something?" Aubrey swept the pile of peelings into the compost bin. "What happened? I mean, you must've been happy at one point, or else why get married? But.... Shit, that's really personal. Sorry."

"It's nothing I haven't asked myself." Not that he'd come up with a satisfactory response. He swirled the remaining wine in his glass for a moment to give himself time to think. Then he picked up a dishtowel to clean up the sugar he'd spilled on the counter. "Honestly, I think what happened is... I retired."

Marty might have cheated on him before that, but Nate mostly wasn't around to notice then, and he didn't want to talk about the cheating with Aubrey. They were having a nice time. He didn't need to go there.

Aubrey leaned back against the counter, hip cocked, his half-empty glass held at his side. "And suddenly you were spending too much time together, or...?"

"No. I know I make it sound terrible, but we actually got along fine."

"I mean, you agreed on that travesty of a vase, so...."

Nate swatted him on the thigh with the dishtowel. "You're hilarious. I think the problem actually was we had different ideas of what my retirement would be like. Maybe we just didn't talk about it enough, or maybe we weren't listening. I mean, we had other problems too, but that's the one that broke us. I thought, okay, retirement, time to start a family. Maybe I'd do some work with the team, but otherwise I'd be home a lot. Only it turns out the whole time, Marty had just been waiting until I hung them up to spring this idea that he wanted to sell the catering company and open a bed-and-breakfast."

Aubrey winced. "Ah. I can see how that would go over poorly."

Nate tossed the dishtowel in the general direction of the laundry room. "Yeah. I was used to having people up in my business in my professional life, but that's different when you literally live where you work. We talked about different things we could try, but ultimately he wasn't any more willing to compromise his dream than I was mine, so we called it quits."

"Sorry. That sucks."

Nate shrugged. "It is what it is. The truth is, we're both better off. He's living out his B and B dream with his new fiancé, and I...."

I have you.

Oh shit.

Whatever was between them felt less like sexual convenience and fake dating all the time. Nate had made himself believe he didn't want another relationship, wasn't ready to fall in love again.

Then he'd gone and done it anyway, and he'd put himself into a position where he couldn't tell Aubrey about it.

"I'm happy for him," Nate stumbled to cover. "It's not like my biological clock is ticking. I have time to figure out what I want." *Which is great, because it's apparently right in front of me and I didn't notice, and now I'm fake dating it.* "It turns out I wasn't really completely ready to retire anyway."

Aubrey was giving him a calculating look, but he didn't overtly call bullshit. "You don't exactly strike me as the type to take well to sitting around doing nothing."

"Spoken like someone without a six-month-old niece."

Aubrey made a face. "You know what I mean. Going from working and traveling October through June to stay-at-home husband and dad is a pretty big shift."

"Yeah," Nate conceded, because Aubrey was right, even if Nate suspected that the B and B plan would have involved a lot of work for him in some capacity—landscaping or cleaning or greeting guests. Maybe giving horseback tours. Marty had always wanted to keep a stable.

"*Anyway.*" Aubrey plunked his wineglass down on the counter with emphasis. "We should eat something, because that turkey is starting to smell incredible, and my stomach is telling me that the Corn Pops were not a sufficient base to layer wine on top of. And then we should make a plan to deal with all of *that.*" He gestured to indicate the cornucopia of vegetables on the counter. "Because we still have work to do."

"I see your point." Nate's stomach growled again. "Let's see what I can come up with."

In the end they resorted to breaking into the charcuterie board Nate had ordered as an appetizer, because neither of them felt like fast food or freezer meals.

"Oh my God, this mustard," Aubrey enthused as he spread a thick layer on a baguette and topped it with a chunk of cured pork.

"We could just eat all this and skip dinner." Nate eyed the platter, then chose a delicate pickle to pair with his manchego.

"Fuck you. I didn't peel every potato on earth for nothing." Aubrey snagged the last pickle. *Oops.* Nate had meant to save some of those for his parents. Oh well; if they ate all of them, his parents would never know they'd missed out. "Besides, potato pancakes."

"You're very fixated on the pancakes."

Aubrey shook the pickle at him and then popped it in his mouth. "I'm goal-oriented."

Nate's ears warmed. He was very aware of how goal-oriented Aubrey could be. "Yeah, I know."

Their eyes met across the table, and he could tell Aubrey knew exactly what he was thinking—and that Aubrey was thinking it too. Nate's parents probably wouldn't be home for another hour and a half. And they already knew Nate and Aubrey were sleeping together.

Nate licked his lips. They'd finished the bottle of wine, and now he was feeling a little parched. Should they open the other bottle of wine? Or just—fall into bed again and—no, that was a bad idea. Nate needed to process his emotions instead of his biological urges—

The timer dinged.

"Shit. I'm supposed to baste the turkey."

The corner of Aubrey's mouth quirked up. "No comment."

"You're hilarious."

"Your mom thinks so."

Nate rolled his eyes and went to attend to the bird.

They never did open the second bottle.

With Aubrey's help, he managed to get everything ready for a respectable five thirty mealtime. At quarter to five, Aubrey slipped upstairs to shower and change just as Nate's parents came in, pink-cheeked and laughing. Nate had just enough sense to be glad Aubrey had thrown his apron in Nate's laundry pile. His mom didn't need an excuse to make any more embarrassing insinuations, no matter how warranted.

AUBREY SHOWERED and shaved and spent the time it took to dry his hair considering his wardrobe for the most appropriate first-Thanksgiving-with-boyfriend's-parents outfit. It was stupid, and it wouldn't really matter what he wore, but if he wore a comfortable sweatshirt with holes in it, at least he'd be wearing a physical reminder of the truth. But he wouldn't disrespect Nate's parents like that, and even Nate didn't really deserve it. He didn't know he'd hurt Aubrey by asking him to play-act a scenario he longed to be real.

So he chose nicely tailored jeans and a button-down shirt in a deep iridescent blue and packed a few more bottles of wine in a cloth bag to bring downstairs. "Just in case," he said at the door as he nearly ran into Nate, who stepped aside to let him in.

"I see you were concerned about the dangers of holiday sobriety," Nate's dad said dryly.

No, I just thought a little social lubrication might help me get through this with my heart only somewhat bruised. Aubrey smiled gamely and handed him the bag so he could take his shoes off. "I need a glass or two to forget it's not October."

He was about to ask if Nate needed help setting the table, but then he realized Nate was still waiting by the door. Before he could ask why, the elevator arrived and a young woman stepped out with a small white box. She saw Nate peering out the door and smiled. "Nate Overton?"

"Thank you so much for delivering last minute." Nate smiled and took the box.

What had Nate forgotten? Had he ordered a replacement for the charcuterie they'd eaten?

"Happy Thanksgiving."

Was that a hundred-dollar bill?

"No problem." The girl beamed. "Enjoy your pie!"

Aubrey caught a whiff of warm cinnamon and nutmeg. As he turned back toward the apartment, he briefly met Nate's eyes.

Nate flushed and turned away, and Aubrey's face went hot. "Well." Nate cleared his throat. "Dinner's on. Let's eat."

While Aubrey was upstairs, Nate had moved everything into serving dishes and set the table, including a nice set of lit candlesticks. He'd set out the second bottle of wine Aubrey had brought earlier. If not for his parents' presence, it would've felt like a romantic gesture.

As they sat around the table, Aubrey looked for a cue as to whether they'd be saying grace. Nate had mentioned his parents were not particularly religious, but once they were all settled around the table, Nate's mom reached out to either side—to Aubrey on one side and Nate on the other—and grasped their hands.

"I know it's a cliché, but I'd like us to take a moment"—*oh no*—"and say what we're thankful for."

Nate blanched. "Mom," he protested. "You can't just spring that on Aubrey when he just met you a couple of days ago."

"Oh, honestly, Nate. He doesn't have to say anything about *you*." Diane shook her head at him and turned to Aubrey. "You don't, dear. It's plain for anyone to see how thankful you are for each other. It would be cheating."

Aubrey wanted to crawl under the table. "Right," he croaked.

Fucking help me, he tried to tell Nate with his eyes.

Sorry, every man for himself, he imagined Nate replying.

"Diane," Elliot broke in, "don't you think you're going to scare him off? They've only been dating a little while."

"I walked in on him naked before we were introduced," Diane said. Nate beat Aubrey to the wine bottle. "If he hasn't run screaming by now, I think he'll be fine. Anyway, I'll go first."

Thank God for twist-offs, Aubrey thought as Nate filled his glass. He continued filling while his mom spoke.

"This year I am thankful for my health and my family's health. For my sweet, adorable *first* grandchild."

Nate and Aubrey locked eyes. Nate filled his glass three-quarters full and then moved on to the next one.

"I'm thankful for homemade meals." Nate finished her pour, and she raised her glass. "And store-bought wine."

Aubrey laughed, grabbing his own, and Diane said, "Your turn, Elliot."

Elliot gamely took his wineglass from Nate. "Well, I am thankful for my wonderful wife and her sense of humor, and for my son and his exciting second career as a TV personality, and that my daughter and Jurgen have settled in the States where I can keep an eye on them." Nate had told Aubrey that Emily and her husband used to be with Doctors Without Borders.

Which brought them to Nate.

He cleared his throat. "Okay. I am grateful for... new opportunities." He didn't glance at Aubrey, looking instead at a spot in front of Aubrey's plate. Fair enough. Aubrey wasn't exactly comfortable being put on the spot like this either. But this had been Nate's idea.

When it became apparent Nate wasn't going to continue, everyone turned to Aubrey.

Thank God he was used to performing under pressure. Besides, Aubrey knew the most convincing lies were the ones with a shred of truth. "Second chances," he said. With his mother, with Jess and the show. If he was lucky, with Nate… though by now that might be a third chance. "And second impressions," he added after a beat.

Nate groaned, but Diane threw her head back laughing, and Elliot raised his glass.

"Cheers," Diane said.

They all touched glasses.

Apparently Nate and Aubrey's chemistry was as good in the kitchen as it was in the bedroom and the studio. Conversation over dinner was mild and pleasant and didn't at all make Aubrey want to stage a freak accident with the carving knife just to escape. But the wholesomeness of it carried its own kind of hurt. His own family dinners had never felt like this. When he was very young, they'd been nice enough, but were they close? The specifics of his younger years were lost on him, and by the time he was twelve, the rift between him and his parents felt insurmountable.

But maybe it wasn't.

Maybe things with Nate weren't either.

CHAPTER SIXTEEN

"WE STILL on for tonight?"

Nate left his stick leaning against the arena wall outside the dressing room and focused on Caley. "Yeah. Why wouldn't we be?"

"I know you have your parents waiting. I want to make sure they don't feel like I'm taking you away from them."

No danger of that. Nate got along well with his parents, but after four days together, they needed some time apart. "Trust me. They've been here since Monday. We're all very happy doing our own thing today."

Caley smiled. She was obviously still riding the high of her beautiful third-period goal, a wraparound which the goalie, a former pro who now coached at the college level, didn't see until three seconds after the puck hit the back of the net. "Great. Usual place, or did you want to try the new place the next block over?"

"The usual. Unless the health department's finally closed it down," he joked.

Twenty minutes later they met up again in the quiet back booth of a bar that would get progressively rowdier as Friday night wore on.

"So, how was your Thanksgiving?" Caley asked, accepting her drink from the server with a smile of thanks.

Nate strangled a laugh thinking about it. First he'd bitten off more than he could chew with the cooking, and then he'd had his uncomfortable realization about Aubrey, and then the gratefulness speeches…. "Nearly averted disaster?" he suggested. "Next year remind me I don't need to cook a whole turkey and stuffing and three side dishes plus salad, hors d'oeuvres, and dessert for four people."

Caley wiped a bit of something pink and frothy from the corner of her mouth. "Honestly, you managed all that? I'm impressed you're not still sleeping it off."

"Ah, well, I had help," he admitted, realizing his mistake only when Caley said, "Wait a minute, four people? I thought it was just you and your parents."

"Uh," he said.

Caley narrowed her eyes and leaned across the table with her arms crossed. "This wouldn't have anything to do with your recent disclosure to Kelly that you're not interested in dating seriously right now?"

Damn it. He could feel the heat rising in his cheeks again. He hadn't blushed this much since he was a teenager.

"So there's a mystery man! I have to admit, you've been skating a little looser for a few weeks. Morgan said you must've met someone, but I thought maybe just having the divorce over with…."

He might as well tell her—except for one thing. "Promise me you won't tell Kelly."

Caley recoiled, blinking like he'd slapped her. "What? I tell her everything. Why wouldn't I tell her this?"

Nate closed his eyes. "Because it's Aubrey."

There. It was off his chest. And maybe, unlike with his parents, he could tell Caley the whole truth. At least then he wouldn't have to suffer in silence.

"All right," Caley said. "Start at the beginning."

Over the next ten minutes, Nate filled her in on everything—from the first frantic night in Winnipeg to the lazy Monday morning that had led to the whole façade. "So now I've realized that I have feelings for him, but I already asked him to pretend to be my boyfriend to my parents, and changing the rules now would make me an asshole. We couldn't date openly anyway, because the show is on the bubble and Jess specifically said don't change anything. And if the show falls apart because we couldn't keep it in our pants, I don't know what I'll do."

Caley shifted in her seat, biting her lip, but whatever was on her mind, she kept it to herself. "Have you considered talking to Aubrey?"

Nate made a face. "That would be the mature, rational thing to do."

"So, no?" She raised her eyebrows. "I hate to tell you, but if you think talking to him about quote-unquote 'changing the rules now' makes you an asshole, not talking to him at all would be considerably worse."

"You're probably right. I mean, you're obviously right, I'm just bitter because you didn't tell me what I wanted to hear."

"Yeah, I'm not known for doing that." She nudged him under the table. "It'll work out or it won't. It's not going to break you. Two years ago you didn't know if you'd ever get over Marty. You can handle this."

Nate exhaled. That was a fair enough comment. He tilted his beer glass at her to accept it.

"And as for the show...." Ah, here it was. "I wanted to talk to you about that. Or, actually Kelly wanted me to talk to you about that. Or, she *didn't* want me to talk to you about that—"

Nate nudged her back. "Caley. Take a breath."

"Right. Okay." She sat up straighter and looked him in the eye. "Kelly got an offer from another network. One of their MLB commentators was scheduled to retire after the coming season, but he took a spill on the golf course and broke both his kneecaps."

Kelly had two Olympic softball medals, so that sounded like a dream assignment for her. "Wow. That's awesome."

"That's what I said." The server dropped off their usual order of poutine, and Caley dove in and gestured with a forkful of cheesy fries. "I think she's a little worried about what you'll say."

"She shouldn't be. First of all, it's business, not personal. Second of all, of course I'm happy for her." He thought that might be the end of it, but Caley's body language said there was more she wasn't telling him. "Caley, what's going on? You're being weird."

"I'm not being weird," she protested. "Just, I had something on my mind I wanted to talk to you about, and I was kind of banking on Thanksgiving small talk as a lead-in. Only that didn't happen, and now I'm trying to figure out how to circle back without a huge non sequitur."

Nate quirked up a corner of his mouth. "How was your Thanksgiving, Caley?"

"Kelly and I are having a baby." The words came out in a tumble, full of so much love and enthusiasm Nate didn't have to ask how she felt about it. "I'm due in May."

"Oh my God! Congratulations." That explained why she'd ordered the fluffy pink thing instead of a beer. They both stood up so they could hug.

Caley flung her arms around his neck and squeezed. "Thank you so much for introducing us," she whispered fiercely. "I'm—you know I love Carter like he's my own, but we wanted a bigger family, and I just... I guess it was the right time."

He kissed her cheek. "I'm so happy for you both. For all three of you," he corrected.

She pulled away and took his hands in hers. "I'm glad to hear that, because we have a tiny request."

"Of course." They sat back down, and Nate grabbed a forkful of fries. "Shoot."

"We want you to be the godfather."

"AUBREY, COME on in."

He stuck his phone in his back pocket and followed his therapist into her office, fighting the urge to fidget. "Thanks for squeezing me in. I know it was last-minute, and with the holiday…."

Theresa raised an eyebrow that said a lot about how well she knew him. "And with the holiday, lots of people need emergency therapist appointments. That's why I keep the Friday after Thanksgiving free." *Which you know because I've mentioned it before every major holiday* went unsaid.

Aubrey nodded distractedly and folded himself into the U-shaped armchair across from her desk. He normally sat on the couch because he liked to sprawl dramatically. Today he wanted something at his back.

He wanted a place to start talking too, but the situation seemed so big.

"I thought you were supposed to be in Hawaii this week?" Theresa said casually as she filled her water bottle from the cooler.

Well, there was his opening. "I was. A friend—" *Fuck.* He was paying for her time, and the whole point was to talk to someone. If he wasn't honest, the whole thing was for nothing. "Nate asked if I could stay and pretend to be his boyfriend after his parents basically caught us having sex."

Theresa didn't react to that right away, which wasn't unusual. It wasn't her job to react to things. Instead she finished filling her bottle and walked back to her desk, where she sat with her feet up. "I see." *Here it comes.* "And how does that make you feel?"

Aubrey sighed and pointed to the jar at the corner of her desk. Theresa rolled her eyes, pulled her wallet from her desk drawer, and withdrew a dollar to throw into it. It was a first-offense-per-session penalty, and every month she donated the proceeds to children's mental health initiatives. "It's complicated."

"The part where you're sleeping with your colleague, the part where you're lying to his parents, or the part where you pretend to be his boyfriend?"

"Yes."

She offered a small smile at that, probably more for Aubrey than because it actually amused her. "Why don't you start at the beginning? At our earlier sessions, you didn't mention you and Nate have been sleeping together. When did that start?"

That wasn't judgment, it was a carefully targeted probe. But it did the job just the same. "The end of October. It wasn't a habitual thing." He shoved his hands under his legs so he wouldn't reach for one of the fidget objects on Theresa's desk. "There was a snowstorm, and our flight out of Winnipeg got canceled, so we went out to a restaurant we'd both been wanting to try."

"That sounds nice."

That sounds like a date, he heard. Well, it hadn't been. "The food was really good, and the cocktails were too. We didn't get drunk," he hastened to add. "But somehow we got to talking about sex."

"Work colleagues do talk about sex sometimes," Theresa said. "Depending on their personal boundaries and the rules of the workplace. It's not automatically verboten."

"Technically I think it is, for us." But that was neither here nor there. "Anyway. I guess specifically we somehow started talking about his sex life with his ex. Which I guess was, um, unfulfilling."

"He must trust you a lot to tell you something like that."

Aubrey opened his mouth to refute that, but then paused. Even Nate had seemed a little surprised he'd confided that. And if he'd told anyone else, well, surely someone would have picked up *that* gauntlet. "Yeah, I guess he does." He shook his head and returned to the story. "Anyway, you know me. Nate is hot. I noticed. He said that, and I basically heard, 'I dare you to do better.'"

That was one of those things he was supposed to be working on in therapy. But even though his failure in this case had led to him needing *more therapy*, he couldn't regret it. He knew how good he'd made Nate feel, at least physically. Maybe better than anyone else had ever made him feel.

Too bad that wasn't enough.

"I'm not going to ask you if you did do better," Theresa said, because it didn't take a trained therapist to spot Aubrey trying to find an opening for a brag.

"We agreed it was going to be a one-time thing. It's… you know, that's my MO, and I sort of told Nate he should get back at his ex by having a lot of hot unattached sex. He seemed pretty keen on the idea." Aubrey bit the inside of his cheek to distract himself from a sudden flash of Nate on his side, writhing under Aubrey's touch. "I didn't realize until afterward that that wasn't what *I* wanted."

Theresa took her feet off the desk and folded her hands on it instead. "Are you saying you've developed romantic feelings for him?"

Aubrey flashed back to dinner last night, sitting with Nate at the dinner table as his parents cleared the dishes—because that was the rule since Nate and Aubrey did the cooking. Looking at him in the candlelight. He'd bought Aubrey an apple pie because he felt bad for not knowing Aubrey's favorite beforehand. He didn't have to do that. He didn't have to find ways to show he was considering Aubrey's wants and needs, but he did. He did it as naturally as breathing.

"Yes." His heart was beating too fast, and his chest felt tight.

Theresa got up and filled one of the plastic cups next to the cooler with water. She set it on the edge of her desk where he'd be able to reach it and then sat down again. "Do you need a break?"

He shook his head and reached for the glass. A few careful sips of water helped.

"All right. So you have romantic feelings for Nate, and you agreed that your arrangement was a one-time occurrence. But it sounds like it happened again?"

"It was an accident. I mean, not 'oops, he tripped and fell on my dick' sort of an accident. We just both went out to hook up at the same bar, and it was easier to go home together than with someone else."

Not to mention Aubrey hadn't *wanted* to go home with anyone else once he realized he could go home with Nate. But he was pretty sure Theresa got the point.

"Well, you probably don't need me to tell you that continued casual sex with someone you have romantic feelings for isn't the best choice you could make for your emotional health." *Oh gee, you think?* "So one thing led to another, and eventually you got caught when Nate asked you to pretend to be his boyfriend? Did he give you a reason?"

"The divorce, basically." It sucked how fast Aubrey had gone from *Yes, he just got divorced, I can fantasize without guilt!* to *Shit, he just got divorced, so he's not ready for a serious relationship.* "He's pretty

Midwestern in his sensibilities, and his parents are the same. Sweet, but… casual sex just isn't in his makeup, as far as they're concerned. He said they'd think he was having a midlife crisis if they knew the truth."

"That must have hurt."

Yes. God, yes. He tried to push it down at the time, but how often had someone thrown around those words about him? Hell, he had been a *few* guys' midlife crisis, hadn't he? Young, a little swishy, a lot flashy, confident, athletic, and undeniably masculine. He'd punched the cards of more than one bicurious thirty-to-fortysomething. But he was more than that. He wanted to be more than that.

"Well, it didn't feel *great*."

Theresa waited for Aubrey to remember he wasn't allowed to use sarcasm as a defense mechanism.

"It hurt," he said quietly.

She crossed her legs, but the calculated nonchalance didn't lessen the impact of her next words. "How do you think Nate would feel if he knew that you'd agreed to do this for him even though it hurts you?"

"I think, if he knew what he'd asked of me, he'd be upset with himself for asking and angry with me for saying yes." Nate was too kind to knowingly hurt anyone like this.

Theresa uncrossed her legs again and put her hands in her lap. "Aubrey, you deserve better than a relationship, real or imagined, that hurts you. And I think you know that Nate deserves to know that he's hurting you too."

Aubrey's stomach twisted. It wasn't like he hadn't known what she'd say, but that didn't make hearing it easier.

He should've felt—something. Some amount of satisfaction. Dammit. He'd grown into a man who could admit that he wanted a romantic relationship. He didn't have to avoid it out of fear.

But it wasn't personal growth, was it? It was Nate. Aubrey hadn't had a choice.

And now he had to give Nate an ultimatum. He might not know how Nate felt about him, and he might not know whether Nate knew how *Aubrey* felt. But he knew that if they kept going like they were, Aubrey was going to end up with his heart shredded. Whatever sins he'd committed in the past, he didn't deserve that.

CHAPTER SEVENTEEN

NATE'S PARENTS flew out Saturday, before the show, which was scheduled to shoot in Chicago because of the holiday. Aubrey was still supposed to be in Hawaii, so Kelly hopped into the cohost seat. Nate hoped it helped the other network understand the depth of her talent, because she did a fantastic job.

Coming home to his empty apartment felt strange. Part of him wanted to feel relief, and part seemed convinced the floor had just dropped out from under his feet.

Or maybe that was just the gut-punch of walking into his apartment and seeing the vase they'd eventually hidden at Aubrey's back in its place in his own living room. Aubrey must have returned it after his parents left.

It felt a little too appropriate. Their arrangement was over. The status quo had returned. There was no new relationship to preempt the ugly vase.

It felt like going back in time.

Nate let out a long breath and leaned against the apartment door. The past few weeks had been…. He couldn't even properly describe them. Aubrey had swept into his life like a whirlwind.

The ridiculous thing was, he didn't want it to stop. Everything felt fine when Aubrey was around, even if he turned Nate's life on its head. It was only now that he was gone that Nate had time to second-guess anything.

He thumped his head against the door a few times for good measure, trying to beat some sense into his stupid brain. Too bad he was punishing the wrong organ.

Before he could do any permanent damage, his phone vibrated. He pulled it out, wondering who would be texting this late, only to see a message from Aubrey. *You still up?*

Nate's stomach did a passable imitation of a roller coaster. *Yeah.*

The message showed marked as read, but nothing new came through. Had Aubrey fallen asleep between one message and the next?

Then someone knocked on the door just behind him, and he almost jumped out of his skin. *Jesus.* Okay, apparently Aubrey wanted to see him, not just text. He turned around and opened the door.

Aubrey looked… wild. His hair was a mess, and he had something—flour? Deodorant?—on the hem of his black T-shirt. His eyes were wide, like he'd had one too many cans of his disgusting canned coffee. "Hey," he said, looking quickly at Nate and then away. "Look, can I… can we…?"

Automatically, Nate stepped aside to let him in.

Then Aubrey finally said, "We need to talk."

Ah. Nate ignored the sinking feeling in his stomach. This was probably inevitable, right? "Okay," he agreed, closing the door. His palms were damp, and he wiped them on his pants. They might as well get it over with.

Aubrey took three long strides toward the living room, ran his hands through his hair, disheveling it further, then turned and said, "We can't do this anymore."

Fuck. Well, there it was. He'd expected it. He inhaled sharply, trying to offset the sting of the words, but it didn't help. His throat closed, and he swallowed a few times. "I understand," he managed, but the words were so quiet, he wasn't sure Aubrey even heard him.

Aubrey went on as though Nate hadn't said anything. "I know who I am, all right? I'm the guy who's good enough to fuck but not good enough to meet Mom and Dad. That's who I've been since I was fifteen. But this time? This time I did meet them."

Nate really didn't need to hear this. If Aubrey didn't want to be with him, he didn't have to justify it to Nate. In fact, right now Nate would really prefer to lick his wounds in peace. "Aubrey—"

"Do you know what that's like? Being introduced to your fuckbuddy's parents like you're someone *important*? After more than a decade of being the disposable guy you pick up at a club?"

Nate didn't know what to say to that, but for the first time, he started to understand that there was more behind Aubrey's fuck-and-go philosophy than a high sex drive. Aubrey had never been disposable to him. Should he apologize? He'd obviously hurt Aubrey somehow, even if he hadn't meant to.

"They *loved me*, Nate." His voice cracked.

Nate felt like he'd been crosschecked. The broken words sucked the air out of his lungs, and his blood drained from his face.

And then he boiled over. Everything he'd been feeling, everything he'd been fighting for weeks to balance, teetered precariously on the scale and crashed over the side. "You're right. They do love you. Everyone loves you, and I—I can't stand it."

Aubrey paused, openmouthed, as though he'd expected Nate to deny it and now didn't know how to respond.

"I can't stand that we keep doing this. That we're telling lies at work and *different* lies to my parents." And it was his stupid fucking idea! That was the worst part. He'd brought this all on his own head—on his own heart.

Now that he'd started talking, he couldn't seem to stop. "Lying so much I can't even guess what's real. What you actually want. The fans love you. My parents love you. And I can't stand that we've lied so much *I* don't get to—"

He cut himself off as realization dawned. He could feel it on his face, feel the blood draining further before rushing back in. Jesus, he was stupid. What was he thinking? Just his idiot luck to realize now, when Aubrey was in the middle of breaking up with him—

But now Aubrey was the one who looked like he'd taken a bad hit. "Finish it," he said.

Damn it. He was the one who said he was tired of lying. Nate's hands were shaking at his sides when he said, "I can't stand that everyone else gets to say they love you. And I don't."

For a moment Aubrey just stared at him, his expression unreadable. He blinked, then looked Nate dead in the eye. "So then say it."

Nate's heart rate kicked up another notch. The conversation had gotten away from him. He hadn't intended—

But maybe it didn't matter what he intended. The show was on the bubble anyway. Who cared if they fucked up their chemistry or if Jess got mad?

"I love you," he said, feeling stupid. "And I can't believe you goaded me into saying it. Actually wait, yes I can."

Nate hadn't considered how Aubrey would respond, since he'd never planned on saying it, but he wouldn't have guessed that Aubrey would just stand there, speechless. The declaration was apparently the one thing that would make him shut up, which was just Nate's luck on so many levels.

Then Aubrey's lips curled up in that familiar smirk. Nate wanted to punch him. Or run. Maybe run was best.

"Then I win," Aubrey said. His eyes were bright.

What the *fuck*. Nate sputtered. "You *win*?" Was this all some kind of sick game? "What the fuck is it you win?"

"Everything." Aubrey took three quick steps forward. Then his hands were on Nate's face so he could haul Nate toward him. "*Everything*." And then he kissed him.

What, Nate's brain said, and, *Wait, I thought he said we had to stop?* But Nate's brain wasn't in charge. He'd told Aubrey he loved him, and now Aubrey was kissing him; that was all that mattered. He lost himself in the bitter coffee of Aubrey's mouth, the softness of his lower lip, the fervent slide of Aubrey's tongue over his own. Everything else could wait.

After a moment Aubrey pulled back, his lips barely whispering against Nate's as he asked, "Am I supposed to say it back? I think I'm supposed to say it back."

Of course Aubrey didn't understand that the nonasshole responses were 1) reciprocate immediately, or 2) put Nate out of his misery, also ASAP. Nate closed his eyes and leaned his forehead against Aubrey's, then pulled back. "You complete fucking asshole. *Yes* you're supp—"

"I love you." His voice didn't quite break, but it had a definite wobble, kind of like Nate's knees. Fortunately Aubrey still held him firmly by the back of his neck. "I have been in love with you for so fucking long, Nate."

How? Nate wanted to ask. How could it have been so long when they hadn't even known each other two months? But he didn't have to ask. He felt the same way. "Okay," he said, aware he was smiling stupidly but not able to do anything about it. "Okay, so does that mean we are, uh. I mean, you came here to say we couldn't do this anymore…."

"Oh, we're not doing *this* anymore," Aubrey said, indicating Nate's apartment with a twirl of his finger. Nate guessed that was supposed to stand in for their modus operandi of the past few weeks. "From now on, we're going to do this *right*." He paused, his expression one of open cluelessness. "Whatever *that* means."

Nate laughed and kissed him again. They could figure it out together.

AUBREY WAITED in the lobby.

He'd said last night they were doing this *right*, and that had meant going back to his own apartment when he really wanted to stay. It was late and their emotions were all over the place, and he felt like he needed an actual reset to start over. But that meant he wasn't there when Nate woke up. He thought about calling or texting, but he needed to be able to see Nate's face. Knocking on the door of his apartment seemed invasive—and repetitive. Work would be worse. The gym felt plain creepy. If Aubrey waited for Nate there, he'd inevitably ogle. Nate's gym shorts did wonderful things for his thighs and ass.

So he waited in the lobby. It had a seating area, and Nate had a strict caffeine-and-pastry schedule.

He'd just lost his seventh consecutive game of 2048 when Nate walked past on his way to the door.

Aubrey started to get up to follow him—which he should have realized was also creepy—but before he could, Nate stopped and turned around, smiling. "Aubrey. Hey. What are you doing?"

Making an ass of myself, apparently. He stood too and picked up his coat and scarf from the sofa beside him. "Waiting for you, actually."

Aubrey was sure he couldn't have been more obvious if he'd simply tattooed *I am in love with you* on his forehead, but Nate had been out of the game for a while. Maybe that was the reason he looked startled.

"Oh," Nate said. God, he was practically beaming. Aubrey hadn't yet done anything to deserve that, but he was determined to earn it now.

"Mind if I tag along for coffee?"

The utterly frigid wind coming off Lake Michigan made talking on the walk to their coffee kiosk an impossibility. Aubrey ordered and paid for coffee and breakfast, then handed Nate his cup and the pastry bag for the walk back.

Nate gave him a questioning look, but he only said, "Thanks."

Aubrey shrugged it off, hunching his shoulders against the cold. Something wet stung him in the cheek, and when he lifted his head, he saw it was snowing—the mean, pellet-like little balls that felt like needles driving into your skin.

"Feels kinda familiar," Nate half-shouted over the wind, the words steaming in the air before whisking behind them.

Aubrey turned and caught his eye. Nate's cheeks were red with wind and cold, and snowflakes spangled his eyebrows and lashes.

He was right. It did feel familiar. Aubrey laughed. "It wasn't this windy in Winnipeg."

When they returned to the apartment lobby, it was otherwise empty. Aubrey set down his coffee—hot this time, because certain things called for it—and tried to rake some of the snow out of his hair.

"Well, that was invigorating." Nate produced the pastry bag from the pocket of his coat. He must have been protecting it from the cold and snow. "Breakfast of champions?"

Aubrey accepted his oatmeal scone, still miraculously a bit warm. *Okay. Now just... say something.* Say what, though? "Thanks."

Nate gave him a funny look. "You paid for it, remember?"

Fuck. Right. "Did your parents get home okay?" There! That was a nice, normal thing to say. It wasn't *Now that we have confessed our love, please go out on a date with me*, but it was a step in the right direction.

"Yeah. Dad's complaining about jet lag, as though there's a huge time difference between here and Michigan. Mom keeps telling him travel exhaustion is not the same thing, but I think they like having something to pretend to argue about."

Aubrey could relate to that, but he couldn't bring himself to say as much to Nate. That seemed too direct, or maybe just too serious. He felt like if he commented, he might as well be saying, *I want to pretend to argue about trivial things with you when we're in our sixties*. They hadn't even been officially together for one day. They hadn't even technically been on a date!

Aubrey hadn't really ever gone on a date with *anyone*. He couldn't believe he was thinking this, but he should have listened to his mother when he was younger. At least then he'd have some experience to fall back on.

"Do you have dinner plans?" he finally blurted.

Okay. This could work. He could do this.

"Not turkey?" Nate answered with a laugh, unwrapping his croissant. They'd put so much leftover Thanksgiving food in his fridge Thursday night that they'd had to relocate his beer.

Aubrey laughed too, letting the openness of Nate's response embolden him. "You want to go out?"

There. That wasn't so hard.

"Mmmf-hmm." Nate nodded around a mouthful of what was obviously flaky pastry. A few little bits stuck to his lips, and he caught those in his hand when he stuck his tongue out to clear them away. "Yeah. What're you thinking? Chinese?"

Crap. Now Aubrey had to research good first-date restaurants with Asian fare. "Yeah, if you want. Pick you up at seven thirty?"

"Sure."

Nate took his coffee back toward the elevators. Aubrey should go back upstairs too, but if he did, he'd be stuck in close quarters with Nate for several more minutes, and the adrenaline crash was starting to hit him.

Nate paused. "You're not going back to your place?"

Aubrey shook his head quickly. "No, I, uh, I have to go out." Awesome. If he didn't want Nate to realize Aubrey had been loitering down here for the express purpose of asking him on a date, he was going to have to go back out into the wind and driving snow and… make up some kind of errand. "See you tonight!"

He ended up walking four blocks to a boutique he liked and picking out a date shirt. He might not know what the hell he was doing, but at least he could look the part.

Hopefully he could fake the rest.

CHAPTER EIGHTEEN

AUBREY TEXTED with the name of the restaurant at six, and Nate called it up on his phone after his shower and perused the menu as he deliberated what to wear. The place looked nice without being stuffy and boasted a menu divided into sections by region as well as type. So, similar to the type of place they usually frequented.

Which made perfect sense, because nothing had changed. Not really. They were just *admitting* that they had feelings for each other now.

Apparently knowing Aubrey loved him didn't prevent him from being nervous about a real first date. By the time Aubrey knocked on his door at 7:29, Nate had changed three times. He'd just put on a custom pair of midnight blue jeans and a lavender sweater and was debating swapping the shirt for a blue linen thing that clung to his shoulders, but the sweater would have to do.

He opened the door.

Nate had always known Aubrey was attractive. Hell, Nate's first impression of him was how handsome he was. But tonight he looked like he'd stepped off the pages of *GQ*.

"Hey," Nate said belatedly, which was better than *Wow*, which was his other thought.

Aubrey smiled, and the supermodel effect only increased. "Hey. Ready to go?"

Nate grabbed his coat from the hook and slid his wallet into his pocket. "Let's go."

Surprisingly, Aubrey didn't push the button for the ground floor when they got into the elevator. Instead he selected a parking deck.

"We're driving tonight?" Nate asked.

"What, you don't think I can drive?"

"Honestly, I didn't even know you had a car." Aubrey glanced at him out of the corners of his eyes. Nate knew that look. He sighed. "How many cars do you have?"

"Here, or total?"

Nate groaned. "How many cars do you need? You can only drive one at a time."

"You're telling me that you, Mr. Hotshot NHL Star, only have one car?"

"What would I do with two cars?" Nate said innocently.

The doors opened on the parking level, but Aubrey didn't get out yet, giving Nate the gimlet eye.

Nate relented. "Fine. I have an SUV and a sports car. The Corvette's in storage until the last snowfall of the season."

"Ha! Beat you." Aubrey raised his car keys, and an engine started about halfway down the lot. "I have three, but only one's in Chicago."

Nate was going to regret asking this, but—"Where do you keep the other ones?"

"Vancouver. But it's not what you think." Aubrey's car was a sleek black Audi S8, which was not at all what Nate expected. "My parents bought me a car to get to the rink when I turned sixteen. I still have it."

Nate envisioned a car similar to this one, only older. "And the other one?"

"Uh, well, it's in a box."

"A box." Nate reached for the door handle. This was a *nice* car. Nate had had nice cars since he'd made the NHL, but this was another level of luxury.

"Yeah, I don't know. I got drunk when I was nineteen and ordered a kit car on the internet. Delusions of grandeur."

Nate grinned. "So three cars, but only two you can drive. Here I thought you trust-fund types were supposed to be either frugal or splashy spenders. What's this moderation about?"

Aubrey slid behind the wheel and shot him an uncharacteristically shy look. "What can I say? I have layers."

Nate wasn't exactly a car guy, but the purr of the S8's engine was *sexy*. "I guess you do."

The traffic was about as light as traffic got at this time in Chicago, and Aubrey pulled into a parking lot fifteen minutes later.

Inside the restaurant, Nate inhaled and immediately said, "Oh my God, I'm starving."

"Gotta say, the reviews were not kidding about the smell in here."

The host greeted them with a pleasant smile. "Mr. Chase! Your table is ready. Please follow me."

The ambiance in the dining room matched the smell. Rich dark wood and red fabric with gold accents made the place feel luxurious. Paper screens had been strategically placed to provide privacy without impeding the flow of foot traffic.

Probably not the kind of place to serve fortune cookies, Nate thought, but he couldn't wait to try everything else.

Their table was a corner booth with a pot of tea and a bottle of wine already waiting. The host handed them their menus and went over a list of specials that had Nate's stomach growling, then let them know their server would be by shortly.

"They've covered every eventuality, I see," Nate said, motioning to the tea and wine.

"I may have made a request when I called for a reservation." Aubrey picked up the bottle. "Shall I?"

"Absolutely." A glass of wine would help settle nerves he shouldn't be having. He'd been out for dinner with Aubrey a dozen times. Besides—Aubrey loved him.

Even if they hadn't had sex in the past week.

Maybe *that* was why Nate felt edgy.

"Any idea what you want to eat?"

"Everything?" Nate said helplessly. "Rice. Noodles. Soup. Meat."

"Meat," Aubrey agreed with feeling. He dropped the menu on the table. "Want to do the tasting menu?"

"You read my mind."

IT WAS probably stupid, how anxious Aubrey felt walking Nate to his apartment door. He could feel his pulse beating in his neck, just below his ear, and his palms were damp.

Well, he'd wanted the full first-date experience. Now he had it. Maybe it was weird to walk a grown man to his apartment when you lived in the same building? But what else was he supposed to do? The night didn't feel like it should end yet.

They reached Nate's door, and he took out his keys and turned them over in his hand. "Well. This is me."

That was such a cliché that even Aubrey recognized it as his opening, but somehow he couldn't get his mouth to make the words he needed. "Right," his brain said instead, calling up some long-forgotten romantic comedy. "I had a nice time tonight."

Oh my God, I am hopeless. Aubrey fought the urge to facepalm.

Nate gave him a look that said he'd seen the movie too. "Me too," he said. "Good night, Aubrey."

"Good night."

In any movie worth its salt, this was where the hero would lean in and kiss the other hero, and Nate would fumble the door open, and they'd knock into things while taking their clothes off all the way to the bedroom. But no one was writing Aubrey's script for him, so instead of a kiss, all he got was the soft click of Nate's door closing.

You utter coward, sneered the part of Aubrey's brain that made him comment on Nate's sex life within twenty minutes of meeting him. *You chickenshit noodle-spined impotent pile of—Virgins on prom night seal the deal every spring, and you can't even get a kiss from a man who's in love with you?*

Fuck. That.

Aubrey could deal with suddenly turning into a person who dated. That was character growth. But becoming a guy people would classify as someone who said, "Not on the first date"? That was a full-on identity crisis.

He crossed the space back to Nate's door in three long strides. He didn't have Nate's key on him, but only thirty seconds had passed. Nate should still be able to hear him.

He knocked. Possibly too loudly and definitely too many times, but once his hand started doing *something*, he couldn't get it to stop.

He had no idea how much time passed before Nate opened the door. It felt like minutes and half a second simultaneously. Time warped around him until the door moved inward and Nate looked at him, raising a brow.

"Did you f—"

Aubrey kissed him.

He could taste Nate's smile under the hint of mochi from their dessert.

Nate brought his hands up to Aubrey's neck and pulled him into the apartment, where Aubrey fumbled comically behind him to close the door.

"I really thought you were just going to go upstairs," Nate gasped when Aubrey broke away from his mouth to lay a trail of kisses down his jaw to his neck.

"I really almost did." Aubrey bit below his ear, rucking up the hem of Nate's sweater. They were still moving, tearing at each other's clothes, but he was pretty sure the bedroom was a pipe dream. They'd never make it.

The flow of time warped again. Aubrey got Nate's sweater off and spent half a lifetime touching his chest, his abs, the cut of his hip. He lost years discovering the way Nate sucked in a breath when Aubrey thumbed his nipples or trailed his fingers into the *V* of his obliques.

But time seemed to be moving differently for Nate. The heat of his mouth on Aubrey's neck lasted only a heartbeat, and the sure, deft strokes of his fingers as he unbuttoned Aubrey's shirt were over almost before they began. Despite the discrepancy in time passage, they were both shirtless when they ran up against the back of the couch.

The First Date part of Aubrey's brain said, *Take him to the bedroom at least, you heathen.*

The rest of Aubrey's brain thought, *Good enough.*

Then Nate fumbled with Aubrey's belt, and it didn't much matter. The time for thinking had passed.

He got Nate's jeans and boxers shoved down to his knees and curled a hand around his cock, earning a low moan and the scrape of Nate's nails across the front of his thigh. A quick jerk of the fabric and Nate took him in hand, sliding his callused palm over the head of Aubrey's dick.

Nate produced lube from somewhere. Had he hidden it in the couch? Grabbed it on the way to the door? Aubrey didn't care. He pulled Nate's leg up to his hip, lining their erections up to brush together, and opened the cap.

He ate Nate's gasps of pleasure and pleas to hurry right out of his mouth, two fingers crooked inside him. Nate's cock leaked against his stomach, and Aubrey's throbbed in response.

Nate was hot and perfect around his fingers, body clenching as though trying to reel Aubrey in. Aubrey was happy to be caught, but when he drew his hand back for more lube and a third finger, Nate bit down on his lower lip, shocking him into opening his eyes.

"Now," Nate said.

Here? Aubrey almost asked, but Nate shoved him back half a step and then turned around and bent over the back of the couch. His ass—his perfectly round monument to a lifetime of athletic training, the kind of bubble that could make a man weep for joy—or a man's cock, at least—stuck out obscenely, inviting Aubrey to look and touch his fill, but mostly to—

"Fuck me," Nate said, as though he hadn't already made himself perfectly clear.

"Yes," Aubrey said intelligently, and applied himself to the task.

Nate pushed back into every thrust. The slap of flesh on flesh layered over the rough sounds of their breathing and the skid of the couch on the hardwood. Fuck, they still had their shoes on. This was not first-date sex. It *definitely* was not I-love-you sex.

Aubrey couldn't bring himself to care.

He fitted his thumbs into the dimples of Nate's lower back, curling his fingers around Nate's hips.

"Just," Nate panted, "a little—" He shifted his feet farther apart, deepened the bow of his back.

Aubrey's eyes almost rolled back in his head at the visual, but that was nothing to how it felt to slide deep into Nate's body. They couldn't keep it up for long. Aubrey was already skirting the edge of orgasm. "Do you need—?"

Nate arched his back, and the sight of it almost sent Aubrey over the edge, but he was only reaching for the lube Aubrey had left on the back of the couch. "I got it," Nate gasped.

Jesus, did he ever.

The air was thick with sex, and despite the chill of the apartment, sweat dripped down Nate's back and down Aubrey's. He could feel it trickling between his shoulder blades, between his asscheeks. He wanted to lean down and sink his teeth into Nate's shoulder, but he couldn't sacrifice his leverage. Next time, he promised himself.

"Close," Aubrey gasped. "You with me?"

Nate made a strangled noise, jerking himself off frantically now. "Uh, fuck—"

That must have been a yes, because it only took a handful more thrusts before Nate's ass tightened around him. Aubrey pushed as deep as he could as Nate milked his orgasm out of him, pleasure coursing through his body. With one last snap of his hips, Aubrey collapsed against Nate's back and finally gave in to the urge to bite his deltoid.

The couch slid under their combined weight, far enough that Aubrey felt the pull in his hamstring. The arm of the couch hit something. He raised his head as a hollow *whoomp* echoed throughout the room, and was just in time to see Nate's stupid ugly vase wobble on the table as if in slow motion and then topple to the ground and shatter with a resounding crash.

Aubrey blinked, his mind comically blank.

For a moment the only sound was their own labored breathing. Then Nate started to shake beneath him. Horrified, Aubrey drew back, scrambling for an apology (and the condom), but a moment later, the sound got louder and he realized Nate was laughing—silently, but it built into a very contagious belly laugh.

"Sorry," Aubrey wheezed into the back of the couch. He'd pulled out and managed to keep the condom from further despoiling Nate's living room, but between the exertion and the lack of oxygen, his legs had given out, and he was sprawled next to Nate across the back of the couch. "I didn't—mean to—murder your ugly vase."

Nate hiccupped, red-faced with tears streaking down his cheeks. "Good fucking riddance," he gasped. "I should've done that years ago."

Aubrey managed a few deep breaths, enough to be able to string together a sentence without pausing. "Why *did* you keep it?"

Nate rolled over onto his back, starfished comically over the couch. "Marty said he wanted me to have it because he knew how much I liked it."

"Nate."

"Hm."

"Do you think he was fucking with you?"

"I couldn't tell." He stood, a little awkwardly, between the lube and the come and the pants around his ankles, held on by his shoes. "I figured if I played along it was as good as fucking with him right back."

Aubrey digested this as he pushed himself to his feet. "Sometimes that competitive drive really bites us in the ass."

"Yeah." Nate looked over at the floor and winced, then looked back at his feet. "But on the plus side, that drive is probably why we're both wearing shoes right now and not in danger of cutting our feet."

"True." Aubrey pulled up his own jeans and buckled them. "All right. Here's the play. We clean this up."

"Uh-huh."

"And then we reward our hard work by going up to mine and sitting in the Jacuzzi tub."

"Sold." Nate looked down at himself and grimaced again. "Just let me do a little personal cleanup first."

CHAPTER NINETEEN

NOVEMBER BLEW into December, along with a lot more wind and snow and a flurry of holiday shopping. Nate liked to get most of his out of the way the weekend after Thanksgiving, but between his parents' visit and sex with Aubrey, he had barely made a dent.

At work, the mood had improved post-holiday, leaving Nate to wonder if everyone simply needed a good meal and some time with their family. Kelly and Caley's news had the studio buzzing—everyone loved good news—and Carl brought photos of his newest pride and joy, grandchild number four.

On the air, Nate and Aubrey were smooth as a newly resurfaced rink and as sharp as fresh blades. The Thursday after Thanksgiving, Jess pulled them aside as Kelly covered the women's game.

"What's up?" Aubrey asked as the door to the office closed.

Jess ditched her earpiece on the desk. "Are you guys doing some kind of mind-reading thing or something?"

Nate glanced at Aubrey. "Mind-reading?" they chorused, turning back to Jess in unison.

She pointed at them. "See! That! That's creepy. I mean, it's compelling television, but it's still creepy."

Aubrey glanced at Nate. "Sorry," they said, in unison again.

Nate felt a smile tugging at the corner of his mouth, but he tamped down on it.

Jess stared at them. For a second, Nate thought she'd actually ask, but after a moment, she shook her head and moved on. "Well, I specifically remember telling you not to change anything, but since you actually got *better*, I can't complain."

"Does this mean we're off the chopping block?" Nate asked.

"What am I, a fortune-teller?" She rolled her eyes. "The meeting's next week. I told you, the network does not like to be rushed."

"So what did you call us in here for?"

"Isn't it obvious?" She smiled, and Nate could have sworn, once again, that she was going to congratulate them. Instead she just said, "Producer stuff. Keep up the good work."

"She knows," Aubrey hissed as they walked back to the set.

Nate figured maybe she did.

As LUCK would have it, their first road trip after Thanksgiving put them in Vegas. Before he and Nate started dating for real, Aubrey had emailed a real estate agent just to take a look around. Whether he took the job or not—whether the show was renewed or not—his contract was up after playoffs, and it might not be renewed. He was keeping his options open.

He was supposed to swing by the Cirque office, maybe take a tour of their facility if he had time.

The problem was how to fit all that into one day without Nate noticing. Not because Aubrey didn't want him to know, but because he felt like he should have told him already, even though he hadn't auditioned. Even though he didn't plan to leave unless the worst happened. Somehow it felt like if he mentioned it, it would be a vote of no confidence on both the show and their relationship.

So keeping it secret from Nate was a problem… or it would have been a problem, except Nate ate the chicken cacciatore on the red-eye they took late Friday night.

To avoid scrutiny, they'd agreed not to stay in each other's rooms on business trips, especially since it had come out in an interview with a local magazine that they'd shared in Winnipeg. So Aubrey didn't find out Nate was sick until the next morning. He woke up to a text message— *Food poisoning. Feel like im dying.*

God, poor Nate. Aubrey was resolved to be a good boyfriend, but he wasn't sure exactly what that meant. Should he go hold his hair back, metaphorically speaking? But Aubrey wouldn't want anyone to see him heave his breakfast into a toilet bowl, *especially* not Nate.

What if Nate needed help getting *to* the toilet bowl, though? That was the least sexy thought Aubrey had ever had about Nate, but he wasn't going to let him suffer. Boyfriends sucked it up and offered their services in situations like this. That was what love was for. Right?

Aubrey was kind of hoping not, but to be sure, he walked down the hall to Nate's door and knocked. He could cancel his apartment showings. "Nate?" he called. "You need anything?"

It took a moment, but eventually Nate opened the door. His face was ashen, sallow, and damp with sweat. Aubrey fought the urge to take a step back. He smelled like stale sweat and vomit. "Front desk is sending up some meds."

They had a call in six hours. "Are you going to—"

He never got to finish the sentence. Nate ran to the bathroom. He didn't even have time to close the door; Aubrey could hear him retching from the hallway.

"I'll tell Jess to send Kelly in your place? We can do a teleconference for the intermission interviews."

Nate retched again, and Aubrey's stomach rebelled. What a time to find out he'd turned into a sympathetic vomiter. "Thanks," Nate said weakly a moment later.

"I'm, uh, I'm going to go," Aubrey said. "Text me if you need anything, okay?"

Nate didn't answer verbally, but he stuck his arm out the bathroom door and gave a thumbs-up.

Aubrey fled and carefully closed the door behind him.

Then he set out house-hunting, even though he was only looking semi-seriously. He stood in the center of the living room of the first apartment. It was furnished, on a fashionably high floor, with huge tinted windows with blackout curtains. It might as well be his apartment in Chicago. The layout was almost the same—one huge bedroom, open floor plan, big bathroom. This one had laundry service instead of an in-suite setup. There was a pool on the roof and a gym on the main floor.

It was very much the sort of bachelor pad Aubrey had always sought out and lived in, and it felt completely wrong.

He gave Sarah, the agent, his best tough-customer smile. "What else have you got?"

The second apartment was better, with a living room that spanned two full stories, a huge private balcony, and enough kitchen counter space to prepare two turkey dinners simultaneously. The walk-in closet with built-in drawers and shelving was big enough to host an orgy.

He hated it... except the closet.

By the time Sarah was showing him the third executive-style apartment, he'd figured out the trend. He could see himself living in these apartments just fine. There was nothing wrong with them.

He couldn't see himself living in any of them *with Nate*.

It didn't even make sense! Nate lived in an apartment very similar to Aubrey's. It should have been easy to superimpose him on any one of these places, to imagine him there with Aubrey as he often was with Aubrey at his actual apartment. But the apartments they lived in now— those were already *homes*. Aubrey couldn't say why it was different, but it was.

The next property, on the other hand....

"I know you're not looking for something with maintenance," Sarah explained as she unlocked the door to let him in, "so I want to assure you that this is a condo. Everything's taken care of in the monthly fees."

"I'll keep an open mind," Aubrey promised.

"It's also rented through the end of the week. We have permission from the residents to show it; they went to a movie. But the point is it's not quite as tidy as an unoccupied home."

"Nor should it be." In truth he liked the way the place looked lived-in. The kitchen was bright and airy, with appliances along the left wall in front of quadruple patio doors and a huge island separating it from an open dining area and living room. There were two glasses in the kitchen sink.

"Master bedroom is this way," Sarah said, gesturing to the right.

Aubrey followed her down a wide hallway to the far end of the house and a master bedroom with a king-size bed and a conversation set. The room also had a walkout to the yard.

"One-way privacy shades to keep the sun and any prying eyes from getting in, but you can still see out." Sarah indicated a control panel next to the bed. "Master bathroom is just through there."

It had every luxury Aubrey expected in a property like this and a few more besides. "Nice place," he commented.

Sarah led them back down the hallway, saying something about the privileges at the development pool, but Aubrey accidentally tuned her out. They were passing another door, which must be a second bedroom or maybe an office? The door was cracked. Aubrey hadn't been able to see in from the other direction, but now.... He nudged it open.

A canopy bed covered in a unicorn blanket took up one wall. Opposite that, a neat white wood desk housed a laptop and a pile of schoolbooks. A hammock overflowing with stuffed animals hung in the corner, and there was an in-progress Lego model of a spaceship on the floor.

It was like something had taken over his body. He stared stupidly, but he didn't see the empty room. He was seeing a full one, three people sitting on the floor, two adults and a kid, putting the finishing touches on a block tower.

Aubrey suddenly realized that he was picking out a new place with the idea that he would be sharing his life. Of course a one-bedroom apartment didn't seem right for that.

But he hadn't realized that he'd also internalized what it might mean for him that Nate wanted children. That wasn't something you could compromise on. Aubrey had never thought about it much himself—he'd been honest when he said that to Nate. But apparently his subconscious had concluded that if he was going to settle down, he'd do it in whatever way made Nate the happiest.

The idea of having a family terrified him. But he'd be lying if he said it didn't also fill him with a sort of warm fuzzy hope and, yeah, that was longing. Time for that identity crisis.

"The home does come furnished," Sarah said, and Aubrey snapped back to the present. "But if you'd prefer to use this room as an office or gym, I'm sure the furniture in here can be relocated."

"I thought you said the complex has a gym?" he said automatically.

"It does." Sarah sounded a little confused, or maybe concerned. "Lots of people prefer their privacy, though."

"Right." Aubrey shook himself, willing the vision he'd had to disappear. Then, out of self-preservation, he pulled out his phone and checked the time, and—"I have to get back to the hotel." How had the day gotten so far away from him? "I've got to be at the arena in an hour and a half."

And he needed at least half that time to get his head back in the game.

NATE SPENT the weekend and half of Monday recuperating. Monday night he felt like himself again, but he didn't see Aubrey until he got an invitation to lunch on Tuesday.

That turned into something else entirely, and then into a nap. So when Nate's phone beeped and dragged him out of a glue-eyed slumber, he didn't panic until he actually saw the time.

Then he peeled his face off Aubrey's shoulder and shook him awake. "Hey. Get up."

"If you wanna go again, I need coffee first," Aubrey mumbled.

Nate shoved his phone in Aubrey's face. "If we don't get in the shower right now, we're going to miss our call."

"Shit!"

Nate scrambled back to his place to shower and met Aubrey downstairs.

"Think we're busted?" Aubrey whispered as they got in the car that had obviously been waiting several minutes. His hair was still damp at the ends.

"At least we don't smell like the same bodywash," Nate muttered back. He was pretty sure that almost got them caught last week.

The car dropped them out front only a handful of minutes later than usual—enough that they could pass it off as bad traffic. But when they stepped off the elevator and into a panic-free studio—a hallway where half the staff were standing around with somber faces and the other half looked about to punch someone—Nate knew.

"Ah, fuck," Aubrey said.

Nate made an aborted grab for his hand but caught himself.

Before they could get any farther, Jess poked her head out of the office, looked up and down the hallway, and sighed. "No keeping a secret in this place. Nate, Aubrey, please come in. The rest of you, I'd appreciate if you could contain your catastrophizing until the staff meeting later."

They closed the door behind them.

Jess didn't make them wait long. "As you may have guessed, Larry was here late this afternoon, and apparently I do not have a poker face. But it's not as dire as you're thinking."

"So, we're not canceled?" Nate clarified.

Jess rubbed her hands over her face. "No. Yes. I don't know."

"Oh, well, that clears it up," Aubrey said sardonically.

Nate shot him a quelling look, but he did have a point. "All right, can you explain in, I don't know, five words or less?"

"The network sold the show."

Nate blinked. He hadn't been expecting that. "Oh."

Aubrey went a little further with it. "Oh, of course they.... They spent weeks harping on us about viewership and ratings and blah, blah, blah, and all the work we put in was just us inflating our value so they could fetch a higher price for us?"

Well, when he put it that way. "I feel like a fatted calf."

"You know the show has always been an experiment." Jess sighed. "The truth is, getting the licensing we did was a coup we only managed because there was a gap in coverage and the show was a guinea pig. Well, phase one of the experiment is over."

Wait— "They sold us to ESBN?"

"Effective tomorrow," Jess confirmed. She looked like she needed a stiff drink, or maybe eighteen solid hours of sleep. "We won't know more about what's happening to us until then."

"Well." Nate's throat felt suddenly thick. "Let's make tonight a good one."

In the end, they got through the episode all right, but even though he and Aubrey were good at their jobs, Nate could tell their banter felt strained. The game they were slated to cover was a gruesome slog, with the total shot clock barely creeping up to thirty at the end of three periods, the score a measly 1-0, and not even a fight to make things interesting.

Kelly's coverage, at least, had more engaging fare to offer. The women's game was tied 3-3 going into the second, and by the time it finished, it had crept up to 9-7.

They wrapped up as they always did, with score updates from around the league. Nate wished he'd had time to come up with something new and different and original to say if this was going to be their final signoff, but he hadn't. The usual words felt hollow and insignificant. "That's all for tonight. Until next time, I'm Nate Overton—"

Under the desk, Aubrey put his hand on Nate's leg. "And I'm Aubrey Chase—"

"And this has been *The Inside Edge*."

CHAPTER TWENTY

NEITHER OF them was in the mood for sex that night.

They also weren't in the mood to be alone.

The nice thing about an actual relationship, Aubrey was finding, was that he didn't have to be alone.

The flip side was that Nate took forever to fall asleep when he was stressed out and not getting laid, and Nate taking forever to fall asleep led to Aubrey being up until the wee hours after he dropped off, staring at the ceiling.

He had only barely managed to ask Nate to go on a date with him. Now he somehow had to gather the courage to have a talk about what would happen to their relationship if he moved to Vegas.

He'd been counting on having a little more time to get used to the whole having-a-boyfriend thing before he had to bring up long-distance versus cohabitation. It was probably too soon to tell Nate he'd been thinking they should move in together, and the show had been sold, not canceled. The new network could replace one or both of them... or change nothing. And there wasn't anything Aubrey could do about it.

He had almost decided to give up on the dream of sleep and go watch TV in the living room when Nate sighed, rolled over, and burrowed his face into the pillow. "Ice cream," he said happily, obviously deep in a very pleasant dream.

Save some for me. If Nate could sleep with this much on his mind, so could he. That competitive athlete drive was still good for something after all, because so resolved, Aubrey finally drifted off.

He woke up to Nate sitting at the end of the bed, fully dressed, holding his phone loosely between his legs.

Aubrey hated feeling wrong-footed before he even stood up. "Hey," he rasped. "Going somewhere?"

"Jess texted," Nate said by way of explanation, holding his phone at chest height and waggling it for effect. "Wants to see me in her office at eleven."

Me? That was probably a harbinger. "Just you?"

Nate shook his head. "Didn't ask. Check your phone."

She wanted to see him at ten thirty. Aubrey winced and looked at the clock. "Me first, I guess."

Nate looked ashen. "You want to ride in together?"

Honestly, if this was going to go down the way Aubrey thought, he'd prefer to go home alone after and sulk. "I'm going to drive myself, I think. Text me after?"

Nate nodded, somber, hands clenching and unclenching around the phone. He looked like he wanted to say something—or do something—but in the end, he just stood up. "I'll, um. I'll see you later, then."

"Yeah." Aubrey swung his legs out of bed, but Nate was already halfway out of the room. "Later."

No one had ever broken up with Aubrey before, but he thought it probably felt a little like this.

The feeling persisted as he walked down the hallway toward Jess's office. The corridor was otherwise deserted. This floor was mostly offices, so Aubrey assumed everyone else was on set of whatever was currently filming. That suited him fine, though. He didn't need any witnesses to what he was sure was coming.

Jess's office door was open, and she waved him inside when he knocked. "Close the door, please."

Yeah, this wasn't going to go well. It had been nice while it lasted, though. He closed the door and took the chair across the desk from her, the same one he'd sat in last night.

"I know you're probably anxious to get started, so I'll cut to the chase. I met with the ESBN show liaison first thing this morning." She had the dark circles under her eyes to prove it too.

"Show liaison," Aubrey echoed.

Jess grimaced. "My opinion? That's what you get when you buy a show wholesale from another network and need someone to implement changes but aren't ready to let the current showrunner go."

"Ouch." Whatever was coming, it wouldn't affect just him. And unlike many other people who worked on the show, Aubrey had a fat trust fund and a job lined up. "So these changes. Let me guess. It's the end of the line for me."

Slowly, Jess shook her head. "I'm really sorry, Aubrey. If it's any consolation, I thought you were great. A lot of people did."

"But ESBN wants to go in a new direction." It came out sounding only a little bitter.

"Technically speaking, I think they want to go in an old direction, but they're afraid the show's new fans will riot if they bring back John."

Aubrey snorted. "Thank God for small mercies, I guess." At least Nate wouldn't have to go back to working with that asshole.

"I guess," Jess echoed. Her shoulders slumped. "I have to say, you're taking this better than I thought."

He was, Aubrey realized with a start. Therapy must really be good for something. "I mean, the writing was on the wall. The good ol' boys at ESBN, they're not ready to cede serious hockey air time to a flamboyant former figure skater. Frankly, I'm surprised they're keeping Nate."

Then again, they didn't know Nate like Aubrey did now. Maybe the new Nate would end up canned just like Aubrey.

"Yeah," Jess said, somewhat grim. But then she made a visible effort to rally. "Look, I know you and I, and you and Nate, got off on the wrong foot. But I just want to let you know how much I appreciate the work you put in since then. The show finally became all the things I knew it could be. It sucks that it's ending like this, but that doesn't mean it didn't feel great to get here."

Aubrey's throat felt suddenly thick. "Thanks for giving me a chance, and then a second chance. This has been… the best kind of challenge, and I appreciate everything you've taught me."

They shook hands.

"What about the rest of the crew?" Aubrey asked. He genuinely liked the staff. He hoped Carl wouldn't be suddenly jobless at his age.

"My understanding is they're keeping everyone until after the Cup Final, just because it's too much hassle to change things midseason. I have the impression they want to move filming to New York or LA."

"LA would make sense if they want to cover all the night's games from start to finish."

"Plenty of studio space there too. HQ's in New York, though."

Would Nate like New York? He barely drove in Chicago; driving in NYC would make him nuts—though he wouldn't really have to. But his staunch Midwestern friendliness would suffocate and die.

Aubrey wondered what Nate would think about Vegas.

"Aubrey?"

He shook himself. "Sorry. I was just imagining Nate relocating to New York."

"Lord. We'll burn that bridge when we get there." She sighed. "Look, this isn't how either of us wanted your stint on the show to go. But that's not your fault. If you ever need a character reference, or if you see a broadcasting job you think a word from me would help you land, drop me a line, yeah?"

Aubrey blinked. "Seriously? After my first day on the job?"

"Believe me, no one's more surprised about this than I am. I don't know what was going on with you that day, but it obviously wasn't representative of who you are. We're going to miss you. Especially Nate, weirdly enough."

For the first time that day, Aubrey had the impulse to smile and mean it. Without the show, he and Nate had no reason to hide their relationship. Maybe something good could come of this after all.

Assuming the idea of him and Nate lasted through the collapse of their jobs together and a potential long-distance relationship, of course.

"Thanks," he managed. "I'll miss you too."

NATE THOUGHT he had prepared himself for the worst right up until the moment he stepped off the elevator on Jess's floor and saw her saying goodbye to Aubrey outside her office.

He didn't want to believe it. But he knew Aubrey well enough, and he knew to look for the cocksure stance, the smirk always hiding around the corner of his mouth. They were missing.

His heart sank.

Aubrey and Jess turned and saw him at the same time. Jess had a decent poker face after thirty years in showbiz, and Aubrey normally did a passable job. But before he could school his features, Nate cataloged the defeat in his eyes, the slump of his shoulders. He even had his hands in his pockets. Aubrey never did that.

He must be trying to keep from a reflexive crossing of his arms—a classic defensive posture.

For the second time in two years, the ground beneath Nate's feet felt like it had shifted, leaving him off-balance and unsure.

Nate was starting to hate not knowing where he stood.

"Tell me you're kidding," he said heavily before he could stop himself.

It wasn't fair. He'd dealt with John for almost three years. Aubrey had been a breath of fresh air. Aubrey had made him really love his job again in a way he hadn't since he left the ice.

Jess took a step forward. "Nate—"

His feet wanted to go backward—back into the elevator, down to the ground floor, out into a Lyft. Home where he could pretend this wasn't happening. Thank God he still had some pride left. He held his ground. "The show is doing the best it's ever done!"

"I know," Jess said.

"Because Aubrey is perfect for this job!" He knew about hockey, sure. But in reality, the cohost's job was to act as a foil for Nate, help the audience learn who he was. They humanized each other—humanized the game. "I just got him broken in."

"I know," Jess repeated gently. "It wasn't my decision. I'm sorry, Nate."

Fuck *sorry*. Nate had never had much of a temper. Even when he was on the ice, even in the highest-stakes games, he generally kept a cool head. But his blood was boiling now. "They can't do that." The words came out hot and venomous.

Jess did a double take, but she recovered quickly. "Didn't think you'd feel so strongly about it, but yeah, they can do whatever they want."

"It's in my contract," Aubrey explained quietly.

Damn it. "But why? Why would they?" Except Nate knew why. Jess knew too. "Right," he said acidly. "That's the bonus of having two gay hosts, I guess. You can fire one and still claim it's not discrimination."

"Kindly watch your tone and your insinuations when you're standing in the middle of the hallway." The flush across Jess's cheeks let him know his anger was contagious. She didn't like this any more than he did, but the steel in her voice made it clear she wasn't going to let him steamroll her either. "This is a little bigger than just Aubrey. Those shows over Thanksgiving, those were part of the test phase. New format. New cohost."

Oh Jesus. "Who in their right mind would rather watch Paul than Aubrey?"

"Nate." Aubrey put a hand on his arm.

Jess's eyebrows hit her hairline.

Mother*fucker*. Nate gritted his teeth. Aubrey's hand dropped to his side.

"Why don't you come in?" Jess said finally, "and we can continue this conversation behind closed doors." Then she turned to Aubrey. "Good luck, okay? You'll be great. And I'll look you up if I'm ever in town."

Ever in town? Where was she going?

Or was the question: Where were *they* going?

Aubrey glanced sideways at Nate, the color washing out of his cheeks. "You better," he said to Jess, and they shook hands. He turned to leave and touched Nate's elbow on the way by. "I'll see you at home, okay?"

He kept his voice quiet, but Nate knew Jess wouldn't have missed it. But he couldn't be bothered to keep up a pretense either. There was no point now. He nodded.

When the door closed behind him, he took a moment to close his eyes and reach for calm. This wasn't Jess's fault. Or Aubrey's. Or his own.

It just sucked.

"I didn't realize you two had gotten so close," Jess said quietly.

Nate swallowed and forced himself to sit, not quite ready to meet her gaze. "Yeah, well. He sneaks up on you."

"I guess so."

He cleared his throat. Whatever else he was dealing with, this was a business meeting, and he was a professional. He wasn't going to quit just because he didn't get his way. "So. Tell me about the new show."

CHAPTER TWENTY-ONE

NATE HAD a long week of meetings ahead of him. The new show liaison, Jim Royce, wanted to meet with him tomorrow first thing, to go over the new format. They wouldn't be able to change everything up immediately—they'd need a new set, among other things—but Royce didn't want Nate to be surprised by anything that was coming. Jess's words.

Nate was pretty sure they just wanted to make sure he knew he wasn't going to get any say in what was going on. He'd heard enough stories about how ESBN operated, and Jess had hinted at what he could expect.

It didn't sound like fun. But it didn't hold a candle to what Aubrey was going through, so Nate sucked it up.

He had his Lyft swing by Luella's for dinner before heading back to Aubrey's.

"Hey," he said when Aubrey opened the door. Nate had half expected him to be wearing grubby sweatpants and a ratty T-shirt, which was ridiculous in hindsight. The closest thing he owned to grubby sweatpants were the ones with PINK on the ass. Instead he was wearing the same suit he'd worn to Jess's office, but he'd ditched the jacket and unbuttoned the top two buttons of his shirt. "Salmon croquettes or chicken and waffles? Or are we skipping to dessert?"

"Are those beignets?" Aubrey took the bag and stuck his nose inside for a sniff. "Oh my God. Come to Daddy." He stepped back to let Nate pass him.

"I know it's kind of early for dinner," Nate said, hanging his coat by the door. "I figured we could heat it up later if you're up to it."

"I'm actually fine." Aubrey put dinner in the fridge and took out a pair of plates for the beignets. "I mean, it sucks. I liked that job. I'll probably want to break something later. But it's not like I need the money."

They were both lucky that way. "I'll miss working with you, though. It's not going to be the same." Why didn't Aubrey seem more upset?

Aubrey handed him a plate and gestured toward the breakfast bar. They sat. "The more things change, right?" Then Aubrey contemplated his beignet. "Oh… napkins."

On second thought, maybe he was a little distracted. "I'll get them," Nate offered.

Aubrey put a hand on his arm. The first and second time he'd done that, Nate had thought he was comforting Nate. Looking at Aubrey now, though… maybe it was the other way around. Maybe this was Aubrey asking for comfort the only way he could.

Maybe beignets weren't what he needed right then.

"Hey," Nate said. "These'll keep another hour, right?"

Aubrey tilted his head.

Nate stood and held out his hand. "C'mon."

Aubrey didn't resist as Nate led him to the bedroom. He let Nate undo the buttons of his dress shirt and slide it from his shoulders, unbuckle his belt and pull it through its loops. Nate kept his touch intimate but not sexual. This was about comfort. Anything else he'd leave up to Aubrey.

"What're we doing?" Aubrey asked finally, as Nate gently nudged him onto the bed.

"Starting the day over. This one blows." Nate left his own shirt over the back of the chair where he'd laid Aubrey's. His pants joined it a moment later, and then he lay down in the bed next to Aubrey in his boxers and curled his body around him. "There. Better."

Aubrey breathed deeply for a few moments. The tension in his back and shoulders slowly gave way until he was leaning into Nate's body. He interlaced their fingers. "I have a question."

"Shoot."

"What kind of heathen leaves his socks on in bed?"

Nate snorted into the back of Aubrey's neck. It must have tickled, because Aubrey hunched his shoulders against it. "Hey, it's December in Chicago. Frostbite is a real concern."

"The heat goes off in your swanky apartment *one time*," Aubrey said dramatically. He sounded better already.

Nate smiled against his skin.

"We could get under the covers," Aubrey suggested.

"Mm-hmm." Despite his earlier comment, Aubrey didn't actually feel cold—no goose bumps—and he generally kept his place a few degrees warmer than Nate did.

"Or," Aubrey said, turning over.

Yeah, Nate thought so. "Or," he agreed.

Their mouths came together slowly, a foregone conclusion without any urgency. Nate traced the shell of Aubrey's ear, the line of his jaw. Their knees bumped; Aubrey adjusted to let Nate slide a leg between his so they could get closer.

Nate kissed Aubrey's mouth, his chin, his cheekbone, and then started over. Aubrey clutched at the back of his neck, then his shoulder. Nate shuddered when Aubrey pressed a hand between his pectorals and slid it down to his navel.

It was easy to let his hands wander. Aubrey arched into his touches, sighing and gasping, letting Nate learn his body. Nate kept his hands light, though, exploring the hard, smooth muscles of Aubrey's back, the curve of his bicep, the dip of his waist. When he slid lower, palming the generous swell of his ass, Aubrey tilted his head against Nate's so their noses brushed, breaking their kiss.

"I want," Aubrey said quietly, but he didn't finish the statement. When Nate opened his eyes, his face was flushed, his eyelashes fanned out against his cheeks. He brushed their noses together again.

Nate stole a handful of quick, sipping kisses. "Okay."

While Nate fumbled behind him for the nightstand drawer, Aubrey wriggled out of his boxers. Nate rolled back with the lube and a handful of condoms, and Aubrey met him with a kiss.

Nate wasn't in any more of a hurry now that Aubrey was naked. They entwined their legs again. Nate took his time working Aubrey open as they kissed, swallowing the sound of his gasps, biting back moans of his own as Aubrey stroked his cock.

He worked up to three fingers, Aubrey undulating against him, his face tucked against Nate's neck. Finally Aubrey curled his leg toward himself and used his knee to push Nate away.

Nate could take a hint. He eased Aubrey onto his back and pulled a pillow from the head of the bed to shove under his hips while Aubrey unwrapped the condom. He rolled it down Nate's erection, then rubbed his thumb in a circle under the head.

He leaned his forehead against Aubrey's as he pushed inside. The tight heat of Aubrey's body enveloped him, sending his head spinning. Aubrey exhaled a soft gasping sound as he tilted his head back and his hips up, cradling Nate with his body.

It was sexy and slick and gorgeous. Aubrey's fingers slid through the sweat on his back, clutching him closer, and his body was hot and grasping around Nate's cock, drawing him in deeper with every stroke. His breath fanned softly over Nate's lips, and he hooked an ankle around the back of Nate's thigh, urging him on.

Finally Nate shuddered and pushed up on his arms, changing the angle.

"Ah!" Aubrey threw his head back, and the tendons of his neck stood out in stark relief. His face was a rictus of pleasure. A rivulet of sweat dripped down his temple.

Nate licked his lips, watching him, focused on his pleasure. His cock was hard between them, full and dripping on his stomach, but Aubrey's hands were busy tweaking Nate's nipples, digging into the flesh of his shoulders to urge him on.

Supporting himself on one hand, Nate reached for the lube and flicked the cap open. He knew he wouldn't last, and he needed to make Aubrey feel as incredible as he did.

Aubrey cried out again when Nate closed his slick hand around his shaft. His eyes shot open, meeting Nate's.

Nate leaned down again until their faces were centimeters apart. At this angle he could barely move his hand, but it didn't seem to matter. Aubrey's breath was hitching, his body coiling like a spring. Clumsy, he lifted his mouth to meet Nate's. Nate's teeth grazed his lower lip, and Aubrey shook just slightly. Then he deepened the kiss, and Aubrey shattered around him, crying out into Nate's mouth.

Nate followed him over the edge, helpless to do anything else.

For several moments they lay panting in each other's arms. Aubrey's pupils were blown, and he seemed dazed, his face slack.

Nate let him recover. It was pretty obvious he'd never felt that bone-deep, soul-deep connection that came from the kind of intimate sex you could only have with someone you loved. It was natural he'd feel vulnerable, and equally so to need time to process.

So he kept his mouth shut and quietly dealt with the condom, leaving it in a wad of tissues on the nightstand. Tissues were not going to cut it for the two of them, but he wasn't going to nudge Aubrey toward the shower before he was ready.

"Nate," Aubrey said finally.

Ah. His brain had finally rebooted. "Hm?"

"There might be something to this whole commitment thing."

Months ago Nate might have bristled. By now he could recognize when Aubrey was deflecting attention from his own vulnerability. Instead of taking offense, he kissed Aubrey's forehead. "I'll have to take your word for it since I don't have a basis of comparison."

Finally Aubrey raised his head and a single eyebrow.

"I tried to have a casual hookup once, but it worked out," he elaborated wryly.

Aubrey smiled and put his head back down. "I'm glad."

"Me too."

WITH THE show undergoing a series of seemingly arbitrary changes, Aubrey suddenly had a lot of time to himself while Nate attended hours upon hours of meetings.

"I wish *I'd* gotten fired," Nate joked one night when he came in the door at eight. They hadn't been filming. He'd had seven solid hours of meetings.

You could retire and be my kept man, Aubrey almost suggested, but that would lead to a serious conversation he wasn't ready to have, and Nate was already exhausted.

"Shower or bathtub?" he asked instead, and afterward they spent a pleasant half hour watching *The Mandalorian* on Disney Plus, because Aubrey was a closet *Star Wars* buff and Nate loved Baby Yoda.

Unfortunately, Aubrey was finding that the longer he went without telling Nate the truth about Vegas, the more difficult it was to broach the subject.

In a twist of events Aubrey never could have predicted, he called his mother for relationship advice.

"Mom, can I ask you something?"

"Please do. Your cousin is a wonderful woman, but I am entirely too old to be expected to partake in bachelorette-party drinking games."

Aubrey laughed. "Come on. You love it."

"Oh, fine." He could hear her amusement. "I could drink any two of them under the table. I just don't go in for lime Jell-O shots. Tell me all your problems."

"Well, they didn't start over Jell-O shots."

"I am already intrigued."

He sat, then stood again, suddenly nervous, like... like a high schooler about to come out of the closet or introduce his parents to his boyfriend for the first time. "The thing is...." He held his breath, hoping the need to expel it would make it easier to say the words. "I met someone."

Dead. Silence.

Well, Aubrey hadn't expected that. When it stretched on for more than a few seconds, he said tentatively, "Mom? Did you hear what I said?"

"I—I heard you." There was a sigh of air and the sound of shushing fabric, like she'd been so surprised she needed to find a fainting couch or something. "You met someone, you said. In a... romantic context?"

Why was she being so weird about this? Aubrey was suddenly uncertain. He'd been sure his whole life that it was his promiscuity his mother had taken issue with, but what if that had been a cover? "That's usually what the phrase means, yes."

"Oh." Now he had a whole new reason to be alarmed. *Oh no.* He'd jokingly told Nate his mother would probably weep tears of joy if he told her they were together. He hadn't expected it to be *true*. And he certainly hadn't expected the waterworks to begin before he even told her it was solid, family-values Nate who'd swept him off his feet—or maybe checked him off them.

"Oh, Aubrey, I'm just—so happy."

He swallowed around a suddenly too-tight throat. "Me too, Mom."

"Oh." Another sniff followed by a zip, and then more rustling. His mother always carried a fine linen handkerchief in her purse. He imagined her dabbing her eyes with it now. "Aubrey, I... I want to apologize to you."

Aubrey had been gearing up to explain falling for his cohost, but this derailed him completely. "Again?"

She laughed wetly. "I haven't apologized for this yet, and it's important."

Aubrey sat again. "Okay."

"I want to apologize for how I scolded you when you were younger, when you...."

"When I slept with any guy who'd look at me twice?" Aubrey suggested.

His mother sniffed in acknowledgment. "I always disapproved of your lifestyle—not your sexuality, Aubrey. I love you, and that includes the fact that you're gay. But I hated that you slept with so many men, and I never made a secret of that. You probably thought it lowered my opinion of you and—well, I suppose it did. I'm working on that. But that wasn't the reason I hated it."

"Okay," Aubrey said again, even more off-balance and unsure how to protect himself against the blow he sensed was coming.

"The truth is I was afraid for you."

Afraid...? Of...? "What, Mom? I don't get it."

She sighed. "When you came out to us, you were already a world-class athlete. You took a lot of pride in your body, and you put a lot of value on it. I worried that if you... if you only ever loved with your body, you would believe your heart wasn't worth anything."

Aubrey was stunned into silence. His eyes burned with tears—at finally understanding his mother's objections and at how close she had been to the truth. He took a sharp breath. "You might have been right to worry." There. Half of the hard stuff out of the way. "If I hadn't met Nate...."

"Nate?" She perked up. "Nate Overton? Your cohost?"

"Former cohost," Aubrey reminded her. "We've been seeing each other for a while." He loved her, and he was trying to repair their relationship, but she didn't need details.

"Tell me about him," she demanded. "I know he's handsome and you have good chemistry, so you can leave that out."

Aubrey smiled, thinking about him. "What do you want to know? He's close to his family. He used to be married, but he's not anymore. I wasn't involved," he added hurriedly.

"Oh, Aubrey. Of course not. I know you better than that."

Aubrey had slept with a few married men, actually, but he hadn't known until after the fact. But those memories were better left in the past; they made him feel used. "Okay. Well. Nate is... he likes to cook? He plays in a coed rec hockey league on Fridays at the rink where I've been skating with Greg." And now to steer the conversation to the advice portion. "He, um. He wants kids."

His mother sucked in a breath. "So it's serious."

Aubrey bit his lip. He flexed a hand at his side to work out some of the tension. "It's really new," he said, which wasn't a contradiction. "But yeah, it's serious. And that's the problem."

"*What's* the problem?" she asked. "That's not a problem. That's wonderful."

"It's a problem because I just got fired, Mom. I'm not staying in Chicago."

"Why not?" she countered. "It's not like you need the work. You could stay if you wanted to."

"The problem is," he said, realizing as he did so that this was the crux of it, "that I don't know if I want to."

"Aubrey! Why not?"

He ran a hand through his hair. "Did I tell you I was helping Greg practice for Cirque? We choreographed a whole routine. Two executives came out to watch it, and I guess they saw us goofing off beforehand. They offered me a spot, maybe a choreography gig." He swallowed. "I can't just sit around, you know? I need to be involved. I'm not going to be able to skate forever, but choreography.... And there are so many other opportunities in Vegas...."

His mother hummed. "But Nate's job is in Chicago."

"Nate's job is in Chicago," Aubrey confirmed miserably. "And it's only been a few weeks. Is that too soon to start something long distance? Asking him to move to Vegas is absurd, right?"

"Absurd is so relative." He could almost see her shaking her head. "You're sure this job is what you want?"

"No!" he exclaimed. "No, I'm not sure. But it's an opportunity that's not going to come around every day. Ever since Greg and I skated for his audition, I've been thinking about performing again. I'm not ready to give it up, I want... I have more to do, more to say, more to contribute. But how do I choose?"

"Darling, I love you very much. But if you think I am the person to ask about achieving balance between your career and your personal life, you might want to reconsider."

Aubrey flopped back against the couch, wincing. "Point taken."

"Since we're on the subject." His mother cleared her throat. "I want to tell you something. When you were little, your father and I desperately wanted to have another baby."

Aubrey was glad he was already sitting down, because that would have about knocked him over. "What?"

"We were so determined, but we just—we couldn't get pregnant. So we started traveling to see fertility specialists. We flew to Toronto, New York, Switzerland…. Anywhere with an experimental new treatment, we went. We'd be gone for weeks at a time, hoping for a miracle."

He remembered being eight, ten, twelve years old, wondering why his parents kept leaving him. Remembered too the way his parents had latched on to Rachel, showering her with love, and how jealous he'd been as an eight-year-old to see a toddler getting that kind of attention.

It had hurt him. But now he understood that his parents had been hurting too.

"Mom."

"Just let me get this out, all right?" He thought she might be trying to sound tough, but in truth, he could hear the edge of tears. "We loved you so much. It wasn't that you weren't enough. We wanted a bigger family to expand on the love you brought into our lives. But we were so focused on it that that we abandoned you when you needed us the most."

Aubrey swallowed. "I'm sorry. I didn't… I had no idea." How different might he have been if he'd had a younger sibling to look after? Sure, it would have further divided his parents' attention. But he'd have had someone to tease, someone to look up to him. He'd maybe have learned some of the balance his therapist had spent the past few months teaching him. He couldn't help thinking he might have been better off.

"That's the way your father and I wanted it. No one knew. We kept our grief very private. The process wrung us so dry that by the time we gave up, we were too burned out to consider adoption."

He could certainly understand that. But… "Why tell me now?"

"Because, sweetheart, I want you to consider the lesson I learned twenty years too late."

He waited.

"Just be careful while you're chasing your dream that you don't sacrifice the blessings you already have."

Aubrey sat quietly with the weight of that advice for a few moments, wanting to give it the consideration it deserved. "I will," he said at length. "Thanks, Mom."

He knew what he had to do.

CHAPTER TWENTY-TWO

"DUDE," CALEY said, jostling Nate's shoulder at the top of the circle, where he'd just sent a puck blistering over the goaltender's shoulder. "You're *angry* tonight. No celly?"

Nate gave a weak attempt at a smile. It was his second goal this game; they were halfway through the second. But he didn't feel much like celebrating.

"All right, all right." She shook her head. "Just try not to run anyone else over, okay?"

He winced. They didn't have a no-checking rule, but the unwritten code was you pulled your hits, since they didn't have medical staff on site. Nate… could have pulled his hits a little more.

"Point," he acknowledged.

She clapped him on the shoulder. "Let's go, line change."

By the time they took a break after the second period, he'd mostly managed to sublimate his work stress. It wasn't that he didn't like Paul. He just wasn't Aubrey, and the new vision ESBN had for the show felt a lot more Barstool Sports than the show Jess had spent so much time creating. It didn't make any sense.

"I just can't help thinking, 'You know who would really like this show? John Plum,'" Nate said gloomily.

Caley dropped her head to the half wall and bounced her helmet off it a few times. Nate realized he might be harping.

"Sorry." He took a deep breath and shook his head. "It'll get better. I just need to try harder and stop sulking."

Caley patted him on the back, and he resolved to wait out the rest of their intermission in silence and let it go. Deep breaths. In, out. He was here to lose himself in physical activity, not bring the office to work with him.

"Hey." This was from Jordan, a defenseman who'd played most of his career in Europe before returning home to his Chicago roots. "What ever happened with those figure skaters?" He was talking to Brigitte, who was sitting on his other side. "The ones who used to have the ice before us. Man, I miss watching them skate."

"Greg?" Bridget squeezed her Gatorade bottle into her mouth. "Didn't you hear? He was rehearsing or whatever for a Cirque show in Vegas. The audition was after Thanksgiving."

"He get in?"

"How did you not hear about this? Yeah, he got in. Word is they both did."

Wait, *what*?

The buzzer sounded. Caley tapped Nate's helmet. "Let's go. Think you got enough juice to finish that hat trick?"

Nate was so distracted in the third that he skated straight into an opposing player's elbow with his head down and ended up flat on his ass with half of his own team laughing at him and the rest concerned. He stared up at the rafters and winced at the light in his eyes, but he knew concussions. This wasn't that. Just a nasty headache and maybe a bruise on his cheekbone later.

"What is with you today?" Caley asked as she hauled him to his skates. Then her gaze got sharp. "Did something happen with Aubrey?"

He wanted to tell her. Maybe over their postgame drinks.

But his head hurt, and his face hurt, and his heart hurt, and he also wanted to sit in his dark apartment and eat a pint of Ben & Jerry's and figure out how he'd done this to himself again.

"I think I'm gonna call it a night," he said. "Obviously my head is not in the game."

Caley frowned at him, but she didn't try to stop him. "All right. You're sure your head's okay?"

"I'm sure."

Back in his apartment, he dropped his keys in the bowl by the door and took off his shoes. The lights from the city shone in through his windows, casting more than enough glow to see by, so he didn't bother with the overheads. Instead he went to the kitchen and pulled out the ice cream and a spoon, then returned to the living room. Before he could sit down, though, something sharp stabbed his foot, and he swore.

He sat down to have a look, left ankle propped on his right knee, holding his phone awkwardly.

It was a small piece of glass from the vase. It hadn't gone deep—he was barely even bleeding. But as far as icing on the shit cake went, it seemed a little much.

When the bleeding stopped, Nate put the ice cream back in the freezer, unopened. Then he went to bed.

Saturday morning he got in the car to the airport by himself. He and Paul were filming this weekend's episode in Vancouver, which just felt wrong. He'd been looking forward to seeing Aubrey's hometown through his eyes. Instead he was stuck in a mental spiral of doubt about why Aubrey hadn't told him about Cirque. Had Brigitte been mistaken? Maybe Aubrey had turned them down and simply hadn't thought it was important enough to share.

When the plane touched down in Vancouver and Nate turned off airplane mode, he got a text from Aubrey: *The downlow chicken shack on main has the best burgers in the city.*

It wasn't an admission of guilt, but it didn't explain anything either.

Work with Paul was fine, but they were never going to connect as friends. Nate could deal with him on the set. As far as dinner companions went, he decided to reconnect with Kelly, who he realized now he'd ditched when he started sleeping with Aubrey.

"Hey." He nudged her as they wheeled their suitcases toward the car that would take them to the arena since they were covering a matinee. "Lunch on me? I've got a line on a great burger, and I hear they deliver."

Kelly slung her arm around his shoulders. "Finally, a man who understands me."

Nate snorted and let his plans with Kelly distract him from everything else.

It worked out pretty well until the puck dropped.

Nate and Paul's set for the game was basically a section of the bar. The majority of the screen time would show the ice, so they'd be audio only for that, but during stoppages and intermission, the cameras would cut to them as they sat on their stools, a green screen behind them to show any replays.

Nate hated it. It felt unprofessional. He didn't think viewers should be able to see his socks. He definitely didn't love that people not associated with the show could watch them tape live. He found it difficult to stay focused on the game.

Tonight, though, focusing was easy, mostly because game play was absolutely blistering. The away team scored to make it 2-2 only eleven minutes and change into the game.

At least, focusing was easy until someone went off after a dirty hit and Paul made a comment about how players weren't "tough" anymore because they didn't want to risk playing with a concussion when it could *ruin the rest of their life*. Then he mocked Nate for using the phrase *performative masculinity*.

Nate stewed all the way back to the airport for the redeye home, until Kelly nudged him with her shoe. "Hey. If you don't stop clenching your jaw, you're gonna grind your teeth into dust. You need a Snickers or something?"

"Or something." Nate thought longingly of the Ben & Jerry's in his freezer. Then he remembered the emergency chocolate bar he kept in the outside pouch of his carry-on bag and dragged it close to dig it out.

He ended up with a handful of paperback instead—the paperback he'd snagged off Aubrey on their last road trip together. He'd never finished it.

Well, now was as good a time as any. He dug out the chocolate bar too and let himself get lost for a few hours.

Coming home to an empty apartment well after midnight felt almost like a repeat of the night before. It was cold and blustery outside. Nate could hear the wind howling, and the light from the windows of his apartment was enough to illuminate the swirling snowflakes. It would have been a nice night to curl up in front of the gas fireplace with Aubrey, if he'd been home.

Between his agitation with work and his swirling emotions about Aubrey, Nate thought he'd have a hard time falling asleep. But he must have been exhausted, because he was out almost the moment his head hit the pillow.

He woke up to sounds in his apartment.

Aubrey must have let himself in. Nate rolled out of bed and pulled on a T-shirt and pajama pants over his boxers. He normally wouldn't have bothered, but he felt naked enough knowing he was going to go out there and see Aubrey and inevitably ask what he was doing talking to people from Cirque.

Not that he couldn't talk to whomever he wanted. Nate just would have liked if he mentioned the potential of moving across the country.

Time to face the music either way.

Aubrey stood at the stove, poking at a frittata that smelled fragrant with tomatoes and basil. When Nate came in, he lifted his head and smiled... but the smile didn't last. "Hey," he said. "Rough night?"

"Rough weekend." Damn it, he'd *missed* Aubrey these last two nights. That just compounded the shittiness. Sometime in the past few months, Aubrey had become the person he talked to when he needed to work things out.

"Is this about the show?" he asked, prodding the frittata again. Then he experimentally jiggled the frying pan handle and, in one smooth movement, flipped the whole thing. It landed perfectly. "I watched last night."

"Painful for you?" The Canucks had ended up losing 7-2.

"Not as bad as it was for you."

"Yeah, well." Nate grimaced. Where would he even start complaining? And could he even vent to Aubrey? That didn't seem fair when Aubrey'd lost his job. Nate didn't want to talk about his work anyway. He wanted to talk about Aubrey's.

Aubrey turned back to the breakfast, and Nate helped himself to a seat. Aubrey had already poured orange juice, and the coffeepot was full, even though Aubrey only drank his coffee from a can like a heathen.

There were fresh strawberries in a bowl on the counter, and Nate popped one into his mouth—surprisingly tasty considering it was December. He'd have to ask about Aubrey's fruit hookup before he moved to Vegas.

Aubrey cleared his throat and filled Nate's coffee cup. Then he slid a plated half a frittata in front of him. "Have you thought about what you'll do if the show doesn't work out?"

Frowning, Nate reached for his fork as Aubrey sat opposite him with his own breakfast. "Why wouldn't it work out?" Did Aubrey know something he didn't?

"You don't seem very happy with the direction the show is going," Aubrey fished.

"It's just growing pains," Nate said. He knew, not even deep down, that it was a lie... but he couldn't figure out why he said it. "I'll adjust."

"Right." Aubrey cut a piece of frittata, but he didn't eat it. It just sat there on his fork, getting cold.

Nate's frittata would suffer no such indignity, he vowed, and shoved a large bite in his mouth, only to nearly burn himself.

God, he was a mess. He put his fork down. Time to face his problems head-on like a grown-up. "Were you ever going to tell me about the Cirque thing?"

Aubrey's knife clattered against the plate. "What?"

"I know they made you an offer. The gossip is all over the rink. I felt pretty stupid that I was the last to know."

Aubrey's eyes were wild now. Clearly he had not expected Nate to take this line of conversation. "I'm sorry. I didn't mean for you to find out like that."

Ouch. "Obviously," Nate said, not bothering to disguise the venom in his voice.

"That came out wrong." Aubrey flushed. "I was going to tell you. I haven't even decided if I'm going to go yet."

I haven't decided.

"Well, you let me know what you *decide*." Fuck it, Nate should have known better than to expect more from Aubrey. He was so tired of the men he loved deciding his future for him without his input or—and he wasn't sure if this was worse—seemingly not caring if Nate was part of their future at all. This was twice now he'd had his heart stomped on. What was he doing wrong?

"You could come with me," Aubrey said. "You hate your job anyway."

"Is there even ice in Las Vegas?" Nate snarked. "Other than the kind that comes in a highball glass."

Aubrey set his coffee can down with enough force to send the orange juice sloshing up the sides of the glasses. "Wow. I guess your memory must be going in your old age, if you've forgotten that I'm a figure skater and Vegas has an NHL team *you played against*."

Nate winced because he knew that had been too mean. A low blow, childish, needlessly hurtful. But damn it, Aubrey hurt him first. "I meant, what am I going to do? I don't have a job lined up in Vegas."

Aubrey spread his arms. "So what? It's not like you need the money. You could come and live with me. See where it goes."

He couldn't just pick up and leave. He'd helped Jess build this show. He owed it to her to see it through. "And what?" he said before he could help himself. He hadn't been truly unemployed since he was a kid. "Be your kept man?"

This was a disaster. This was exactly what had happened with Marty. He didn't want to tag along in someone else's dream. He had aspirations and plans of his own. He wanted a partner, not a sugar daddy.

He could see the moment Aubrey realized it too. His face went from cajoling and hopeful to resigned and hurt.

Fuck.

"No-go, isn't it," he said heavily.

Nate poked at his frittata, suddenly not very hungry. "I mean, it's too soon to move across the country together anyway." As if the real problem wasn't that he didn't want to.

Aubrey put down his fork. "If you say it is, probably. I wouldn't really know."

Nate exhaled and closed his eyes for a moment, scrubbing his hands over his face. "So where do we go from here?"

"I don't *have* to go anywhere. I told you, I haven't decided if I'm going."

"Haven't you?" Nate challenged. For the first time, he really took in the breakfast table. There was a tablecloth and linen napkins, and Aubrey had poured the orange juice in champagne glasses. Or maybe those were actually mimosas. He'd dressed nicely.

He'd obviously been buttering Nate up for something. Nate felt a little twist of guilt in his stomach for not noticing sooner. He might've missed out on Aubrey actually coming clean about Cirque and a much more productive discussion.

Aubrey dropped his gaze to his plate. That was answer enough.

Fuck.

"Look. Opportunities like this probably don't come around that often, am I right?"

Aubrey gave him a weak smile. "There are only so many shows and a lot of retired athletes who can still skate."

That was what Nate thought. Still, his heart sank. "And this is what you want to do? As opposed to, I don't know. More broadcasting work. Maybe a stint on *Dancing with the Stars*."

"I would be incredible, thank you for recognizing that." The smile didn't get much stronger, though. "Yes, this is what I want, at least right now. I'm only going to be this recently retired once. In a year or two my window will have closed. So, if I want to do it...."

"Now's the time." Nate understood. Hockey had felt like that too, in the later years. He'd had to choose between trying to find a spot on a team with a strong shot at the Cup or staying and playing with the team he loved, knowing they were in the middle of rebuilding and wouldn't have a chance.

Marty's business was in Houston. Nate stayed.

"Yeah." Aubrey bit his lip. "But if it came down to you or Cirque... I'd stay."

Nate couldn't stand being the reason Aubrey missed out. Nothing was worth that. "Don't."

Now Aubrey closed his eyes. The corners of his mouth turned down, and crow's feet appeared in the corners of his eyelids as he squeezed them shut. His brows drew together. "Nate—" His voice cracked.

Fuck. "Not, I'm not...." Nate forced himself to take a sip of coffee to wash away the lump in his own throat, took a deep breath, and tried again. "I love you," he said roughly. "So I can't be the thing that holds you back from following your dream. You should go."

Aubrey swallowed visibly and opened his eyes. He looked sad... and scared. "I don't want to break up."

Oh, thank God. "Me neither." Nate had to clear his throat. "It won't be easy. But it's not like I've never had a long-distance relationship before." Being gone half the time was just his default state of being. "It's not that bad. We can figure it out." He could fly to Vegas on a Saturday redeye or an early morning Sunday flight and be back in Chicago by four on Tuesday. It wasn't much, but it was more than nothing.

"You think so?"

In truth, Nate didn't know, but he wasn't going to give up without a fight. "It'll be Christmas in a couple weeks. We'll have a few days off where we can see each other. There'll be other holidays.... Isn't it worth trying, at least?"

"Yeah, no. Yes. Absolutely."

Great. Now that they had that sorted.... Nate picked up his fork again, but when he took a bite of his frittata, it had gone stone cold. "Hey. I'm sorry I ruined your special breakfast."

"No, I think I get at least half the blame for that. I should've told you about Cirque sooner."

He should have, so Nate didn't argue. "Let me take you out to breakfast instead to make it up to you?"

But Aubrey slowly shook his head. "Rain check?"

Nate blinked. "O... okay?"

"Don't get me wrong, I just think...." He ran a hand through his hair, mussing up a style that must have taken him ten minutes to perfect. Nate had seen him fuss with it often enough to know. "I came over this morning to ask if you wanted to come with me to Vegas, and instead we got this." He gave a tight, unhappy smile. "I need some space."

That stung, but Nate couldn't blame him. "Okay. I understand." He took a breath, more challenging than it sounded, since it felt like tight bands had wound around his chest, constricting his lungs. "Text me later to...." To what? *Let me know you're okay? Confirm you're not mad I said no?* Aubrey had every right not to be okay, or to be upset Nate turned him down. "Just text me later?"

Aubrey stood up, rapping his knuckles on the table. "I will."

CHAPTER TWENTY-THREE

IT WAS a good thing Aubrey was rich, because he apparently needed a lot of therapy. "I fucked up," he admitted to Theresa as soon as she could fit him into her schedule. He was pretty sure she was working through her lunch hour, and she definitely charged extra for last-minute appointments. It was worth it.

She clicked her pen, never taking her eyes off him. "What makes you say that?"

"I didn't tell Nate about Cirque, and he got mad."

She sat back in her chair a little. Her face didn't offer anything in the way of judgment, which.... Was that what they taught in therapy school? How to keep a poker face? He made a mental note never to play her in Texas Hold'em. "Did you escalate?"

"No. I told the truth." He paused, considering how to phrase his next admission. Fuck it. "I asked him to come with me, and he said no."

Again, no reaction. "Then what happened?"

"Then we talked, I guess? He's not ready to move to Vegas. But he said I should go." That was what Aubrey kept getting hung up on. They loved each other, didn't they? They'd said as much. Maybe they didn't say it all the *time*, but they said it. He was pretty sure they meant it. Wasn't that supposed to make all the other problems go away?

He felt like romantic comedies had been lying to him.

Theresa tilted her head to the side. "It sounds like he's supporting your dream."

Aubrey made a face. "Cirque isn't the *dream*... but I'm not ready to be done skating professionally. I should've known that by halfway through October." Instead he'd gotten distracted by his attraction to Nate, and then sex with Nate, and then his feelings for Nate. Bantering with him gave Aubrey the same sort of thrill he got on the ice.

In retrospect, maybe it was no wonder he hadn't noticed that he really wanted to be doing something else.

Apparently her last comment hadn't steered him where she wanted him to go, because she changed tactics. "Did you break up?"

No, they hadn't. The problem was that he didn't know how they could be together and apart. "I don't think so, but I... I don't even know how to be a good boyfriend in person. How am I going to manage long distance?"

That finally got her sitting forward again, leaning across her desk. He'd given her something she could engage with. Yay. "Being a good boyfriend isn't a singular skill set, you know. It means different things for different people. If you and Nate are going to try long distance, he probably already thinks you're a good boyfriend."

"Yeah, but his ex-husband sucks. The bar is too low to trip over."

Now she pursed her lips. "I think you're selling Nate short. He can't be a pushover. In fact I know that he's not from how you came in here after you met, complaining about him busting your balls."

Fine. He let her peel away that excuse as well. That just left him with a plain, honest fear. "I just... I don't want to mess this up."

Theresa didn't say anything. Aubrey fell into the trap as usual, trying to make her understand. "When I first started coming to see you, I couldn't imagine being in a relationship. I lied to myself about not wanting one, but the truth is, I'm too needy, I always have to be the center of attention. I knew that, just like with my parents, I wouldn't feel like I was important and I'd mess it up.

"Nate makes me—he's just always paying attention, you know? Even when he's not. He buys me my favorite crappy pulp paperbacks in airports before flights. He knows my coffee order. I mean, he's hot and kind and funny, but so are lots of people. He never makes me feel ignored. He's perfect for me."

When he finished, Theresa had a hand over her mouth, but it didn't do much to hide her smile. Maybe he was safe to play poker with her after all. "What?" he asked.

She took a moment to compose herself and then placed her hand flat on the desk. "First let me say that I don't want to minimize what you feel for Nate. It's wonderful that you've found someone you're so compatible with."

Aubrey sensed a *but* coming.

"However, your reasoning is flawed. Broadly speaking, people were never ignoring you. Their behavior hasn't changed. Your perception has." She tapped the notebook in the corner of her desk—the same one Aubrey had written his assignments in. "*You* put the work in. *You* made having a relationship possible, not someone else. And if it came to it, I am confident that you could do it again."

AUBREY COULDN'T put it off any longer; the offer was about to expire. At one in the afternoon on Monday, he was in his agent's Chicago office, signing the paperwork.

An hour after that, he confirmed his rental.

Now all that was left was packing up his life. He had four days to make the drive to Vegas. That basically gave him twenty-four hours to say goodbye. By the time Nate went to work tomorrow, Aubrey would be on the road.

How could he make the last day count? There were so many things he wanted to do with Nate—make him buy something fabulous and just out of his comfort zone on the Miracle Mile, take in an exhibit at the Art Institute, spend a day at Shedd. Neither of them was from Chicago. They could play tourist.

And then there was skating in the park. It was a cliché, but apparently romantic relationships were actually full of those. Besides, they both liked skating.

What else did they both like? Aside from *The Cutting Edge*. Did Nate like other romcoms? Was he too much of a jock to enjoy musical theater?

It felt like Aubrey still had so much to learn. That feeling led to a sense of inevitability. How were they ever going to get to know each other when he was in Vegas? Maybe this was as close as he'd ever get.

Maybe—

Aubrey blinked as he stepped into his apartment. The table was set for two—wineglasses and San Pellegrino, a bottle of Chateauneuf du Pape in a bucket. The kitchen emitted some familiar wonderful smells— garlic and ginger and soy, and something with a strong sense of heat that cleared Aubrey's sinuses.

That heat was practically glacial in comparison to the sight in front of him, though. Because Nate was decked out in a full tuxedo, hair freshly cut and styled, jacket buttoned. He looked like he'd come right out of a Tom Ford catalog.

"Wow," Aubrey said. He didn't mean to say it out loud, but his brain was having trouble doing more than just committing Nate to memory.

He felt like his phone when it got stuck in an infinite reboot cycle. "I mean.... Hi."

Nate's eyes sparkled like in an actual fairy tale. Aubrey had the giddy thought that he'd be writing about this in his diary later, because he'd apparently reverted to a teenager. "Hi. I hope you don't mind I took a few liberties."

"For future reference, if you ever need to get away with something, just put on the tux." Nate could politely rob a bank in that tuxedo and no one would lift a finger to stop him.

Maybe that was why Bond wore them.

Nate smiled, and Aubrey's brain rebooted again. "I'll keep that in mind."

The reboot finally completed, Aubrey cleared his throat. "What's all this?"

Nate rubbed the back of his neck, and the Bond persona evaporated. Thank goodness. Bond was hot, but Aubrey didn't love him.

"Uh, well, I figured *a*, I owe you for raining on your breakfast yesterday, and *b*, you're leaving tomorrow, so I thought I'd recreate our first date. Our first real date, anyway. I wasn't sure I could arrange for a blizzard, and even if I could, you'd have to drive through the mess it left tomorrow."

That was why everything smelled familiar. "Did you get the whole tasting menu?"

"Yeah, but I only got the two bottles of wine."

"My liver and I thank you for your restraint."

They sat next to each other at the table, and somehow Aubrey ended up with Nate's foot hooked around his ankle.

He didn't fuck Nate over the back of the couch this time, but although it was slow and sweet, the desperation felt the same. He needed to make every second count.

Afterward Nate fell asleep with his head on Aubrey's chest, breathing deep and evenly. Aubrey's last thought before he followed was that he didn't know how he could ever give this up.

IT WAS stupid to feel like the building was empty because one person had moved out of it. There were twenty-one stories; Nate was hardly alone. But lying in his bed after Tuesday's show, trying not to grit his teeth over

Paul's continued glorification of "old-school hockey," he missed Aubrey. It was like Nate could sense that the apartment upstairs wasn't occupied.

He sighed and rolled over, thinking maybe if he wasn't *staring* at the ceiling, he'd stop pretending he could see through it, only to find the light on his phone blinking.

Aubrey, with his first check-in.

Nate debated only for a second—using his phone in bed always made sleeping more difficult afterward—but then he snatched it up. He wasn't going to be sleeping any time soon at this rate anyway.

Made it to Lincoln, the text read. It was dated seven minutes previously. *Fun fact, the state flag of Nebraska kind of looks like a big white dong.*

Nate googled it, found he did not disagree, and navigated back to the text thread to say so, only to find another message. *Nebraska, the Moby Dick State.*

The corn fields are just a metaphor for the ocean, Nate replied, vaguely impressed with himself for remembering what a metaphor was. Tenth-grade English was a long time ago. *Weather hold out?*

As though he hadn't checked it three times since Aubrey left.

Nothing but a few flurries, he confirmed. *Think I'm going to hit the hay, though. Another 11 hours tomorrow.*

Drive safe, Nate wrote back.

I will. Then, a few seconds later—*I love you.*

Nate smiled, stupidly tracing his thumb over the words as though he could feel their warmth. *Love you too.*

He was tired but too keyed up to sleep, so to distract himself, he flipped over to Instagram and scrolled through his private feed. His friends' kids were growing up before his eyes. The dogs too, and Kaden's cat.

And then he scrolled past an ad, blinked, and scrolled back up. *Huh.*

Seized by a sudden wild hair, Nate clicked the ad. Aubrey had left a copy of his rental agreement just in case. He could get the address from that.

When he finally put his phone back on the nightstand a few minutes later, he had no problem falling asleep.

THERE WAS a box on Aubrey's front step.

Not just any box either. It was four-and-a-half feet high and maybe twenty-two inches square. It had a cheerful red-and-yellow

DHL sticker and a fat customs form taped to it. When he picked it up, it weighed a ton.

Had he ordered something and forgotten? He hadn't been sleeping well the past few nights. He was used to Nate's deviated-septum breathing at night, and now he needed a white-noise machine or something. He'd been meaning to order one online. Maybe the lack of sleep had caused him to do some late-night impulse shopping, but he didn't remember it.

Weird.

He took the box inside.

Finding a knife that was actually sharp took some doing. Aubrey hadn't done a lot of unpacking, and the knives provided in furnished rentals had notoriously dull blades. But finally he managed to get something that would cut through the thick tape.

The box had layers, like an onion. Slice by slice, his living room became a cardboard graveyard. Inside the two exterior boxes was an actual honest-to-God wooden crate that said FRAGILE THIS WAY UP in Italian. Aubrey didn't have a crowbar, so he carefully pried off the lid with a butter knife. Well, two butter knives; the first one bent. Then there were packing peanuts. Then bubble wrap.

He was starting to doubt there was anything actually *inside* the box when he found the semi-sharp knife back in the pile of packing material and sliced through the tape holding the bubble wrap.

It fell away slowly, dreamily, leaving behind a four-foot-tall mustard and puce glass sculpture that looked… that looked….

It looked like a giant whale penis with a really nasty skin infection. Just looking at it, Aubrey knew it must have cost several thousand dollars, never mind the cost to get it to the States. It was the kind of color that would only appear in nature if nature were very ill. There was no hope that it would ever match Aubrey's décor, because Aubrey was not a cave-dwelling gremlin who'd had his taste surgically removed.

What the fuck. It looked just like the hideous vase they shattered at Nate's apartment, only larger and orders of magnitude more hideous.

It had to be from Nate. No one else would spend that kind of money on something so singularly unattractive. But what kind of message was it supposed to send? Aubrey didn't think it was a callback, intentional or not, to Nate's relationship with Marty. Nate was definitively over that. It seemed like an unsubtle reminder of what had happened to the first vase.

The shape was right, anyway.

The kicker of it was, Aubrey didn't want to get rid of it. Sure, it was ugly, but it was hilarious.

While he was cleaning up, he found a card in the mess of packaging— typed rather than handwritten, probably because Nate had bought this on the internet and never seen it in person. *Happy housewarming!—N.* Very understated. He could hear Nate saying it too, see the warm, smug curl of his mouth around those words as he handed over a supremely useless gift. That fucker.

Aubrey set the sculpture on the breakfast bar in the kitchen. Maybe he could get matching plates.

He took a picture of it there, with his left hand in the frame, flipping the bird, and sent it to Nate.

Fucking Nate. What an asshole.

Aubrey loved him so much. *Wish you were here*, he started to write, but then he paused and erased. He didn't have the right to say that, did he? He'd asked Nate to come, and Nate had said no. It wouldn't be fair for Aubrey to keep reminding him, would it? To keep asking?

Nate should be here, no question. And maybe one day he would be, but it had to be his decision.

You're an asshole, he said instead, and softened it with a laugh-crying face. Really, the sentiments came from the same place.

CHAPTER TWENTY-FOUR

NATE WAS not a romantic gift-giver by nature. He always defaulted to the practical. When he needed to give someone a gift, he asked the recipient what they wanted. With Marty they'd gone so far as to purchase the items together and use them immediately rather than wrap them and wait for the occasion, be it birthday, anniversary, or Christmas. NHL money made it easy to buy extravagant gifts, and extravagance could make up for the lack of romance and surprise, Nate often found.

But Aubrey wasn't Marty. Aubrey had never been in a romantic relationship before Nate. And Aubrey also wouldn't be impressed with simple extravagance; he'd grown up with that. No, the way to please him would be to surprise him with something that showed how well Nate knew him. Nate was going to get him a romantic, thoughtful gift if it killed him, goddammit.

If the holiday crowds were any indication, it might.

He went to the bookstore first. With a clerk's help, he found a few prospective series in similar veins to those he knew Aubrey liked, all in paperback, and bought the first two books in each set.

He was turning away from the cash desk when a child of about five or six ran into his leg and looked up with that expectant expression that children get when they look at their parents, which turned to easily read horror when he realized Nate was a stranger.

"Jimmy," called a woman about Nate's age from close to the door. She had a stroller as well, and a man wearing a similar coat to Nate's stood next to her. "Sorry," she said to Nate as Jimmy ran toward her, relief plain in his posture.

He shook his head and smiled. "It's fine."

Jimmy took his father's hand and they walked away.

Cute kid, Nate thought wistfully.

Maybe someday.

After the bookstore, he puttered around the mall for an hour and popped in and out of stores, searching for inspiration. Aubrey had mentioned that the knives provided at his rental weren't up to snuff, so

Nate picked up a nice set, but that didn't really count. He was tempted by a gorgeous cream sweater in an upscale department store, but it was a thick cable knit. Wouldn't Aubrey roast wearing that in Vegas?

Instead he found himself fingering a very fine silk shirt in navy, with a pattern of tiny martini glasses. He liked the whimsy of it, and it reminded him of that first night in Winnipeg. Aubrey would've had something to say about it. He would have teased Nate until Nate blushed and suggested they could recreate that night once they got home. The thought made Nate feel suddenly very alone, but he bought the shirt anyway because Aubrey would love it.

But it wasn't *romantic*. It didn't feel like enough. Aubrey had asked him to move across the country, and he'd said no. He needed something *good*, something that would let Aubrey know, in no uncertain terms, that he wanted them to have a future together.

He paused in front of a swimwear shop, lost in thought.

And then he had an idea.

AUBREY HADN'T worn a harness since his first jump, when he was eight or so. And that had been nothing like this. He certainly had never landed a triple axel only to leap again and twirl midair to end up dangling crotch-first from an arena ceiling while acrobats on long cloth apparatuses performed aerial feats on either side.

He couldn't *wait* to do this in front of an audience… except for one thing.

When the show started, he'd have even less opportunity to spend time with Nate.

With performances three nights a week and Nate needed in Chicago for filming three nights, the odds of them finding time to be together in person seemed stacked against them.

Aubrey missed him.

He'd never lived with a boyfriend—obviously, since he'd never had one—and his only roommates had been temporary ones at competitions. He was used to being alone… or he had been. These days he found himself turning on the television just so the house felt less empty. He had Greg over for dinner one night because he missed cooking and couldn't muster the enthusiasm to make dinner just for himself.

Greg took one look around, raised his eyebrows, and immediately opened the wine he'd brought. But he didn't made Aubrey talk about it, so that was nice.

The tech in charge of Aubrey's wire lowered him smoothly back to the ice, moving him laterally so he could transition seamlessly into skating. After that, it was just one more spin and that segment of the program was over.

The gymnasts dismounted as well. One of them, Kyla, must have spotted someone she knew, because she hopped off the ice and right into someone's arms. They spun her around, and she laughed with joy. Apparently she didn't get enough twirling in the air.

How did people do it? How did they make relationships work? Most of the professional athletes he'd trained with were either single or married to their training partner. The ones who played team sports seemed to fare better—at least they'd be home about half the time and their spouses would have each other for a support group when they weren't. But those athletes could be traded at any time. Then what? Their families were just supposed to pick everything up and trail after them? What about their schools, their friends, their jobs?

It seemed like a lot to sacrifice. He was starting to understand that.

Aubrey was still turning that over in his brain when he walked past Kyla and realized the person who'd twirled her around was Greg, who must've been waiting for the next segment.

Greg waved at him as he passed but otherwise didn't pull his attention from Kyla. Had they known each other before Greg moved out here? Or had they somehow forged a connection in the past two weeks?

Aubrey unbuckled his harness, handed it back to the prop master, and retreated to the locker room. Reflexively, he checked his phone. No missed calls.

Well, Nate knew his practice schedule by now. Aubrey would call from the car on his way home, like he usually did.

He just hoped he could steer the conversation away from any Christmas plans. He wanted to spend time with Nate… but his mother had specifically asked him to come home to attend his cousin's wedding and spend the holidays with his family. Aubrey couldn't remember the last time he'd done that, and he'd been at odds with them for so long… he felt like he had to go.

Aubrey had convinced himself he didn't need Nate to put him first. He'd taken the job instead of putting Nate first, and Nate stayed in Chicago instead of putting Aubrey first, and now Aubrey might not see him at Christmas either.

How did people actually do this?

Maybe I should just give up.

But as he was reaching into his locker for his towel, the light on his phone blinked. He reached over and swiped to unlock.

It was a text message from Caley—no words, just a picture that took a moment to download. When it did, he was treated to a photograph of Nate and Carter Ng mid pillow fight, Nate with his weapon raised over his head and Carter in the process of a wide sideways swipe, inches from making contact.

A moment later, a text message followed. *He misses you.*

Aubrey enlarged the picture, memorizing the smile lines around Nate's eyes.

What was it like for Kelly to leave her family every weekend? Aubrey imagined she must hate it. He'd seen how close the three of them were, and it would be worse now that Caley was pregnant.

On the other hand, while she was gone part of the weekend and two weeknights, she had the rest of her days free to spend time with Carter, bring Caley lunch at work, cook family meals…. There was a happy medium there somewhere.

Aubrey just didn't know how to find it.

"ARE YOU going to tell me what's going on with you or am I going to have to guess? I haven't slept through the night in a week because an embryo the size of a goldfish cracker has moved in to the apartment above my bladder, and my patience is shot."

Nate blinked at Caley. Hadn't it only been two days ago that he'd been at her and Kelly's place, having a pillow fight? How had they gotten to this? "Uh. Hi to you too."

She pushed past him into his apartment and handed him a tub of ice cream. "Spoons," she demanded imperiously, holding her own ice cream under one arm. "Chop-chop. Also I'm using your bathroom."

Well, that was why she was the captain.

Nate procured spoons as well as napkins and glasses of water, and when Caley emerged from the bathroom, she picked up right where she left off. "So you're a miserable sad sack, and it's making Kelly cry. Not literally, she doesn't cry, but you're upsetting my wife and I'm pregnant. I need to have dibs on the mood swings. What gives?"

He huffed. "Aside from the obvious?"

Caley rolled her eyes. "Look. The past couple weeks have been challenging. I get it. But humor me. Pregnancy brain is real. Is this about the show or about Aubrey leaving?"

Nate didn't know that he was emotionally capable of separating the two right then. But apparently he really did need to talk about it, because he offered hesitantly, "Yes?"

"Oh good, an easy one." Caley dug a prodigious scoop of ice cream from the carton. "Do you want to elaborate, or am I going to have to play Twenty Questions?"

They'd run out of ice cream long before they came to any useful observations that way. "I didn't expect the show to be sold. I thought it'd be canceled or go on as it was. I wasn't ready for this."

Caley nodded and licked ice cream from her thumb. "That's fair. It's a big change."

But not the worst of it, actually. "I don't like the direction the show is taking. It feels like a betrayal of everything Jess and I worked to make it. And I know the network is forcing her out of her role."

"And Paul is an asshat."

"And Paul is an asshat," Nate agreed.

"But this still doesn't explain the depth of your sulk." She gestured with the spoon. "You forget, I knew you during the John Plum years. He was even worse than Paul, and he never got to you like this. Which leads me to believe this is actually mostly about Aubrey. So. Do I need to put a hit on my countryman or what?"

Nate blew out a breath. "No, I... no. I'm just upset he left so fast, without a lot of warning that he was planning to go."

"Maybe he didn't."

"What?"

"Maybe he didn't plan to go. Maybe he would've stayed if the show hadn't been canceled."

Yeah, Nate had gotten that impression. "That's what I thought too, but—then he said he wasn't ready to stop skating. He wanted to get back on the ice."

Caley gave him a calculating look. "And that surprised you."

"Yeah, I guess?" he said, feeling unaccountably defensive. "I mean, this isn't the first TV gig he's had, so…."

Something like understanding dawned in her eyes. "It's like déjà vu all over again, eh?"

Nate blinked.

"Because that's what happened with Marty, isn't it?" she pressed. "You retired, and then he sprung a dream on you that he'd never shared and you broke up. Now here's Aubrey, by all appearances Marty's actual goddamn polar opposite, doing the same thing. That has to hurt. Want to talk about it?"

"All I ever do is talk," Nate muttered and shoved a spoonful of ice cream into his mouth.

"Well, maybe you're saying the wrong things, then."

Ouch.

"You're upset because Aubrey didn't tell you he wanted to perform again. It especially hurts because Marty didn't tell you he wanted to run a B and B after you retired."

"Yeah," Nate said, wondering where this was going. Why was she telling him things he already knew?

"Yeah, well, here's the thing." Caley jabbed her spoon into the ice cream carton so forcefully it broke through the bottom of the container. She gave it a forlorn look and then set it on the table. "You could've asked."

Nate stared at her. "I…?" Was she blaming him?

"You could've asked!" she repeated. "Honestly, Nate, I love you. I think you're a great man, and believe me I do not say that about a lot of men. But did you honestly never talk about what your significant others wanted for their futures? One time I could dismiss, I mean, maybe Marty hid it from you on purpose, I don't know. But twice? That's not a coincidence."

Very carefully, Nate set down the ice cream before he could drop it. His palms were damp, and he didn't think it was condensation. "You're saying it's… that I…."

Caley took his hand, apparently heedless of the clamminess. *"You didn't ask, Nate.* Do you know how long it took me and Kelly to talk about our dreams for the future? How many kids we wanted, where we wanted to live, how involved we wanted our parents to be in our kids' lives, what our professional goals were and which ones we were prepared to sacrifice?" Nate squirmed. "It's a little different for us because, to be frank, unlike you and Aubrey, we don't have piles of cash sitting around. And also because we're lesbians."

Nate rubbed at his forehead with his free hand, easing another sudden headache. He'd had a lot of those since Aubrey moved to Vegas. "I mean." He sighed. She had a point, but.... "I've only *known* him a couple of months. When were we supposed to have that talk?"

Caley paused a moment as she considered this. "I guess that's fair. And here I thought we moved fast." Then she shook her head. "The point is, it only takes one person to fuck up a relationship. It takes at least two to make one work. Why didn't you know your husband's dream? Why didn't you know Aubrey's?"

Fuck. Was Caley right? Nate was the common denominator here. He scrubbed his hands over his face. Finally he said, "Marty… had a habit of keeping things from me." He raised his eyes to meet Caley's, hoping she would understand that he wasn't going to answer questions about that. "So even if I asked him directly, I don't know that it would have made a difference." He blew out a breath. "But I don't have an excuse for Aubrey."

Not a good one, anyway. Fear. Complacency. Was it better to try and fail, or to fail without trying and be able to believe you could have succeeded?

It was a stupid question, and he knew the answer, but that didn't make it any easier to implement the obvious change of behavior.

Caley nudged him with her elbow. "Just wanted to bring that to your attention. I've got to pee again, but you want to watch a movie?"

"HE SAID *what* on the air?" Aubrey half shouted over the Bluetooth, making the final turn into his driveway. He'd spent the past three days meeting everyone involved in the show and planning out choreography, including learning the various apparatuses that would be used and skating to the point of exhaustion, so he'd missed the last episode.

"Oh, he tried to walk it back," Nate said, sounding like he needed to break something. "But it was obvious he meant women's sports are never going to 'measure up' and they shouldn't ever expect national audiences."

"I hope Kelly puts a fastball through his windshield."

"At *least* let the air out of his tires."

Aubrey put the car in Park and closed the garage door. Then he grabbed his phone and went into the house.

"Anyway, that was my day yesterday. Christmas shopping today. Spoiler—it sucks, so I went home and bought everything online."

"It's a jungle out there," Aubrey agreed, closing the door behind him. Then he crossed to the patio doors and went outside. He liked Vegas in general. It suited him better than the frigid wind and bitter cold of Chicago in the winter. And the idea that he could spend time outside in his own yard in December without risking frostbite, wearing only a light sweater… delightful.

"Try blizzard," Nate said ruefully.

At least Aubrey knew Nate wouldn't be driving in it. "Sad for you. It's seventeen degrees here. Uh." Aubrey grimaced, doing the math. What was it, multiply by nine, divide by five, add thirty-two? That was a lot of mental math. "Like, sixty? Not a cloud in the sky."

"You're a cruel man," Nate sighed. "I never minded the cold until I hit thirty-five. Now it drops below fifty and I swear I can hear creaking from every one of the bones I've broken."

Aubrey smiled. "That's just the wind off Lake Michigan."

That made Nate laugh, and Aubrey's heart clenched a little because he'd missed that sound. "Asshole," he said fondly. Then he cleared his throat. "So I was talking to my mom…."

Something in his tone made Aubrey sit up straighter, wary. "She and your dad are okay?"

"They're fine," Nate soothed. A beat passed, and he cleared his throat. "Look, I know… you just moved and you've got a lot going on. She just wanted to make sure I officially invited you to Christmas." He paused again. "So this is me, officially inviting you."

Ah, shit. Aubrey closed his eyes, feeling that sinking sensation in his stomach. He should've known. "I can't."

"Going home?" Nate asked quietly.

Aubrey let out a deep breath and nodded because he'd forgotten Nate couldn't see him. "Yeah. Uh, I haven't been home for Christmas in…." Longer than five years, definitely. But it hadn't been ten yet, had it? The sensation in his stomach turned into something heavy and sour when he couldn't remember for sure.

"I understand."

The words were quiet and gentle, but they cut anyway. Aubrey dug his fingernails into his palm as he clenched his fist. This was so—stupid. He wanted to invite Nate to come to Vancouver. Aubrey's parents *would* love him, and now… now Aubrey thought he could maybe stand that, instead of resent it. Hell, part of him thought he'd even enjoy it. *See, Mom? I did okay, didn't I? Isn't he great?*

But this was Nate's niece's first Christmas. He'd been looking forward to it for weeks.

And Aubrey didn't know what he'd do if he made that offer and Nate turned it down.

"I'm sorry," he said helplessly and wanted to kick something.

"It's okay," Nate assured him, though he sounded disappointed. And then he cleared his throat, and Aubrey knew the conversation was over. "All right, I have to go. Caley and Kelly's holiday party is in an hour and I haven't even bought wine. I'm a disgrace."

"Truly a failure as a gay man," Aubrey agreed, trying for a levity he didn't feel. Good thing he was a natural-born performer. "For shame."

"I shall diminish, and go into the west," Nate quoted. "Call me tomorrow?"

"Of course," Aubrey agreed, and they hung up.

For a few minutes, he simply sat in the sunshine, which was growing cooler by the minute. Finally he couldn't stand his own company anymore, so he went back into the house to grab his keys and gym bag. He was still sore from the physical challenge of work—learning new skills and the various apparatuses the show employed took training and effort—but right now he needed the meditation of exercise.

Too bad Nate was in Chicago and Aubrey was here. Sex would've been a really great way to get out of his head.

CHAPTER TWENTY-FIVE

AFTER THAT Saturday's episode, Nate needed a few minutes to himself. Preferably to break something that wasn't his own teeth.

So it didn't help much when Paul found him in the green room, pacing and working on aforementioned teeth breaking, and said, "Hey. Can I talk to you?"

The answer was a blatant *no*. Before they had to work together, Nate hadn't minded Paul's company. They weren't ever going to be best friends, but they were both amiable enough, or so Nate thought.

But ever since Paul stepped into Aubrey's shoes, Nate's general tolerance for the man had taken a nosedive. Still, he couldn't exactly have a temper tantrum in front of him. He didn't want to be *difficult*. He knew well enough what happened to bad sports in hockey—in the media as well as on the ice. So he worked on pulling his shoulders down from around his ears, straightened his spine, and affected an open, inviting posture he absolutely did not feel. "Sure," he said. "What's up?"

Paul closed the door behind him and scratched behind one ear. He reminded Nate of a mangy dog.

Then Nate second-guessed himself. That wasn't fair to dogs.

Damn it. He was going to shred his reputation for being easy to work with, and there was nothing he could do about it.

"So, I know the whole point of the show is for us to have some spirited discussions." Paul helped himself to one corner of the single sofa in the room. "Or did I get that wrong?"

In that moment Nate utterly despised him. "You didn't get it wrong."

Paul spread his hands. "Okay. Then maybe you can help me understand. The point of the show is spirited discussions about topics hockey fans care about. So how come every time I try to start one, you act like I just pissed on the flag or something?"

A vicious, insistent throbbing started up at the base of Nate's skull and then immediately migrated to his temple and frontal lobe.

Nate had only ever been in a handful of hockey fights. He prided himself on his equilibrium. He had *patience*.

Or he *used* to have patience until he had to work with Paul. "Paul. Seriously?"

Paul made another, broader shrugging gesture, as though he truly did not understand. "What? Like, I never got the impression you wanted to wring Chase's neck during the show, no matter how hard the two of you went at it"—Nate grimaced internally at the word choice; Paul didn't know they were dating, and Nate sure as fuck wasn't going to tell him now —"but me? You fucking hate my guts, dude."

If I do, it's your own fault. He took a deep breath. "Aubrey and I debated the finer points of hockey contracts, pros and cons of trades, play styles."

"Isn't that what *we* do?" Paul challenged.

"It's what *I* try to do," Nate clarified. He was pissed now, and Paul was literally asking for it. "*You* want to talk about whether women's hockey has merit! You want to talk about whether it's okay for guys to use homophobic slurs on the ice, Paul, you fucking asshole. It's the twenty-first century, and I'm gay, in case you forgot."

Paul gaped as though it had never occurred to him that his shitty homophobic behavior could offend Nate. "Oh, come on. You don't think I believe that, do you? It's just entertainment."

Just entertainment. Nate's frustration, Nate's pain—? "Entertainment?" Nate thundered. "You're gonna let every queer kid watching a stupid fucking talk show about *hockey* know the game isn't for them, that the game itself *hates them*, because it's *entertaining*? Jesus *fucking* Christ."

"Hey," Paul protested. "Take it down a notch. Queer kids aren't exactly our target audience."

Nate's jaw dropped. He could not come up with a single thing to say.

Paul either didn't notice or didn't care. "And look, you think I don't know what I'm doing? You think the name Mitchell is a coincidence? My father's on the network's board of directors. When I came to him three months ago with the idea for the show he was all. Over. It."

The *idea* for the *show*? "The show that was *already on air*?" Nate said. "Wow, I hope you didn't strain yourself coming up with *that* one."

Of fucking course. Nepotism at its finest.

"I think I'm done here," Nate said coldly. And he walked out of the arena and hailed a cab.

"Where to?" the driver asked without giving him a second glance.

"Airport," Nate said shortly. He wasn't spending another second in Paul's company.

THERE WERE a lot of calls he needed to make, but he didn't want to talk in the car. He felt like he needed some small measure of privacy, and as contradictory as it might be, the airport seemed like a better place for that.

He checked in and went through security, then found an out-of-the-way seat near a coffee cart—at this time of night the airport was sleepy anyway—and sat down to dial.

Despite the hour, his dad picked up on the second ring. "Nathan?" he said. "It's a bit late, isn't it? Shouldn't you be on a plane?"

"I'm at the airport," Nate answered. "Sorry for calling so late."

"It's fine." He could practically see his father brushing this off. "You know your mother and I are always here for you. What's up?"

Nate took a deep breath, difficult with the lump in his throat. He hadn't really even thought the words to himself yet, but it was time to admit it all out loud now. "I know you're always saying you raised me to persevere against the odds." Professional athletes didn't stop when things got hard. They'd never make it if they did.

"We did. Your mother and I are proud of everything you've accomplished, your determination…." He trailed off, sounding uncertain. "What's this about?"

"I…. Dad, I'm not a quitter, but I hate my job." There. He'd said it. Pushing the words out seemed to loosen something in his throat, and more followed after. "I was so proud of everything Jess and I did, and Aubrey made it all feel like it clicked. Then the network sold us out, and ever since then—well, you've been watching." Ratings in their previous demographic had dropped, though they'd picked up a few points in other areas. Nate was more miserable now than he'd ever been when he was John's co-anchor. "Paul is a troglodyte. I feel like we're catering to a completely different audience who wouldn't like me anyway. I don't have any creative control, and I miss Aubrey."

"Nate...." He could almost see him shaking his head. His gut churned. Disappointing his parents was something he absolutely could not do. Not when they'd sacrificed so much for him. "I don't know where you got this idea that not being a quitter meant suffering through a job that's making you miserable."

Nate's breath came out in an unexpected rush. "I...."

"You want to keep your hand in in the sports-anchor world or in the entertainment world, then your mother and I expect you to put your best effort into that. What we don't expect is for you to continue doing this show." He paused, and Nate could hear something vague in the background. "Your mother says, 'Please tell him to quit so we don't have to watch this garbage anymore.' Direct quote."

Nate barked a surprised laugh that brought a tear with it. Did he have a Kleenex or something somewhere? He checked his pockets. "All right. Thanks. I—"

He paused and pulled a tiny piece of paper from his pocket. It was crumpled—had it gone through the wash? Absently, he smoothed it out.

Follow the middle path. Neither extreme will make you happy.

"I have... some more news," he said roughly. What a stupid time for an epiphany, but— "I'm not coming for Christmas. Tell Emily—tell her I'll make it up to her, I promise, whatever she wants. I'll take everyone on a vacation somewhere, just... I have somewhere else I need to be."

"I understand," his father said, and Nate didn't think he was imagining the approval in his voice. "Say hi to Aubrey from us."

Nate laughed a little incredulously. "I will."

In retrospect, an airport on December 23 was a stupid place and time to come to a decision. On the other hand, at least he'd finally made one.

The idea of getting back on a plane with Paul, who wasn't Aubrey, going home to Chicago, where Aubrey wasn't, dropping off his bag at home and then flying on to Michigan to meet his own parents, finally made something inside him snap.

This was stupid. He was stupid. But he had the resources to *stop being an idiot* and do what he wanted with his life.

He sent a text message to his agent, because this was going to get messy. He sent another to his mom, because she deserved an apology of her own.

Then he found a ticket counter and prepared to pay through the nose to change his flight to somewhere he actually wanted to be.

Chapter Twenty-Six

Aubrey had once had his own apartment in Vancouver, of course, but considering the difficulty of finding housing there and the restrictions on vacant real estate, he'd leased it out. So, for the first time in forever, he was staying with his family—albeit in his parents' guest house instead of the main building.

His family. How strange. He couldn't remember the last time he'd spent a holiday with them and actually enjoyed it. And sure, things weren't perfect, but Rachel's wedding was fun. He didn't feel jealous, at least not of the attention heaped on her. The serene happiness she projected everywhere and the obvious adoration in her new husband's eyes... those he could envy.

His mother must have noticed, because she'd reached over and squeezed his arm. "Give it time."

He'd already tried getting Nate to move in with him. The ball was in Nate's court now. Giving it time was all Aubrey could do.

Meanwhile, it was already the morning of December 24, and the tree needed decorating.

"No professional this year?" he asked as his father set a dusty box of ornaments on the floor next to the tree.

"Your mother's therapist suggested it would be a good family activity."

They looked at each other, then at the box, then at the tree, which was nearly tall enough to reach the fourteen-foot ceiling.

Aubrey said, "Does Mom's therapist know you're afraid of ladders?"

"Where's your sense of adventure?" his mother chided, coming into the room with a stepladder that one of them might, generously, use to get decorations two-thirds of the way up the tree.

"I hung upside down from a roof last week with knives strapped to my feet," Aubrey pointed out.

"Which reminds me we'll be needing tickets to your first show."

Aubrey smiled. What did they think he got them for Christmas? "We'll see."

They hadn't done much more than open boxes when the doorbell rang. Aubrey's mom set down the garland she was holding and headed to the foyer. "That'll be Rachel and Tim."

"We brought mimosas," Rachel said cheerfully as she and Tim entered a few minutes later.

"And cinnamon buns," he added.

"I'll put on another pot of coffee," Aubrey's dad said. It did not escape Aubrey that he was conveniently going to be away from the ladder for the next several minutes.

The advent of booze and breakfast—and, Aubrey found to his own surprise, company—improved the decorating experience immeasurably.

"I think if I get the angle right, I might be able to land this in one of the upper branches," Tim said idly, hefting a glass ornament the size of a softball.

"And if you miss, you can land in my mother's bad books indefinitely," Aubrey pointed out. Then he shoved another piece of cinnamon bun into his mouth. God, it was still warm. *Bless* his cousin and her foresight.

Tim's face fell.

Aubrey licked his fingers clean of the last of the cinnamon sugar and held out his hand. "Give it here. I'll do it."

Rachel laughed into her mimosa, flush-cheeked, grinning, and happy, and Aubrey relished it. His childhood should have been like this. He spared a flash of bitterness that it hadn't been, but he couldn't do anything about that now. He *could* make sure he had more holidays like this one.

It was almost perfect, with just one thing—one person—missing. Nate would be on a plane again now, if not already back in Michigan with his parents. He'd been looking forward to seeing his niece. Aubrey would call him later… maybe on Skype. Nate was pretty irresistible with children, and it was Christmas. If Aubrey wasn't going to see him in person, he should get to see him with a baby.

An hour or so later, they'd run out of ornaments and ambition to attempt reaching the top of the tree. As a result, the decorations mainly clustered around the bottom two thirds, leaving the top naked and sad.

It was still kind of nice, though.

"So next year," Aubrey said, turning to his mother. She was lounging with her feet up, mimosa in hand, and she raised her eyebrows in invitation. "Hire the decorator and we'll just do the mimosas. Therapists don't know everything."

Now she raised her glass as well. "I always knew you got my brains."

Aubrey's dad accepted this with a mild smile, and Rachel and Tim exchanged grins as well. Which just figured. Maybe next year he'd get to be something other than the fifth wheel.

If he could convince Nate they were worth fighting for, at least.

But before he could get any further into his own self-pity, the doorbell rang again. "Who else did you invite?" he asked his mother. Maybe she was going to have someone deliver an actually decorated tree?

"Nobody," she said, shaking her head. "Everyone's here."

Well, obviously not. Aubrey heaved himself off the couch to answer the door. Maybe someone had ordered a last-minute gift?

But when he opened the door to the drizzly Vancouver morning, it wasn't a beleaguered delivery person on the doorstep.

It was Nate.

Aubrey's mouth dropped open.

"Merry Christmas," Nate said, dripping ice water from his eyelashes. "I hope your mom loves me as much as you think she will."

"HOW DID you even find us?" Aubrey asked, ushering Nate into the guest house on his parents' palatial estate. Nate guessed this must be where Aubrey was staying while he was in town, which was kind of hilarious. He easily could've taken a room in the mansion and had enough privacy that he wouldn't have seen another soul unless he wanted to.

"Honestly? Luck. I ran into Jackson Nakamura in the airport." He managed a partial smile as he worked off his boots. It was the polite thing to do in Canada, and his socks were wet through.

Aubrey helped him wriggle out of his coat. That was soaked as well. "Was that your rental car in the driveway?"

Nate winced, not relishing the way his shirt and jacket clung to him or the way he smelled after so much air travel. His eyes felt like sandpaper. But there was a manic energy humming beneath his skin too.

"What, you don't like it?" It was a bright green Kia Soul that had barely made it up the steep driveway. "It's December 24. Options were limited."

He paused as they both absorbed that. They hadn't actually addressed the elephant in the room yet.

Nate hoped the past two weeks hadn't changed Aubrey's mind. "It's okay that I came, right?"

"Yeah!" Aubrey said a little too loudly. Maybe he was having flashbacks to their first I-love-you; God knew Nate was. But he could relax now. "Yeah, it's—I would have asked you, but, uh." He blew out a breath. "I was afraid you'd say no."

"I might have," Nate admitted. His priorities had been confused. "But it would have been the wrong decision."

They were still standing too far apart, but after flying God knew how many thousands of miles, Nate didn't know how to close the last two feet. This wasn't how he'd imagined it. The arrival he envisioned had less talking, no rain-soaked clothes, and a lot more kissing.

"I just...." Aubrey was staring at him like he'd never seen him before. Nate couldn't tell if that was a good thing. "I can't believe you're *here*."

Oh—and *there* was the kiss, Aubrey's fingers in his hair, his warmth against the damp chill of Nate's body, his smile against Nate's mouth. Nate put his hands on Aubrey's hips and held on, reveling in everything he'd missed for the past weeks.

Finally Aubrey pulled away and said, "Okay, I love you, and I'm thrilled you're here, but you're freezing. Do you want a shower?"

"Do you want to join me?" Nate countered.

Nate thought he was pretty enthusiastic, but Aubrey still dragged him toward the bathroom.

"So," he said afterward, when he was dressed in borrowed clothes because everything he'd brought on his trip was dirty and overly formal anyway, "I've been thinking."

Aubrey was in the process of putting his sweater back on, and he struggled for a moment to get his head through the neck.

Nate tried to breathe evenly and calm the butterflies in his stomach, but it wasn't easy. "I hate my job."

Aubrey sat down on the bed, all traces of levity gone. "I'm listening."

Nate exhaled slowly. "I talked to Jess and Kelly, and I made my decision. I'm going to quit. But it's kind of complicated."

"Legal trouble?"

Of course he'd be familiar with the issues. "Technically under contract until the playoffs are over," Nate confirmed. "I have my agent looking into it. If I have to pay to get out of it, I will, but obviously I'd prefer not to."

"Obviously," Aubrey agreed, and he stood up again and went out to the living room.

Nate wasn't finished talking. "Where are you going?"

"Getting my shoes on." Aubrey stuck his head back in. "My cousin's husband, Tim, is in the house with my parents, and he's an entertainment lawyer. You want to make friends?"

Well, in that case, the rest of Nate's news could wait. "I guess it's time to meet the family."

When they entered Aubrey's parents' living room a few minutes later, Aubrey's family were all sitting on the sofas, ostensibly engaged in their phones and not in gossip. It reminded Nate of that scene from *Pride & Prejudice*, and he had to smother a smile. Aubrey's parents were definitely not the Bennets in this scenario.

"So, this is Nate," Aubrey said, as everyone jumped to their feet in unison. "Nate, this is my mom and dad, my cousin Rachel, and her husband, Tim."

Aubrey's mom actually cried, wrapping Nate up in a hug so tight he thought he might need help with extraction, but finally she pulled away, wiped her eyes, and said, "We're so glad to have you here."

Aubrey's parents apparently were having lunch catered, and there was plenty of food for everyone. Nate ended up sitting with Tim in a corner of the living room, discussing options and strategies until Tim and Rachel had to leave around two to travel to his parents' for the holiday.

By that time Nate was flagging, and Aubrey must have noticed.

"Mom, do you mind if Nate and I head back to the guest house?" He flicked his gaze over to Nate, who tried and failed to get his eyes to open past half-mast. "I think he's going to pass out on the couch."

"Oh!" Aubrey's mom looked initially disappointed, then contrite, and then compassionate. "I think you'd better, actually. But bring him back tomorrow."

Nate managed a genuine smile despite his exhaustion. "Wild horses couldn't keep me away." He glanced at Aubrey's dad. "Even if I have to justify every goal I've ever scored against the Canucks. Again."

Aubrey's dad barked a laugh. He'd spent ten minutes giving Nate a hard time earlier. "I like you," he said cheerfully, clapping Nate on the back. "Have a good nap."

The emphasis he put on the word made Nate's ears burn, but all things considered, the whole day was a win.

All the same, it was a relief to take off his boots—still wet—and borrowed socks—wet again—in the tidy living room of Aubrey's parents' guest house and just collapse on the sofa. His eyes felt gritty, but he had more he wanted to say before he gave in to sleep, so he reached out his arm for Aubrey, who dropped next to him and leaned his head on Nate's chest.

"I didn't get anybody presents." Oops. That wasn't what he'd meant to say. "Yours are probably waiting for you in Vegas, but even the Duty Free at the airport was closed at three in the morning. Just inconsiderate."

Aubrey kicked his feet up on the couch and arranged himself further with Nate as his pillow. "It's all good. It's not like my parents actually need a two-thousand-dollar bottle of scotch."

"How's it going with them?" Everything had seemed okay today, but families could put on a pretty convincing front for outsiders.

"Good, actually." Aubrey rolled so he was facing the ceiling, and Nate could see the way his brow furrowed. "It's... I have a hard time trusting it, still. I keep waiting for the rug to get pulled out from under me. I don't know if that'll ever completely go away, but it's been really good so far."

Automatically Nate threaded his hand in Aubrey's hair and massaged his scalp. God, his whole body was in overload. He'd never felt so skin-hungry as he had these past two weeks.

He never wanted to feel like that again.

"So, not to bring up a potentially sensitive subject." He tried not to hold his breath. His heart suddenly felt like it was beating way too loud, but he'd put this off long enough. "I was wondering if you know anyone in Vegas who might be looking for a roommate?"

For a moment Aubrey only blinked at him, and everything seemed very still.

Then he sat up so fast Nate had to lean back to avoid cracking their heads together.

"Are you serious?"

Nate had a moment of doubt. "I mean, if you changed your mind—"

Aubrey cut him off with a kiss, hard and fast and fervent, that basically left him sitting in Nate's lap. Nate wasn't complaining. "I haven't. Yes, you can still come live with me." He paused. "Actually, I insist. If I have to subject myself to that vase...."

Nate laughed, and Aubrey leaned down to touch foreheads with him. "There's that competitive streak biting me in the ass again."

"Rude," Aubrey said. "That's my job."

He was such a brat.

"I was worried," Aubrey admitted quietly a moment later.

Nate leaned back into the couch, taking Aubrey with him, and maneuvered until they were lying side by side. "About?"

He shook his head, obviously searching for words. "Us? Everything? I don't know. I thought, I didn't want to give up Cirque for you, and you didn't want to give up the show for me, and where did that leave us? How could we make that work?"

Nate got it. He ran his hands absently up and down Aubrey's back while he worded his response. "I needed more time," he said finally. "I already knew I didn't like my job anymore, but I hadn't accepted it yet. And I knew getting out of my contract was going to be a pain. But it was never...."

"It was never the show or me," Aubrey said quietly.

"Yeah. Though this new version of the show wasn't hard to give up once I finally admitted the truth to myself."

"What about in the future, though?"

"Well, I have it on good authority that Vegas has an NHL team now. Maybe they need some off-ice personality."

Aubrey shook his head. "I meant—what about after Cirque is done? What if you have a job there and my work is somewhere else?"

"Then we make that decision together." Nate lifted a shoulder in an awkward shrug. "I've been lucky my whole life to have a job I've done because I love it. Doubly lucky because I could quit now and never worry about money again. But if it came down to a job I love or the man I love?" He cupped the side of Aubrey's face. "Easy choice."

Aubrey's eyes were suspiciously shiny. "It's me, right?"

Nate gently pulled him closer, until his lips were kissing distance. "It's you."

CHAPTER TWENTY-SEVEN

"YOU'RE SURE this'll work?" Nate asked, doing his best not to telegraph his anxiety through body language. Keeping unnaturally still seemed just as likely to give him away, but at least it didn't carry the same connotations as fidgeting.

"No," his agent said. "But it probably will. The strategy you and Tim worked out is sound. And chances are, if they want to continue the show in this vein, you're giving them an out anyway."

Nate snorted a little. "Until they hear my caveats."

"Carrot first, stick afterward," Maddie reminded him, and then the door to the conference room opened and the network crew filed in.

Everyone stood for handshakes and introductions, and then Gary Mitchell gestured for them all to be seated.

Nate was glad they were doing this on the neutral ground of his agent's office—just one of the perks of the network not having a major presence in Chicago.

"Gentlemen, Ms. Chapel." Maddie nodded at her, and Nate caught her eyes across the table, trying to telegraph, *Sorry for dragging you into this*. "Thank you for coming. We appreciate that this is taking you away from time you'd rather be spending with your families."

Maddie could have invited someone to eat shit and die and they'd have thanked her politely. Best agent ever.

Gary looked a little off balance as he answered, "Our business associates are family for us too."

Backward. Nate made his family his business associates. But he kept his mouth shut.

Maddie smiled pleasantly, acknowledging the sentiment. "Mr. Mitchell, my client and I have no desire to waste your time. Mr. Overton is here to tender his resignation, effective immediately."

The man to Gary's left—he was the network's in-house counsel, Nate remembered—put a hand on the table as though to forestall anyone else on his side from speaking. "Mr. Overton is aware, of course, that the penalty for early termination of his contract is two million dollars."

"Mr. Overton can read, thanks," Nate said before he could help himself.

Next to him, Tim put a restraining hand on his arm. Right. This was why he'd hired a specialist. "My client is aware of the fine print," he said smoothly. "However, given the particulars of the situation, my client would like to propose an alternative settlement."

From the sour-grapes look on his face, Gary didn't like that much, but the lawyer didn't seem surprised.

"Such as?"

That was from Royce, the show liaison. Nate didn't think he particularly cared whether Nate was on his show or not, except for the fact that Nate had brought in part of a certain audience and now he was at risk of losing it. Good. He should be nervous.

Tim nodded to Nate, so he guessed that was his cue. "Since the network's acquisition of the show, the format has become a challenge for me. I've gone from considered analyses of trades, salaries, and strategy to barstool coaching—from professional debate to antagonistic bickering." *And your son's a homophobic dickwad.*

Jess's mouth twitched briefly in an expression Nate interpreted as *Give 'em hell.*

"In short," Maddie said before anyone could respond, "this is no longer the show Mr. Overton signed a contract for."

"A court may not agree with you," Gary's counsel pointed out.

"Maybe not," Tim allowed, "but my client is willing to take that chance."

Nate was, but he wasn't done either. "To be honest," he said, "I'm not even sure why you want me on the show. It seems pretty obvious that my cohost has an agenda that is anathema to my existence. So I can only speculate that I'm still around because you knew you couldn't take over a show and fire both gay hosts without backlash."

Direct hit. A muscle twitched at the corner of Gary's jaw, and his temple throbbed visibly. "Mr. Overton, if you're threatening us—"

"With what?" Nate said before he could help himself. "Telling the truth?"

Tim put a hand on his arm, but before he could speak, the network's counsel stepped in. "I think we can guess where this is going." He glanced at Tim. "You indicated your client has an alternative proposal?"

"Indeed." Tim opened a folder and slid it smoothly across the table. "These are the particulars. In short: Mr. Overton will announce he is taking a personal leave of absence that will last until his contract expires. Of course that will leave his position open and the network in the unenviable position of losing two high-profile gay hosts within a single month. In order to avoid further public relations challenges, the network will promote Kelly Ng to co-anchor for the duration. As a bisexual woman of color who is married to a female hockey player, promoting Ms. Ng is an obvious statement that the network values diversity in broadcasting."

Nate had talked to her about it. Baseball season opened just as the NHL playoffs geared up. Her contract didn't have an expensive exit clause, though. He wondered if she'd negotiate to stay until the NHL season ended or tell the network to take a hike in no uncertain terms. It wouldn't be difficult to get a pinch-hitting host for playoff coverage. They might even get an active player whose team hadn't made the cut.

Mitchell looked like he'd been fed a mouthful of nails, but he kept his mouth shut at a motion from his lawyer.

"And what's to stop anyone from speculating on the true reason for Mr. Overton's departure?" the counsel asked.

Nate took a deep breath and cleared his throat. "I plan to announce my engagement to Aubrey Chase."

Mitchell's face turned a gratifying shade of purple, while Jess lost any semblance of ability to keep a straight face. "Congratulations!" she said, beaming.

"Yes, congratulations," Royce said grudgingly.

"Nate and Aubrey are prepared to be very honest, Mr. Mitchell," Maddie said. "Not only about Nate's treatment on the show these past few weeks and particularly at the hands of your son, who replaced Aubrey as co-anchor, but also about the details of their relationship, which began during their tenure together."

In other words, they could release true information that would make it look as though Aubrey had been fired specifically because of their relationship.

"Of course, they are also prepared to omit certain details and focus on another truth—that Mr. Chase was offered an opportunity to participate in a figure-skating show across the country and that Mr. Overton made arrangements to follow him as soon as was prudent, and that no one at the network had any knowledge of their relationship."

It took another twenty minutes of hashing out details before they agreed on a course of action similar to what Nate and Tim had laid out. Nate had wanted to insist the network hire a diversity consultant, but they hadn't managed to get them to agree to that stipulation.

Maybe this would teach them and they'd hire one anyway, but he had his doubts.

When it was all over, Nate slumped in his seat at the conference table. "Well, that was unpleasant."

"But necessary." Tim patted him on the shoulder. "I've got to go catch a flight back to my family. You want me to send Aubrey in?"

"Please," Nate said pathetically.

Maddie smiled. "I'll just give you the room."

The door closed behind them, only to open again a second later. Aubrey stood in the doorway, his hair a disaster that spoke to how many times he must have run his hands through it. "So? How did it go?"

"My retirement fund is safe."

"Oh, well, thank God." Aubrey sagged into the chair beside him. Their hands found each other automatically.

Nate snorted. Aubrey had offered to simply pay the fee and be done with it. He hadn't quite brought himself to ask exactly how rich Aubrey was, but he got the feeling two million was chump change. "You were worried, huh?"

"Obviously. Weddings are expensive." He nudged Nate's knee with his own. "At least the honeymoon's paid for."

On Christmas Day, Nate had printed out a copy of his gift to Aubrey—a two-week all-inclusive stay at an exclusive resort on Oahu for two, with flexible dates so they could go whenever the show had a break. Aubrey had opened it and spent a moment in quiet reflection with his mouth slightly open, then looked up and said, a little faintly, "We should get married."

Nate found himself unable—and unwilling—to disagree.

"Well, a man has priorities," Nate said.

Aubrey squeezed his hand. "Yeah, he does."

Epilogue

INSIDE EDGE COHOSTS GLIDE TO ALTAR

CHICAGO, ILLINOIS—It's wedding bells and slot machines for Nate Overton and Aubrey Chase, former hosts of the surprise sports news sensation, The Inside Edge.

Chase, a Canadian figure skater with impressive hockey cred, and Overton, a fourteen-year veteran of the NHL, first met the day Chase replaced former host John Plum. Despite a rocky start, they immediately captured the attention of a wide audience and gained something of a cult following on Twitter—unusual for a show featuring analysis of professional hockey.

Overton and Chase have faced their fair share of changes in the past eight months. In November of last year, the unexpected cohosts found unlooked-for love. Then their show was sold to another network, Chase landed a dream role in a Cirque production in Las Vegas, and Overton had to make a choice.

"I was fortunate that the network was willing to let me follow my heart, and that they had Kelly [Ng, who previously worked on The Inside Edge as a correspondent] to fill in," Overton admits.

The pair, who became engaged in December, have wasted no time settling into their new lives in Las Vegas. While Chase was busy practicing with the troupe, Overton landed a dream job of his own, working in conjunction with the Las Vegas Board of Education and PBS to develop SportsTalk.

"Nate is a natural with kids," Chase says. "It made perfect sense."

SportsTalk is a short-format educational web series that focuses on highlighting young talent, demonstrating key skills, and promoting healthy exercise for children. Proceeds from the show's ad revenue directly benefit community sports programs for at-risk youth.

"It's the best job I've ever had," Overton says with obvious sincerity.

"And it's good for him to be the one who has to try to copy the skills sometimes, instead of teaching them," Chase teases. *"Keeps him humble."*

"Not a problem my fiancé has," Overton replies, never one to cede the upper hand.

The couple will tie the knot in September at Chase's family home in Vancouver, Canada.

ASHLYN KANE likes to think she can do it all, but her follow-through often proves her undoing. Her house is as full of half-finished projects as her writing folder. With the help of her ADHD meds, she gets by.

An early reader and talker, Ashlyn has always had a flare for language and storytelling. As an eight-year-old, she attended her first writers' workshop. As a teenager, she won an amateur poetry competition. As an adult, she received a starred review in Publishers Weekly for her novel Fake Dating the Prince. As a matter of fact, there were quite a few years in the middle there, but who's counting?

Her hobbies include DIY home decor, container gardening (no pulling weeds), music, and spending time with her enormous chocolate lapdog. She is the fortunate wife of a wonderful man, the daughter of two sets of great parents, and the proud older sister/sister-in-law of the world's biggest nerds.

Twitter: @ashlynkane
Facebook: www.facebook.com/ashlyn.kane.94
Website: www.ashlynkane.ca

DREAMSPUN
DESIRES

FAKE DATING THE PRINCE

Ashlyn Kane

A royal deception. An accidental romance.

A royal deception. An accidental romance.

When fast-living flight attendant Brayden Wood agrees to accompany a first-class passenger to a swanky charity ball, he discovers his date—"Call me Flip"—is actually His Royal Highness Prince Antoine-Philipe. And he wants Brayden to pretend to be his boyfriend.

Being Europe's only prince of Indian descent—and its only openly gay one—has led Flip to select "appropriate" men first and worry about attraction later. Still, flirty, irreverent Brayden captivates him right away, and Flip needs a date to survive the ball without being match-made.

Before Flip can pursue Brayden in earnest, the paparazzi forces his hand, and the charade is extended for the remainder of Brayden's vacation.

Posh, gorgeous, thoughtful Prince Flip is way out of Brayden's league. If Brayden survives three weeks of platonically sharing a bed with him during the romantic holiday season, going home afterward might break his heart….

www.dreamspinnerpress.com

HEX AND CANDY

Ashlyn Kane

True love's kiss can break the curse...
but then what?

True love's kiss can break the curse. But then what?

Cole Alpin runs a small-town candy store. He visits his grandmother twice a week. And sometimes he breaks curses.

Leo Ericson's curse is obvious right away, spiderwebbing across his very nice body. Though something about it worries Cole, he agrees to help—with little idea of what he's getting into.

Leo is a serial monogamist, but his vampire ex has taken dating off the table with his nasty spell, and Leo needs Cole's companionship as much as his help. When the hex proves to be only the beginning of his problems, Leo seeks refuge at Cole's place. Too bad magic prevents him from finding refuge in Cole's arms.

Cole's never had a boyfriend, so how can he recognize true love? And there's still the matter of the one responsible for their troubles in the first place….

www.dreamspinnerpress.com

WINGING IT

ASHLYN KANE &
MORGAN JAMES

Gabe Martin has a simple life plan: get into the NHL and win the Stanley Cup. It doesn't include being the first out hockey player or, worse, getting involved with one of his teammates. But things change.

Dante Baltierra is Gabe's polar opposite—careless, reckless... shameless. But his dedication to the sport is impressive, and Gabe can overlook a lot of young-and-stupid in the name of great hockey. And Dante has a superlative ass in a sport filled with superlative asses.

Before Gabe can figure out how to deal, a tabloid throws him out of his comfortable closet into a brand-new world. Amid the emotional turmoil of invasive questions, nasty speculation, and on- and off-ice homophobia, his game suffers.

Surprisingly, it's Dante who drags him out of it—and then drags him into something else. Nothing good can come of secretly sleeping with a teammate, especially one Gabe has feelings for. But with their captain out with an injury, a rookie in perpetual need of a hug, and the race to make the playoffs for the first time since 1995, Gabe has a lot on his plate.

He can't be blamed for forgetting that nothing stays secret forever.

www.dreamspinnerpress.com

CPSIA information can be obtained
at www.ICGtesting.com
Printed in the USA
LVHW021802260121
677550LV00014B/1892